Other Books by Bette

The Organ Harvesters
The Organ Harvesters—Book II

Books in the Gina Mazzio RN Medical Series with J. J. Lamb

Bone Dry
Sin and Bone
Bone Pit
Bone of Contention
Bone Dust
Bone Crack
Bone Slice
Bone Point

Other Novels by Bette Golden Lamb & J. J. Lamb

Sisters in Silence
Heir Today …
The Killing Vote

THE RUSSIAN GIRL

THE RUSSIAN GIRL

BETTE GOLDEN LAMB

Two Black Sheep Productions

Novato, CA

The author acknowledges the historical basis for THE RUSSIAN GIRL, but the novel does not necessarily conform 100% to history—it is a work of fiction, as are the narrative's names and personalities. The story is a result of memories passed onto me, leaving much room for human error and improvisations. Yet, the essence, the inner core of my mother's life as depicted here, is real.

www.twoblacksheep.us

ISBN: 978-0-9984643-2-9

Cover and Interior Design: Sue Trowbridge, www.interbridge.com

Dedication

For my mother—I think I finally understand.

J. J.—You are and always will be the love of my life.

My sons, Clifford & Michael—With all my love forever.

Author's Note

So ... it all began one day during a lunch break, normally the time of day when I would hurry to my car and write fiction. It was always an exciting moment for me.

On this particular day, having just finished writing one book, jumping into a new project seemed daunting. I decided to read instead.

I was heavy into a magical cosmic book by Stephen Hawking: *A Brief History Of Time: From The Big Bang To Black Holes,* when out of nowhere, my mother (who had been dead for many years) came to me.

I was stunned.

She mouthed the words, "Tell my story."

It was pretty strange.

Only a wisp of time, but I was really shaken. I forced myself to pick up the book and start reading again.

Within a few minutes my mother was back again, repeating, "Tell my story."

I'd had plenty of years to discover just how stubborn my mother was in real life. I knew if I didn't agree, she would haunt me forever.

And thus, *The Russian Girl* was born.

—Bette Golden Lamb

Chapter 1

Albuquerque, New Mexico
Early 1980s

The door squeaked open.

Just a crack.

The sound drew her. Made her stop, turn around.

She studied the doorway and inched closer. Her eyes widened, then narrowed into suspicious slits.

More sounds. Her head jerked, raspy breaths whistled in her throat, giving off an alien wheeze.

Agitated, she tugged hard at her pink robe. Balls of fuzz floated and settled, leaving a cottony spoor on the terra cotta hallway floor.

The door squeaked again.

A quick jab and the crack widened. A flash of light streaked in and was gone before she could grab onto the vision.

Jab again, pull back, jab again. Each time the door settled back into a slender crack.

Something was hidden in there. Maybe a segment of lost time—she'd slipped through those corridors before. But *they* always brought her back.

They. Them. They.

Always.

Brought her back.

She looked around.

Still alone. Her and a beam of sunlight shafting through a window.

The light landed on the floor. She slid a toe into a glittery scrap of rainbow. It slashed across her slipper. She smiled at the colors, reached a veined hand out to the light. Motes of dust floated like delicate seeds.

She looked back at the crack.

Someone would come soon. Make it disappear.

But the nurses' station was empty. The corridor with its red and green pictures of funny-looking fruit was deserted.

Why was it so quiet?

Then she heard the buzz of a radio.

KOB UNDER BEAUTIFUL CLEAR ALBUQUERQUE SKIES WISHES YOU A GREAT NEW MEXICO MORNING. HEY, HEY, HEY, IT'S GONNA BE A SCORCHER AGAIN TODAY. TEMPERATURES UP TO A TORRID 115 DEGREES. EVERYBODY HEAD FOR THE POOL!

Why did they talk so fast? Couldn't grab onto what they said. Just static and meaningless garble.

She turned away from the buzz, held out a dirty fingernail and worried the door opening again. The crack yawned a little wider this time before she pulled away.

A flash of memory brought back her mother and father—she stood watching them. What was she watching?

Perspiration bubbled and streaked her thin, white hair.

She looked up and down the corridor again.

Empty.

With both hands raised, she shoved hard at the crack and wriggled through.

Chapter 2

Bobruysk, Russia
Early 1912

Dancing flecks of light winked through the darkness. She squinted, imagined lightning bugs on the far, far side of the village where the *goyim* lived.

Blink, blink. She froze the moment in her mind.

Snuggling down into the leafy tree, she ran a callused finger over the bark's roughness and stretched for a moonlit peach bigger than her fist. It plopped into her hand and her teeth pierced its flesh—sugary spurts of juice dribbled down her chin.

Blink, blink. Time stood still.

Lightening bugs.

Voices:

"Minna darling, MINNA! Come to Mommy! We have to go! We have to go now!

A gruff voice. Daddy: "No time for your silly games, little girl. Come or we go without you."

"Go. Go away," she whispered to the probing moonlight that searched the leaves for her hiding place. She squeezed her eyes shut to wall out her parents' sounds that were like the summer lightening storms that crackled and hissed outside her window. When she peeked through her fingers again they were gone, carried away by dancing moonbeams.

Distant lights grew closer, but she snuggled into the comforting arms of the tree and munched her peach. Luminous moon-eyes stared at her until she turned from the brightness and searched the sky where stars could glitter through the airy glow.

Mommy had named the different points of light, said they were like sparkling diamonds.

Diamonds?

Mommy said not to worry about things I would never have. Diamonds must be very beautiful. Mommy had that funny look in her eyes when she said it.

With a finger she traced the outline of the Big Dipper, crisscrossed Orion's belt, and jabbed at the Seven Sisters through the warm evening air. She hummed and sucked loudly on the peach pit, finally spat it out and watched it vanish in the darkness.

Later, they would scream at her. Mommy would pull her hair—face as red as summer borsht, while Daddy would tug at his frizzy carrot beard, strike out at her and almost hit her, but miss. A twelve-year-old should be more responsible, do their chores: feed the chickens, milk the cows. Be like her brothers and sister.

Them?

They called her a witch. Four of them—Sarah, David, Moishe, and herself—and *she* was the only one who could heal the cows like Mommy.

Why did they have to be so mean, push her around, make fun of her? It hurt when they laughed at her.

She took a deep breath and let her mind jump like a grasshopper.

They didn't laugh when the *goyim* paid money for the healings.

They didn't laugh at her shiny yellow shoes, or throw away gifts of clothes for the family—gifts they wouldn't have without her. No, they smiled and cuddled the sweaters and pants, then shouted dirty names at her almost in the same breath. Well, all except her brother Moishe who was in America. Mommy said Moishe was a doctor. Soon he would bring them all to America to live.

Not me.

Let her stupid brother, sister, and father go. She and Mommy would stay.

She smiled when she thought of how sick and dying cows would turn from death when she stroked their matted hair, whispered special words in their ears.

And the *goyim*? They treated her like something special.

Sure they called her a dirty Jew but she never came home with a shredded lip or eyes stained a creeping purple. How often had Sarah and David run from the shouting, kicking crowds of boys, run home to hide under their beds like whipped dogs? Minna knew there was no safety there—the *goyim* could follow any time they wanted and beat them until their screams bellowed through the straw roof of their own house.

She never ran.

When jeering crowds surrounded her, she planted herself firmly on the ground before placing one shaking leg in front of the other. Head held high, she stared into their fiery eyes and soon a path would open until she was beyond raised fists, sprays of spit that showered the air and slimed her face. Only she heard her heart pounding unbearably loud; only she knew that fear gagged her as though a snake was coiled around her neck.

Yes, *goyim* were afraid of her.

Afraid of Mommy, too.

Afraid of their powers.

Afraid.

She looked towards the village again. The distant sound of hoofs echoed in her head, fireflies changed into twirling torches riding the darkness like floating puffs of blue and orange.

She sat up, feet dangling on either side of the tree limb.

Flickering lamps, wick by wick, lit up neighboring homes. She sniffed at the heavy air.

Sweaty horseflesh.

Sweaty riders.

Villagers erupted out of their homes, running toward her like a gush of water racing downstream. She curled into the tree, an explosion of terror shooting through her bowels.

Foaming, snorting, wild-eyed horses with flying manes crested the hill carrying uniformed giants. Torches flew, houses burst into flames and a sudden wind carried thick spirals of smoke that tortured her throat. She stifled a chest full of coughs and clutched hard at the tree.

Were these the devils her brothers and sisters whispered about? Russian Cossacks. Creatures that rode the night sucking Jewish blood until their hearts burst like overripe plums.

She swallowed a cry of terror, clamped her eyes shut. The ground trembled under her and screams of neighbors pierced her ears. She forced her eyes open to stare at the glare of orange flames that encircled the fleeing masses.

Beneath her, Cossacks chased after shrieking mothers and fathers who squeezed their babies to their chests. *Bubbes, Zaydes* with old, crooked backs yanked at their grandchildren who stood like startled deer. The giant devils with their billowing clothes became darting ghosts fading in and out of the clouds of thick smoke.

She covered her ears against the deafening roar of the horses rearing up, crashing down onto huddled clots of people. The swords became a blur, like spinning tops, swishing, slashing faster than her eyes could follow. Blood spurted everywhere as clutched hands of parents were sliced free from their babies who were tossed in the air and spiked.

Rabbi Bender's legs and praying arms were whacked away from his body, leaving him covered in a river of blood. The heads of her friends, Eli and Ida, flew through the air, sailing inches past her face. The Cossacks bellowed, laughed, hacked over and over at the heaped bodies until nothing moved.

She covered her eyes, silent screams filled her head.

Mommymommymommymommy.

Chapter 3

Two Years Later

Large cow eyes stared hard.

Round liquid eyes.

Pleading eyes filled with pain.

Minna knew even Mommy would have trouble healing Bossy's leg. It was a gushy mess of pus with shifting clouds of flies buzzing back and forth over its smelly stickiness. It was bad, very bad.

Minna hated the Spenovics' dirty run-down farm, hated the filthy grunting pigs that ran loose in the squishy mud. Last time a huge sow chased her, bit her as she fell in a pile of liquid shit. The stringy farmwoman and her big drooling son had laughed until Minna punched the pig on the snout, beat it with her shoe. It ran away squealing as loud as Mrs. Spenovic who shrieked curses at Minna for killing her animals.

The woman and her son stood behind her now.

Watching.

Minna turned her thoughts away from them and soon the ugly memories faded.

She and Bossy were alone. They deep-searched each other's eyes. Minna passed her 14-year-old secrets to the cow while they floated together in an eerie, golden airiness.

Was it God that held them between heaven and earth?

Was it God that gave her the magic to heal?

Over and over she rubbed at a white clump of hair on Bossy's forehead. Fingers raked, raked, raked.

Round

and round.

Five strokes one way.

Six the other way.

Eyes fused, explored. She willed the healing words to fill her head.

Nothing.

The golden light faded and left behind a scary emptiness. She grabbed for any words, made up sounds in her head.

Nothing.

She let the panic ebb. Waited. The cow was motionless, crusty eyes intense.

"Bossy, Bossy," she whispered.

The cow turned to slurp her arm where she had spread tiny crystals of salt.

"Bossy, Bossy."

Lick, lick.

The black animal suddenly shifted, bellowed a hoarse moo of anger at the sky, then hobbled away, favoring her sick leg.

"Noooooo, Bossy. Come back! Let me see your leg. Let me make the sore better." She went after the cow, petting its rump, pressing hard to make it stop, but the cow swatted her face with its tail. Tears stung her eyes. When she tried to follow, Mrs. Spenovic's high-pitched voice stopped her.

Minna turned to face the woman, who was breathing as though she'd lifted a bale of hay. The son stood next to his mother, staring at Minna's chest, smirking.

"So it's true. Baby Goldmich has lost the power."

"No, it's not true. It takes longer but I can heal Bossy's leg."

The woman snagged her by the ear and yanked hard until Minna kicked out at her.

"Filthy Jew! Who the hell do you think you're kicking? Get out of here! Send Mama Goldmich to fix Bossy. Send her now!"

"I can do it. You won't let me."

"Careful how you talk to me, Baby Yid."

"I'm not afraid of you," Minna said.

The woman suddenly laughed. "I know where they hide you and the rest of the Goldmich yidlettes when the Cossacks ride." She pointed a finger. "You'd better be afraid."

A spike of terror stabbed through Minna's heart.

"You're lucky your mama's the village cow healer. You can thank God for that, or you'd be dead."

The son laughed; phlegm rattled in his throat. "Your mamma better heal Bossy, heal her good—or else."

Minna's heart boomed. Just the word *Cossack* terrified her, made her remember the devils who had killed her friends, killed her people.

What would she thank God for? God had let the Cossacks steal her magic.

"Get out of here, filthy Jew bitch."

Minna turned and ran toward the tiny grove of trees that separated the *goyim* from the Jews. The sun, a large orange dot, hung low in the sky. She would have to hurry or be out in the dark alone. Mommy would be angry.

Angry about Bossy, too.

It was shadowy among the trees as her feet crushed the dry pine needles.

Footsteps.

Footsteps behind her.

She turned as the Spenovic boy grabbed her hair, shoved her to the ground. Sour breath exploded in her face; he fell on top of her, hands moved up and down, pushed at her underwear.

"Jew animal. Spread your legs or I'll cut your heart out." He held a knife above her head.

He tried to pin her but he was weak, clumsy with the gutting knife.

She yanked loose, punched his nose, but he laughed and sat back hard on her stomach. She beat at his legs, his chest, but it was as useless as a lone fly pestering Bossy. He made silly faces at her and put the knife down, opened his pants.

"I've got a present for you, little Jew girl."

"Donhurtmedonhurtme!" she screamed. Pee ran down her legs. Her hands became claws. She reached, gouged, pressed hard at his eyeballs until they were tight little eggs in her fingers.

He howled and rolled away.

On her feet, she grabbed a jagged rock and smashed it against his head, again and again.

He lay very still. Very still.

Her panting slowed.

Blood dripped down his cheek and onto the ground.

• • •

Samuel Goldmich paced around the kitchen table, his hands clenched behind his back. Every few steps he would stop to pull at his beard and hurl a fiery glare at Minna.

Frieda Goldmich stepped protectively in front of her daughter, her harsh voice a frigid blast of anger. "She must leave tonight, Sam."

"And tell me how we are to pay for this trip to America."

Mumble: "I have money."

He cupped a hand around his ear. "What? What did you say?

Louder: "You heard what I said."

His face swelled with anger and a voice she hardly recognized bounced off the walls. "Am I not the man of the house?"

"Yes, Samuel."

Red-faced, spittle flying, the words seemed to catch in his throat before he screamed again, so loud Minna covered her ears. "Am I not the one to decide where our money goes?"

Frieda's chin jutted stubbornly. "Stop wasting away in the synagogue and break your back on the farm like the rest of us. *Then* it will be our money. Now, it's *my* money."

"I am your husband. Do you hear yourself? An abomination before God—"

"God can strike me dead as long as my daughter lives. Can you understand that, you fool?"

Frieda's words hovered, then sagged like a blanket covering the room. David and Sarah hid in a corner, clutched each other's hands. No one dared speak. They barely breathed.

Finally, Samuel said: "This is what we get for spoiling her, letting her hide in trees, do whatever she wants." He pointed an accusing finger. "It's your fault. Everything is your fault, you crazy woman."

"Go ahead. Blame me. She still goes."

"Look at her. She looks like a sixteen-year-old. What boy wouldn't want to pull her tits?"

"Samuel, you're worse than an animal. This is what thirty years with the Czar's army has done. Tough soldier. No heart left even for your own daughter?"

"At least I'm still alive, still a Jew."

"Better to die young than become an old man with all the juice sucked out of you."

He sat down heavily at the kitchen table and fingered the spoon in his tea, rattling it against the glass. Minna stopped crying. She looked from her father to her mother, back to her father again.

"Friedaleh, how can you talk to me like that?"

"Because you don't care about our Minna. And you don't care because she's not the son you wanted." Her eyes bored into his until he was forced to look away "Don't you understand? We don't know if the Spenovic boy is dead or alive. If he's dead, the *goyim* will tear her apart."

"If he's dead, no one will know she cracked his skull."

Frieda turned to look at Minna. She pulled a piece of shredded cloth from her housedress pocket and dabbed gently at a renewed gush of tears running down her daughter's cheeks. Sam was right about one thing: She did look like a sixteen-year-old, and that meant sooner or later someone would hurt her. Why couldn't she be small like her older sister? Frieda suddenly reached out and hugged Minna to her chest, whispered: "*Maideleh, maideleh.* Don't cry. Don't listen to him. It will be all right."

"We can't let her go. Who will do her chores?"

Frieda turned back to her husband and stared in disbelief. "What is wrong with your rotting brain that you can't understand that the *goyim* will kill her? Already she comes home a bloody mess. They're not afraid of her anymore."

"They would leave her be if she would heal."

Frieda studied the old man's wrinkled face and tried to remember the handsome man she had fallen in love with. The memories of that time were almost gone, first replaced by indifference, and now by hatred.

"Can't you see, she may never heal again?" Frieda eased into a wooden chair opposite her husband while Minna remained standing, continuing to shift from one foot to another. "If only she'd been with us that horrible night. If only we'd waited, found her."

"She's had two years to be finished with that night." His mouth tightened into a stubborn straight line. "She stays here where she belongs."

Frieda glared at him until he shifted in his seat, then she sighed and rubbed her shoulder where bouts of occasional pain had changed into a constant companion. "I suppose you can't help being what you are."

She stood, walked up to him and picked up the bread knife and began slicing a loaf of fresh black bread. Her voice was soft but menacing. "You will let her go or I will kill you."

His lips formed a perfect circle of alarm. "Friedalah! Stop this now!"

"I will kill you, you selfish old man. Maybe not today. Maybe not tomorrow. But you will die by my hand."

"You don't mean that, Frieda."

She looked at her trembling daughter, then back at her husband. "I do, Samuel. I swear before God, I do."

Chapter 4

Albuquerque
1980s

The sidewalk heat burned through her slippers; sweaty feet made each step a slip, slide, stumble of motion.

Step, step.

Slide, slide.

She jerked to a stop, let the heat singe her feet as she shoved a finger between the buttons of her bathrobe to scratch an itch. She stared at her yellowed nails before raking deeply into dripping, slimy skin. The maddening prickle continued.

She wanted to jump, scream, yank everything off. Instead, she lifted the pink robe just enough to study a patchwork of purple clusters and a string of wide blue rivers that snaked around her snow-white calves. She wrinkled her nose, let the robe fall back into place.

A sudden dust devil sand-blasted her. Blinded, she covered her face and rubbed at the grit and pools of salty tears while sounds of whizzing traffic reminded her of something she couldn't remember. Scratching herself again, she peered at the blur of colors that spurted by. Then there was nothing. Only silence.

She could see again. See the undulating heat waves down the street, across the sand in the distance.

Where was everyone?

Not an animal.

Not a person.

Just her and the endless flow of apartment houses on both sides of the street— row after row of stacked white and tan boxes.

Boxes and more boxes.

Adobe boxes surrounded by walls to protect the adobe boxes. She stared at the barriers that continued like a solid matte ribbon of clay. She'd lived in one of those boxes before she went to the place with the funny-looking pictures on the walls.

Where are *they*?

When she needed them, they never came. When she wanted to be left alone, they were all around her: combing her white hair, wanting to dye it, fussing about her colorless nails, nagging her to wear dresses, take showers. Do this, do that, until she screamed at them to leave her alone.

Why didn't they come now?

Wanted her lunch.

Thirsty.

Wanted her soda. Her Coke.

She scuffled along and when the sidewalk ended, she stepped onto a field of broken glass glittering on the gray-white sand—a jagged piece knifed through her slipper. She cried out and tried to reach the stabbing wound but fell onto her rump.

Confused, heart racing, she looked to the sky. "What should I do, mommy? Tell me what to do."

The high noon sun blinded her, seemed to answer her plea with a renewed blast of heat.

It was hot.

She was hot.

Boiling hot.

Pushing onto her knees, sweat running between her legs, her breasts, she strained and struggled again and again before she lifted herself.

She limped to an overpass where splotches of purple, splatters of yellow, heavy strokes of blue and red paints screamed names at her like a rush of daggers. She stepped onto the walkway. Her wounded foot traced the words:

Carmelita loves Michael.

Alfredo loves Maria.

Maria's a cocksucker.

A cement arroyo was below. No water, only papers, broken glass, scrub brush rooted in large deposits of dirt. Someone had sprayed the concrete with bold black letters:

NO ONE CARES

A jolt of pain reminded her of the glass in her foot. She sat on the edge of the bridge and removed the pointed shard. She stared hard at the slipper filled with blood, her foot smeared a sticky red.

She started to sing:

"You are my sunshine, my only sunshine."

What was that in the distance? Was it a flash of lightning?

She pulled herself up and limped along, drawn to the far-off light like a moth lost in the dark.

BARNEY'S DRIVE-IN

She squinted and read the winking sign, tugged at her leathery skin while the sun beat down on her neck.

Didn't like New Mexico's sun leached land—it made her feel small, made her feel lonely, made her feel empty. She studied the desert from horizon to horizon, asked herself why she had come.

The drive-in parking lot was empty. A pimply-faced teenager stared out at her from behind a closed glass window.

She tapped hard on the glass.

"What'llitbe, lady," he said, barely cracking the window. A rush of cool air washed over her face.

"I want a Coke."

"Large or small?"

"Large, please."

He shut the window, but she could see him filling a cup with ice, then shoving it under a spigot.

"Dollar fifty," he said, thrusting it towards her.

Her fingers touched the cup, its iciness made her parched mouth water.

"Dollar fifty! Are you deaf, old lady?"

"Want the Coke."

"No money? Fuck you." He stuck his tongue out at her and slammed the window shut.

Confusion made her head heavy. She knocked on the glass again and again but all she could hear was the blast of a radio:

ARE YOU FRYIN' YET, FOLKS? IN CASE YOU HAVEN'T NOTICED, HA, HA, IT'S HOTTER THAN HADES. ME, I'M SITTIN' IN THIS NICE COOL STUDIO WITH A TALL, COLD ONE. TEMPERATURE'S 115 OUT THERE. YOU HEAR THAT, FOLKS? DOWN THAT WATER OR WHEREVER'S YOUR PLEASURE. TAKE CARE. YOU HEAR ME. TAKE CARE.

No matter how hard she pounded on the window, the boy never came back.

"Where is everybody? Where are they?"

She circled the building several times before taking off through drifts of sand behind a huge dumpster. Each step sucked her deeper and deeper into the desert. She concentrated on placing one foot in front of the other to keep from falling, but she toppled over anyway. Hand over hand, she crawled across the sand; when she finally stood and looked over her shoulder, the red dumpster was far, far away.

Tired. She was so tired. She stopped, forced herself to look at the glowing sun.

Oh, bright.

Her eyes slammed shut. Random, meaningless, and

disorganized thoughts took her from one vision to another until a luminous twinkle of green dots bounced up and down. Funny little marbled green faces winked back from the darkness.

She laughed, pointed a finger at the swirling balls and sang:

"Lazy bones
sittin' in the sun,
when you hope to get your
day's work done?"

"Hey, ole lady!"

"Lazy bones—"

"I'm talkin' to ya. Who the fuck you yackin' to?"

The harsh voice made the whirling green bounce into emptiness.

Her eyes blinked open. A boy, his skin reflecting the glow of the hot sun, stood close to her. She watched large droplets of sweat roll into the creases of a mean grin.

"What's your name, little boy?"

"I ain't little, old lady. Fourteen ain't little."

"Do you have some soda?"

The boy howled and held his hands out from his side. "Does it look like I got soda on me?"

"Do you have soda?"

"You got money?"

He suddenly shoved his hands into her bathrobe pockets. When she pushed at him, he ripped off the pockets; a wad of tissue and a large, clear marble fell to the ground.

Her hand grabbed for a small golden Jewish star around her neck. She stared at the torn cloth. "Why did you do that, little boy?"

"Give me that thing." He yanked the star from her fingers and pulled until it snapped free.

"That's mine. Give it back!"

"Jew bitch! I ain't giving you nothing. My mama said it's you people that steal all our money."

She started to cry, pulled at her hair.

"Sh-eet. You ain't rich. You ain't got dog shit." He pocketed the star, picked up the marble and tossed it in the air a few times.

She grabbed at his arm, digging her nails deep into his skin. "Give that back to me!"

He shook her loose, shoved her roughly. She hit the ground hard and rolled down a steep incline, stopping with a jolt in a ditch. He threw the marble at her.

"Fuck you, bitch!"

• • •

Shimmering layers of heat, liquid vats of molten gold spinning in circles of fire.

Circles, circles.

Round and round.

She stared at the burning sun until it scorched a fiery pathway to the top of her head, sizzling her eyes, flashing in her brain.

Blink, blink.

She narrowed the light to a slit of heat, a crack of wavering yellow. Just a tiny crack of gold.

Chapter 5

Russia

1914

"Come down from that tree right now, Minna Goldmich." Her father's voice was shrill, demanding. "Don't make me send your brother after you."

"I'll break his stupid neck."

"Minna!"

"I'm not going."

"Ignoramus. The *goyim* will kill you. You have to leave." He leaned heavily on his cane, shook a clenched fist. Fiery eyes pierced hers, veiny cheeks a blur of ruby dots.

She tore a handful of leaves from a branch, shredded them into long thin strips and stared back at him in disgust.

Why wasn't his beard white? He was old. The hair on his face should be floating drifts of snow like the rest of her friends' fathers, not a hot flaming red like her own curly hair.

Mean old man. Hugged or kissed her only when dribbles of wine like drops of blood stained his beard.

Then he would notice her.

Then he would smile and pat her on the head like a stray dog.

A tremor of rage pulled at her, and sap from the torn leaves leaked through her fist. What kind of papa was that?

"Foolish girl! There's no time for this. Come down! Now!" He shook his cane at her so hard his yarmulke slipped from his head onto the ground. Her sister, Sarah, immediately scooped it up and helped him place it back on his head.

Minna's eyes traveled the length of his body. Time had crushed his back into an ugly crooked S. His eyes were runny and clouded, and his voice cracked when he was angry.

There was no pity in her heart.

She was *glad* when he cried out in pain each morning as he struggled out of bed or got up out of a chair.

Glad that he needed that knobby stick to get from one place to another.

Glad he was weak while she was young and strong.

Glad he was old and would die soon.

"I hate you, Daddy, I hate you!"

"Rotten child! More trouble than you're worth, nothing but trouble."

The first rays of dawn sent a shaft of light past the horizon. A scattering of clouds turned a feathery pink and the rising sun turned the distant hills a fiery red. Mysterious sounds of the night hummed on and the sweet smells of hay and manure filled the air.

How could everything be so beautiful? How could all this wonder, all this beauty continue when she was so miserable?

She caressed the peach tree's trunk, explored each crevice with her fingers. She knew its every turn, understood every knot, loved every scar. This tree was her *real* papa. This tree held her, fed her, protected her—not that old man looking up at her, not that old man who would be happy to never see her again.

Minna turned toward the barn door as it slammed shut. Her brother was carrying a ladder and her mother was close on his heels, struggling to keep up. Minna's eyes filled with tears as she watched her mother: wrinkled housedress stained with last night's supper, knotted wild hair. "Mommy! I'm not going!"

The clunk of the ladder against the tree trunk made her heart shudder as if she'd been smashed with a fist.

"Mother, let *me* go," David shouted He gave Minna a hateful glare. "I'll get her out of there."

"Go stand with your father!" Her mother yanked the back hem of her dress between her legs and tucked it into the neckline. She slowly pulled herself up the steeply slanted ladder.

Minna squeezed her eyes shut, covered her ears to blot out the wheezing and groans as her mother climbed higher.

"Mommy, don't! Please Mommy, don't!"

When she opened her eyes, her mother was straddling the same large limb. Minna inched toward her.

"Crazy woman, get down from there," her father shouted. "Let the *goyim* have her. Better that than you should break your neck."

Frieda's arms spread wide. Minna scooted until her head was enveloped by the sounds of her mother's heart pounding rapidly like a woodpecker's peck, peck, peck.

She was a tiny child again.

Safe from her father who continued to croak at her from below.

Safe from being fat and ugly.

Safe from David and Sarah and their cruel taunts.

Safe in a hidden universe where miracles were as much a part of everyday life as the wonder of the stars that shone at night.

The cows began to moo with a whining strangeness that brought a fresh gush of tears to her eyes.

"Shush, *maideleh.* Everything will be all right."

"I don't want to go, Mommy."

"You have to. Uncle Herschel will be here soon and he won't leave you until you're safe on the ship." Her fingers played with Minna's hair, smoothed it over and over.

"Think of the big ship, think of the ocean … deep and blue as your beautiful eyes." She held Minna at arm's length. "You have your grandmother's eyes … bright, bright blue."

"Mommy—"

"Best of all, you'll be with your brother Moishe in America."

"I don't remember him."

"But, you'll know him when you see him. Think of it: a whole new world."

"But what if that boy is alive? Can't I stay then?"

She hugged Minna to her again. "It doesn't matter anymore. That Spenovich idiot makes no difference." She shook her head slowly. "The *goyim* still hate us, will kill us every chance they get."

"But what will they do to you?"

She laughed softly in Minna's ear. "*Bubeleh*, our family lives because I have the gift just like your grandmother. They would never hurt me. Who will heal their sick cows? Where will their milk, their cheese, their butter come from?" She spoke quietly, brushing the hair from Minna's forehead. "When they look at me, they don't see *my* face. They see themselves: hungry, starving in the iciness of a long winter. But when they look at you, they see a Jewish child that fooled them, made them think she had the gift. They will have to kill you. *Need* to kill you." Tears covered her cheeks "I've lost two little babies already …"

Minna hugged her mother tighter. "I know, Mommy."

"I won't let them have you." She squeezed Minna until she could barely breathe. "Do you hear me? They can't have you."

"But maybe they'll hurt David or Sarah."

"You'll be the one they want. Why can't you understand? You'll be the one they want because you made them think you had the magic. *They* were afraid of you. *You* should have been afraid of them."

"Mommy—"

"You *were* at the Spenovichs' farm. You were right there. Oh yes, they will come for you. What was I thinking? Should never have let you go to that horrible farm." She rocked Minna back and forth, then held Minna at arm's length again and her face lit up with a wide smile. "Just think, *maideleh*. You're going to America."

Minna shook her head. "I'll heal again, Mommy, I promise I will. I can do it. I know I can."

"Too late for that now."

"But this is my home. What will happen to my trees, my animals?" She caressed her mother's cheeks and stared into her large brown eyes. "How can I leave *you*, Mommy?"

"You must!"

A jolt of fear tightened Minna's throat. "How will I know who I am? Know what's right? Know what to do, what to be? Who will teach me?"

"You will learn."

"No, no, I can't."

"You can, Minna. Have I taught you nothing? Have you learned nothing?"

Minna stared blankly.

"As long as you breathe, there is hope. Life is hope."

"I don't care anymore. I want to die."

Her face stung as her mother slapped her. "Never say that again! Never! Do you hear me?"

Minna was silent.

"You will hang on with all your might. Do you hear me?"

Minna's stomach cramped, her world tilted into a slow spin, and vomit flew from her mouth, splattering the tree. Hiccupping, crying, she said, "I'm so frightened."

"And I'm frightened for you. But you have to be strong for both of us. Do you hear me?"

Minna nodded.

Her mother gently rubbed her cheek. "Don't you see? I have to know you're safe."

Minna's voice quivered so much she barely understood her own words. "What will I do without you? I can't do anything without you, Mommy." Tears ran down her face. "Not without you."

"Listen to me. Listen!" She lifted Minna's chin. "You will hang on alone or brokenhearted. You will hang on."

Frieda Goldmich removed a small golden Jewish star from around her neck and placed it onto Minna. "Grandma's good luck piece is now yours." She kissed her on each cheek. "Never take it off, and I promise you'll be safe. Remember, you were chosen by God to survive."

Minna rubbed the star gently between her fingers and stared into her mother's eyes.

Chapter 6

Silvery spikes poked from under Uncle Herschel's sun-streaked cap. He eyed Minna from the driver's perch of his rickety delivery cart while his seat creaked and groaned in rhythm to a sad melody he hummed over and over. Minna burrowed deeper into her mother's bulky sweater and watched the late spring gusts drive wisps of her uncle's beard against his face like old white moss clinging to a tree.

The cart, which was usually tightly packed with water-filled tin canisters, was now empty. Only piles of moldy hay remained from the long winter. Its smelly roughness protected Minna from the harsh breeze, but even with the padding of hay, wooden slats poked into her bones with every bump in the road.

Her father made fun of her uncle for selling what any person could tote for themselves. Yet Minna couldn't remember her father ever hauling water or doing any heavy labor. But he laughed, laughed at her uncle, made fun of his muscled body, his clumsiness, his rough hands, called him stupid in a high-pitched voice that made Minna cringe. Heshie never fought back.

"It's a living," is all he would say and gaze with humid eyes before the two brothers drank their schnapps with a toss of the head.

It puzzled Minna because she knew that without Heshie there would be no farm, no extra rubles to pay the taxes on the land. There would be no room where she and David and Sarah could squeeze into their lumpy straw mattress to keep warm in the long, freezing winter, and no time for her father to sit and study in the *shtetl* day after day while the rest of the family shared the farm work.

Instead of thanking Heshie, her father called him an irresponsible revolutionary who had lost the path to God, a socialist who would end up as bloody fertilizer along with his comrades, tossed like hay across the steppes.

Her uncle would stare straight ahead then roll his eyes and say, "You more than anyone should know that to be born a Jew is to live dangerously."

Minna flushed, remembered how Mommy had screamed at her when she criticized her father.

"You should be proud of him. Rabbe says he understands the wonders, the hidden meanings of the Talmud beyond *anyone* in the *shtetl*. Is that not something wonderful? Can't you see that we would be nothing without our history, our traditions? Learn to be strong, Minna. Work hard for our family. That is God's work, too. Do you understand?"

No, she didn't.

All she understood was that her father hated her because she wasn't the third son he had wanted, and he said it was her fault there were no more children.

But Heshie made excuses for his brother, said being a soldier had taught her father to hate.

"Fought for the royals, the enemies of the people. Killed for the Czars, the exploiters of the proletariat. What good did it do that they crushed the Turkish devils? What good did it do your father? Death oozed into his bones, turned a gentle man of the land into a murderer. No different than the Cossack who slaughtered Jews in the name of the Czar. He should have run away with me, lived in the woods until the soldiers stopped looking for us."

Why couldn't Heshie be her father?

He no longer had a wife. She had died in childbirth along with their baby, leaving every *shadchen* a desirable male to hound. How could such a desirable catch remain single? *They* would fix him up, fix him up with the most beautiful woman in the *shtetl*. The marriage brokers begged, nagged, never let up throughout the years, but he always refused.

Minna became the daughter Heshie never had, and he became the most important man in her life. Unlike her father, he was a man of action and fun: talking, chewing, spitting sunflower seeds, sucking on soggy cigarettes, teasing her, grabbing her, squeezing her until she was drowning in his musty tobacco reek and her face was raw from his scratchy woolen tunic.

Heshie coaxed the tan mare like a little child.

"Alexdrova, my darling. Fly! Fly with the wind!"

The wagon continued to clatter with its emptiness, and the horse kept the same slow deliberate pace as though the cart was still laden with heavy water canisters.

Minna began to cry again. She remembered how David and Sarah had leaned against the wagon, strangely silent as they watched Mommy give Heshie the coins for her trip to America and explain to Minna where extra money was sewn and hidden in her clothes.

She had turned toward her father, stared at the small, silent man whose eyes were fiery, mouth drawn into a pale slash. He'd tried to say good-bye, had reached out to touch her hair. She'd spat in his face, said she never wanted to see him again. Then in the same breath, she'd begged him to allow her to stay. In the end, she had clutched her mother so tightly that David and Sarah had to peel away her fingers. Minna had tried to see it all in that final moment: cows, trees, her mother, father, brother, sister.

Heshie held her seated as the wagon pulled away.

"Mommy!"

Her mother stood in the road, chin high, tears glistening on her face.

"Mommy!"

She'd shouted until she was halfway to the village and her voice croaked, then silently she'd climbed into the back of the cart.

• • •

For a long time after they left the farm, Heshie had laughed and greeted neighbors and customers, calling out their names in a happy, roaring voice.

Minna stared hopelessly through the wagon slats, studied the land along the roadway, memorized every tree, every farmhouse.

Vegetable gardens were being tended in almost every field they passed. Minna thought about the tomatoes, cucumbers, and peppers she had planted. In the last few days, tiny seedlings had broken through the ground. They would all grow and feed her family, but she would never taste any of it.

If only she could jump from the wagon and hide among the peasants. Instead, she meekly watched parcel after parcel of farmland roll by.

"*Nu shain*, little girl? When are you going to come and keep your old uncle company?" He patted the seat next to him, smiled at her with large, liquid eyes.

"I don't want to, Uncle Heshie."

"Put the *shmates* down and come up here with me!"

Minna sat up, shook her head, and kept her sheet-bundled clothes crushed to her chest. She rubbed the Star of David between hot and sweaty fingers and thought of her mother. She started to cry again.

When they reached the *shtetl*, with its crooked streets and bunched-up houses that circled around the small market place,

Heshie stopped many times to speak softly to a number of men. She couldn't hear what was said but her uncle's face now held a dark expression.

The sun climbed higher in the sky. Minna lay stunned in the back of the wagon, still refusing to sit up front.

She tried not to listen to the clackity-clack of wooden wheels pounding the duckboards that kept them from sinking into the muddy streets. She shut out the noise of the peddlers and beggars that became a layer of sound smeared over the haggle of the grocers and artisans.

And then, it was gone—the village, the *schtetl* that held her school, the land that held her home and her family. They were all gone.

After awhile she stopped crying and listened to Uncle Herschel's hacking cough.

• • •

Piercing sunlight jumped around her ... a floating cow drifted by, its legs walking on air, eyes glowing a strange yellow. She reached ... reached ... the cow's tail slid through her fingers, its eyes widened into saucers of fear. A human voice shrieked from the running cow "GO AWAY!" A sudden gush of blood rained down on her, leaving her hair full of sticky, dripping clots of red.

"Mommy! Help me!"

Her mother: "Minna! MINNNAAA! Look for the golden light."

"Gone, Mommy. Everything is bloody. Everything is dying. The golden light is gone. I'll never heal again."

"Look for the light ... look for the light."

"AFRAID."

Minna awakened with a start.

35

"Comecomecome," her uncle said gently, "Put your things down and sit with me." He pulled hard at the reins.

"Whoa!" The mare neighed, snuffled complaints, and clopped her hooves into the mud. The wagon inched back and forth, and Minna tucked her hair into a large babushka. Reluctantly she left her belongings and climbed up to the front.

Her stomach growled with hunger, but she refused to ask for something to eat. Heshie laughed, reached out, and squeezed her to him before reaching into a cloth sack filled with food. He tore off a handful of black bread and cut a large chunk of cheese, passed both over to her. Greedily, she ripped off a piece of bread with her teeth, chewed slowly.

"You were dreaming?"

Minna nodded.

"Golden light?"

She looked at him, puzzled, taking a bite of the hard cheese.

"You cried out in your sleep."

She ate the rest of the food before she spoke "I need the light to help me."

"This light you need … this light … without it, you can't heal anymore?"

She nodded.

"Maybe it will return some day."

Minna refused to speak, stared into the distance. After a while her uncle broke the silence "What a beautiful babushka. Such large red flowers."

Minna nodded, said nothing.

He finally gave up conversation and they rode in silence as the miles drifted by.

She hugged herself inside the brown sweater, her mother's scent still strong in the fibers of the wool. She closed her eyes and let the aroma wash over her.

. . .

On the darkening horizon, a vast sprawl of houses and a clutter of churches with soaring onion spires became the jagged skyline of Minsk.

Twilight tossed a flush of purple across the sky as Heshie drove toward circles of campfires that surrounded the city. Minna's eyes drooped as she watched the flickering flames throw fistfuls of sparks at the moon.

"Stay close to the wagon," he said.

"Is there something wrong?" Minna asked. She looked at the shadowy figures around the campfires. He took her hand and pressed his fingers against hers.

"From now on you will have to be a brave woman."

"I'm not a woman. Mommy's a woman."

He nodded slowly. "Being a girl who hides in trees will not save your life."

She looked at her uncle: his eyes were pools of darkness that reflected neither the light of the moon nor the glow of the campfires.

"Uncle Heshie, please let me go. Let me hide in the forests like you did. *I* could do that."

He reined in the horse until he was barely moving. Several moments passed before he spoke "Tomorrow we will take a train to Hamburg."

"Where?"

"A seaport in Germany where you will take a great ship to America."

She yanked her hand away from him. "I don't want to go to Germany. I don't want to go to America. You can't make me!"

He grabbed her, pulled her roughly against him, his voice husky and tense. "Do you think we want you to leave? Do you think your mother's tears were tears of joy?"

He was so close, strands of beard slid across her face. She could smell the sharp odor of salted herring and onions.

Until that moment, she had refused to think about America. Her voice had disappeared in a tight clutch of muscle around her neck.

"Minna! Look at me!" Heshie's eyes were darker, scarier. "The Spenovich boy… "

Shivers started at the base of her spine and zigzagged across her body, her teeth chattered as though it were winter. "Did he tell on me?"

Heshie suddenly released her arm. "*Gott in Himmel*! He's dead, Minna! He's dead!"

Emptiness, then a sudden rush of questions: "But how do you know for sure? Mommy said we couldn't know for sure. We've been riding for three days. Who could have told you?"

"The day we left the *shtetl*, the word was everywhere … the boy's mother claims you killed him. She went to the village officials. The elders have warned this will not go away without time and money. Thank God, no one saw the two of you together in the woods." A long deep sigh made his lips quiver. "Money under the table will make them forget that miserable boy. But it's much too late for you, Minna. You have to go now!"

A fist of terror clutched her insides. "Will they send the Cossacks after me? Chop off my arms and legs like my friend Elie?"

Heshie rubbed her cheek with a callused finger. "Once you're on the ship to America, you'll be safe."

"Heshie—"

"You have to trust your Uncle Heshie. Have I ever let you down?"

She shook her head slowly.

"We must be careful, *maideleh*." He reached for the Star of David hanging on her sweater. "Hide that inside your clothes until you reach America. If someone sees that out here—"

Her teeth were chattering again "They'll chop me to pieces."

"Maybe. Maybe not. Better to be safe."

Heshie was lost in a coughing spasm. He tore the smoking stub from his lips and tossed it over the side of the wagon, but he still hacked and struggled for air, his chest rattling with every breath.

"Why do the *goyim* hate us?"

"People always hate what's not there," he said, his chest wheezing.

"How can you hate what's not there?"

"Look at your father. He hates that my *pais* are not there bouncing against my face." He pointed to his cheeks "That I'm not there with him in *bet midrash* studying the torah day after day. And if that's not enough, think of the years he spent as a soldier—his youth gone with all those wasted years. Minna, what's not there can make a person hate."

"But why does that make the *goyim* hate *us*?"

"Point enough fingers at the Jews, generation after generation, and they'll feel nothing when the Cossacks burn or kill us. Blame us for stealing their food, work, money, land, and if that's not enough, blame us for every dead baby they have, that we suck the lifeblood from their children."

"But—"

"Does it change anything to blame us for the things they don't have? No! Because what's not there is not the Jews' fault. We are just the scapegoats. *Gott in Himmel*, it's the royals that are the parasites! Them and the bourgeoisie bleed our country dry, then point their fingers at us to distract the masses from the real reasons."

Minna watched her uncle light another cigarette with shaking hands. Large puffs of smoke hovered around him as he wiped his face on his sleeve.

A rush of sound engulfed them as they approached a large ring of campfires: laughter, yelling, singing, children screeching at each other, mothers screeching at children, fathers screeching at mothers. The only distinctive sound was the strum of a balalaika.

"Who are all these people, Heshie?"

"Nomads. Poor peasants who have no land, no home."

He brought the wagon to a halt, pulled out a large knife. He tested the blade, barely touching his finger. A thin trail of blood grew wider.

"Tonight we will rest in the wagon. You will sleep and I will make sure no one steals the horse."

Chapter 7

Albuquerque

Aaron Lubin shouted into the telephone. "What the hell do you mean she escaped? I'm not paying friggin' top dollar to some fancy, lockdown nursing home so my mother can *escape* and wander around in a 115 degree heat wave. Christ, she's eighty years old."

He paced back and forth behind his desk, a mess that he compulsively stopped every few seconds to rearrange with nail-bitten fingers.

"Damn right, I'm upset!" He listened a beat. "Yeah, sure. As soon as you find my mother, I'll apologize for my foul mouth." He yanked a handkerchief from his back pocket and sopped up a pool of sweat erupting on the top of his balding head. He covered the mouthpiece and yelled to his secretary. "What the hell's going on with the air conditioner, Rita? I'm roasting alive."

Rita ran into his office, a look of panic tightening her mouth. She fingered the thermostat, shook her head, and raced out again. He knew she was headed for her telephone. It was the third time in a week the air conditioner had died.

Aaron's stomach rumbled in frustration and a sharp pain blossomed in the middle of his chest. He concentrated on hugging the phone to his head while lighting a fresh cigarette with the one still smoldering among ash-coated butts. Sitting down gingerly, he inhaled the smoke deeply. The gnawing pain hadn't eased.

"How long has she been missing? Jesus Christ," he muttered. "Four hours? How the hell could an old woman wander around in a bathrobe and slippers and not be spotted?" He took another deep drag. "Have you called the police?"

He positioned his feet on the desk and nodded impatiently. At least they'd done something right.

"Okay. You have my cell phone number. Call if you hear anything at all. I'll start looking for her, too."

He hung up and immediately punched in a call to his wife. As he waited for her to answer, he stared at the family picture on his desk and couldn't help noticing how much his daughter Leah looked like his mother.

"Cynthia, Mom's gotten out again."

He sucked a final lungful of smoke and stubbed it out. "She's too smart for her own good. Could find her way out through a mouse hole if she had to."

A tapping finger poised in mid air. "Cynthia, I'm not calling Frieda. You know my sister. Nothing is ever simple. She'll blow it up into a big deal. No sense calling her until we have more information."

He reached for a couple of Tums and chewed them slowly while he listened. "Uh-hum." He rubbed hard at the center of his chest and rolled his eyes.

"You know, Cynthia, I don't have time to discuss my late hours right now. I'm going out to look for Mom, and the truth is, it'll be a helleva lot cooler in that damn car than it is in this sweat box."

Now he was really angry. He slammed the phone down. "Goddam bitch!"

• • •

Minna lay on her back. She lifted a hand to shield her eyes but the sun still beat down on most of her face. She inched her tongue over parched lips and felt a string of painful blisters.

"Get up," she muttered. She rolled onto her stomach, cried out from the searing heat of the sun-baked sand against her face.

Her hand flew to the flat of her chest. She remembered: A boy had pushed her down the hill into the arroyo, stole her mother's Star of David, threw away her magic marble.

She pushed up to her knees and rested before she forced herself all the way up. The world took a spin—the sun, a large molten eye, whirled in space. She almost fell over again.

"Where am I?" she muttered to the sun, which finally settled in a descending orbit toward the horizon of the desert flats.

An old newspaper lay at her feet. It took two tries before she could snag it, then held it over her head. The instant shade made her eyes feel better. She stared at a huge gash on her naked foot and spotted a bloody slipper half buried in the sand. She grabbed it, shook it out, and dropped it onto the ground. She stepped into it and shuffled on.

Soon she forgot about the pain.

Chapter 8

Minsk

1914

Minna and Heshie drove into Minsk on a gust of chilled air that brought back memories of the long harsh winter. The roads were still muddy in spots, but most people ignored the crowded duckboards and walked in the street, circling around the wagon.

There were people everywhere in the city, so different from Minna's village with its small *shtetl* where she could skip everywhere, even in her sleep, and still know exactly where she stood.

Her gaze jumped from one place to another. One moment she was panicked by the loud buzz of noise, the next dazzled by the swirl of colorful clothes with exotic designs she'd never seen before.

Six men, topped by tall, velvet hats, strolled near the wagon. The wind lifted their long robes off the ground. Flowing hair and beards whipped around their cheeks as their pasty faces floated toward her. Silver crosses hung from heavy chains, slung low on their chests.

One of the men turned to her, pierced her with cruel eyes.

I didn't mean to kill him, Mister. It was an accident.

Her heart pounded in her ears as he held her in his sight. Did he *know* she was a murderer? Was she covered in blood that only others could see? The stink of fear burned her nostrils as he glared until swallowed up in the shifting crowds.

Handsome soldiers wearing flashy medals trailed the frightening men, then a chattering group of children her own age. Some of the girls had shiny braids intricately layered on the top of their heads, others wore curls tied in colorful ribbons that covered their ears. As if on signal, they all turned at once and stared briefly at her. She slid down into the seat.

Why couldn't she be like them?

They were rich.

They had homes to go to.

A sudden explosion of sound burst around her. "*Boshestva moi,*" she cried, clutching her uncle's arm. The horse reared, legs chopping wildly at the air, eyes large with fear.

"Alexdrova!" Heshie yelled. "Don't be afraid, I will protect you."

The loud, bleating noise repeated; the horse reared again. Minna turned. A large, bug-eyed creature that squawked like a wounded goose was behind their wagon. She was stunned. A man and woman, dressed in clothes she'd only seen in picture books, sat within the frightening thing, looking confident and bored.

"Uncle Heshie! Look! They're riding a dragon!"

He laughed, patting her hand. "There are no dragons, Minnaleh. That's just a machine, a horseless carriage that carries rich people."

Street crowds circled the creature: barefooted women with babies, rich men with trimmed beards, peasants with clothes and hair caked with dried mud. They weren't afraid.

"Eh, just a contraption. Better to fear the *burzhui* parasites riding in it ... that's where the real danger is. Look at it! A useless thing that's supposed to replace my beautiful Alexdrova." Heshie reined the horse over to the side of the street away from the automobile. He laughed so hard tears started rolling down his cheeks. "I hear they are more temperamental and sickly than the mangiest nag alive." He flipped the reins and called out to the horse: "Don't you worry, my darling, I'll never let anything happen to you."

The horseless carriage pulled around them, parting the crowd.

As it edged past, Minna eyed the woman inside. An open, fur-collared summer coat revealed a dark, high-necked silk dress, and perched on her head was a large hat with a brilliant red flower held in place by piles of black netting draped across the wide brim. The morning light made the woman's face glow with a soft, pink radiance that was framed by wisps of hair like curling fingers caressing her cheeks. The woman turned and looked right through Minna, then tipped her head so her elegant features turned up to face the overhead sheets hanging from building to building. She laughed at something the man said and flipped the hem of her dress. A flash of delicate lace appeared for an instant, then was snatched away.

Minna stared at her own wrinkled, badly stained cotton dress. She delicately fingered the colorful flowers she had embroidered around the neck, then looked down at her dirty boots. Tightening her babushka, she tilted her head, tried to sit straighter in the seat. But in a moment the pose slipped away.

Minna nudged her uncle. "Isn't she beautiful?"

"No more beautiful than the fleas that crawl through your clothes, or the mosquitoes that leave your skin with lines of welts to drive you crazy." He shooed cigarette smoke from his eyes in a quick motion. "Don't be taken in by that young smiling face or the fancy suit of that arrogant man. They may not have flames shooting from their faces, but they can chew you up and spit you out worse than any dragon you can imagine."

Still, Minna kept her eyes on the automobile until it was gone from sight, then she craned her neck to follow the rise of the onion spires on churches that climbed into the cloudless blue sky.

"Not like our little synagogue, eh, Minna?"

"They're so beautiful. See the colors sparkle against the sky?"

"*Goyim* seem to need that fancy *drek* the way your father needs his *pais* bouncing on the side of his face. I guess they think it will capture the eye of God."

"You make it sound so bad."

"Not bad. Worthless."

"But, Uncle Heshie—"

"Forget the grand buildings, Minna. Better to carry God in your heart, and help our comrades … keep them from starving to death."

"But it's so pretty to look at."

"Think hard, Minna. Is that all you care about?"

"Noooo!" She hesitated, not liking her uncle Heshie at that moment.

"Look beyond the surface of things, Minna. Look deeper. Use your head!" He rolled and lit another cigarette, sucked on it a moment. "If only the streets of the city could talk to you, they would tell you stories to break your heart. They would tell you about scores of dead bodies. About men, women, and children collapsing in their tracks, and the bourgeois stepping over them like chaff from wheat." He pointed to a raggedy man led by a small, sickly-looking boy, then pointed back at the churches. "Wouldn't it be better to spend the money on people, help that blind man survive? He can't see the fancy church, but he knows the taste of food and can understand the joy of a full belly."

Minna nodded, but she didn't want to think about being hungry or dying. She only wanted to go back home.

When they reached the marketplace, vendors and buyers were everywhere. Shopkeepers, artisans, and peddlers stopped people to sell their services, while beggars held out their hats. Heshie had to calm the horse again, spooked by the constant sputter of noise.

Finally, her uncle pulled up to a post in front of a small coffee house. It was crowded with long tables, and lines of benches on either side were filled with chess players and kibitzers. The traffic continued to swell and flow as he jumped down and tied up Alexdrova, taking a moment to murmur in the horse's ear and pat its flank.

To Minna: "I'll be back soon. The shoemaker down the street is a good man and a comrade. He'll keep Alexdrova and the cart while we're on the train."

"Can't I go with you, Uncle Heshie?"

"You have to stay with the horse. You should be safe here. I'll be right back."

"But, Uncle—"

He waved his hand as though chasing a nasty fly. "Don't be a foolish girl. How many times have I told you, we can't just leave everything and walk away?"

In a moment, the crowd ebbed and flowed around Heshie. She concentrated on the peak of his cap until it vanished.

Blink. Blink.

When she realized he was gone, her stomach burned with fear. Then she was angry with herself. *Now* was the time to run. Run and hide until it was safe for her to return to her farm, to her mother. She reached quickly for her clothes, but was interrupted by a young man who sidled up to the wagon.

"Hello!"

Minna sat up. "Hello," she said, studying the man: early twenties, baby face with blue eyes like hers, a soft fleshy mouth that made her think of Heshie.

"You look as though you need a friend." His smile was warm and sweet. She couldn't help being drawn to the white tunic that draped across his chest—she could see the rise and fall of his breathing, the outline of a strong body. She was frightened by the sudden weakness that spread through her as his eyes slowly traveled across her body.

Pulling himself up onto the front wagon wheel, he boldly reached out and caressed her cheek, then ran his finger slowly across her lips, leaving a flash of heat in her belly.

"Go away! I'm … I'm waiting for my uncle. He'll be back in a moment."

"So, why don't we walk around until he gets back—"

Suddenly Heshie was there, yanking the man down and flinging him hard against the wagon. The stranger's blue eyes slammed shut as he slid to the ground. But in a moment he was up and running. A Cossack high on his horse sneered at the tussle. A few people stopped to watch, but most kept walking.

Heshie's eyes burned with anger, then cooled to stone.

"I didn't do anything, Uncle Heshie. He was just talking to me."

"What does a man like that want with a girl like you?"

"He wanted to show me around."

"Listen to me, Minna Golmich." He pulled himself up onto the seat of the wagon, then coughed until his chest rattled. When he was able, he lit a cigarette and spoke through tight lips. "Aren't you in enough trouble without trusting a stranger who flies in with the wind? Again, what would a man like that want with a peasant girl like you?"

"Can't somebody just be nice to me?"

"These 'nice' men, they … use women. Take them away and make them slaves."

"Slaves? But he was so friendly."

"Why shouldn't he be friendly? He was about to snag you and a pocket full of rubles! He would sell a strong young girl like you to the highest bidder … no different than leading cattle or sheep to slaughter." He grabbed both her shoulders; his eyes blazed again.

"If anyone tries to take you ... fight! Bite their ears, gouge their eyes! Never let them just *show you around*."

"You mean hurt them like the Spenovich boy?"

"If you must ... yes."

Her eyes filled with tears. "If that's what I'm supposed to do, why is everyone so angry with me? And that horrible boy, he's ... " She could barely say it. " ... dead."

"Forget Spenovich, Minna." The rasp of his voice hurt her ears. "Trust no one. NO ONE!"

. . .

In the crowded Minsk terminal, they wandered from one peddler to another, buying food and water for their trip.

"Would you like some tea? It'll be our last warm drink until Hamburg."

Minna nodded, numb with sadness. She accepted a cup from the woman peddler, who looked like her mother in her flowered housedress and long white apron. They sucked their hot drink through a hard lump of sugar while Minna's fingers traced the delicate swirls of the largest samovar she'd ever seen. The fierce eyes of the peddler soon warned her hand away. They stood, silently finishing their drink, surrounded by the frantic shouts of people dressed in strange clothes, speaking words she couldn't understand. As the time drew closer for the train to arrive, everyone began to push, shove, and fall over others sitting on their bags.

Minna fought the crushing bodies that tried to punch her away from the train steps. She clutched her sack and finally shouldered her way inside. Heshie had warned her to grab a seat immediately once they were in the compartment, no matter how much they were separated. It was only after trading seats several times that they finally ended up sitting together. Then, exhausted, she immediately dozed off, lulled by the clacking rhythm of the train's wheels.

The ride to Germany was long, and the dull ache of loneliness was as much a companion as Heshie and the pounding sounds of the steel wheels. Five days, jammed into an overcrowded box, breathing the same stale, smoke-filled air—only stepping out of the train to relieve themselves when told.

Much of the ride was stop-and-go, with hours spent fixing breakdowns while screaming babies with their stinking pee-and-shit-soaked rags were only silenced when given the tit. Minna clutched her belongings to her chest and tried not to notice the odors of her own stench. It was her time to bleed and in three days of the journey, she'd gone through all the rags in her sack.

But most of the time she dozed. All of her dreams were about her farm, her family, and the life that had been snatched away from her in the blink of an eye.

Peace came only on her final night when she fell into a heavy sleep. She floated back to her farm and settled in her tree, surrounded by her healing light. Even in sleep, her mouth watered at the vision of her teeth piercing the yellow skin of a warm peach. Finally, she was happy.

Someone sneezed in her face as peach juice dribbled down her chin. She awakened with a start, her face covered with phlegm. Confused, her mind tried to hold onto that fleeting feeling of happiness.

Heshie growled at the sneezer and mopped her face gently with his sleeve.

"Come, *maideleh*. It's time to go."

Chapter 9

Hamburg, Germany

Herschel cupped his hands around a wavering flame and lit another cigarette. A two-hour wait standing across from the ticket office had created a pile of grimy butts that lay scattered around his dusty boots. He toed the cigarettes stubs into a neat pile then kicked them into a disordered mess again.

They had been at the rooming house a week—a week of eating poorly and barely washing, and the last two days he'd saved most of the landlady's stingy ration of water for Minna. As he stood in a warehouse doorway, the smell of sour sweat, dirty clothes, and splattered dog piss were constant companions.

Poor child. Letting her have the extra water is the least I can do.

The rooming house was a nightmare. Minna and he shared the same lice-filled mattress under the kitchen table. The room stank of cabbage soup, onions, and spoiled herring—every breath brought the acrid reek of alcohol and vomit. Roaches were everywhere—even the light from the wicker-covered lanterns didn't discourage them—and he'd bitten back a scream when he saw a rat's steely eyes glaring at him from behind the stove.

At first he'd squeezed himself against the wall to give Minna more room on the moldy mattress, but she'd awakened with a shriek when the bastard who slept at the other end of the room crept up and put his filthy hands between her legs. Herschel muscled him out onto the street even though he had to pay for the loss of a night's rent when the fool demanded his money back. After that, Minna huddled against the wall and cried herself to sleep—he kept his fingers curled around his knife and barely slept.

The landlady's fat legs were the first things to greet them before dawn, followed by a rush of smelly farts in a rhythm that seemed to help her stoke the stove. Minna and Herschel forced themselves out of bed, sucked weak tea through a lump of coarse sugar and ate their stale black bread slowly to make it last.

They had been in the rooming house only two days but the look of desperation on the faces of the other boarders made Herschel uneasy, made him think of piles of useless, rotting wood. There was no turning back for anyone here—returning home meant an immediate death sentence. Most were Russian and Polish Jews and his heart cried out for their suffering. Only desperation could drive people away from their homes to waste away in some miserable hovel like this, waiting until there was a spot in steerage on a ship bound for America.

This is what the royals did to all of us: turned the decent, the hard working into hungry and dispossessed masses.

He vowed this would not happen to Minna.

This morning he'd walked Minna to a coffee house several streets away from the warehouse doorway where he stood now.

"Please let me go with you," she'd said after he seated her in the crowded room.

But he'd shook his head and she'd sipped the coffee reluctantly, then made a sour face.

"You will stay here. You will play chess. And you will wait." He'd tried to offset his sternness with a gentle pat on her shoulder. "Do you understand?"

Instead of arguing as he'd expected, she merely nodded. But he felt her eyes on his back as he left. He told himself she would be safe in the crowded room. She'd always been a good chess player and time would pass quickly.

A rush of fear made him clench his teeth. What if he didn't come back?

He shook off the tension. He *was* coming back. He would have to.

Lifting his cap, he rubbed his forehead to ease a stabbing headache, never taking his eyes off the entrance to the Hamburg Line ticket agent's office where crowds of people milled about.

Well, he was waiting too. No sense in being impatient. Ivan Nicolas Ilevich would come out when he came out. That was that. And when he did, Herschel would be there.

He thought back to a time when Ivan had been a dear comrade. Had that only been six years ago when they'd met on the outskirts of Minsk at the first secret meeting of the Marxist Social Democrats? Together they had become not only drinking companions, but dedicated messengers for the movement.

The last time he'd seen Ivan was at a gathering in a rat-infested warehouse in Brussels before the group was discovered and rousted by the police. By the time they reassembled, Ivan had vanished.

Heschel had mourned for his friend, knew the Mensheviks must have killed him, or worse, hacked to pieces by the Cossacks. Either way, he knew Ivan was gone forever. Later the horrible truth surfaced—Ivan the Bolshevik was really Ivan the traitor, a Romanoff spy and a skulking expatriate living in Germany.

Tears sprang to Herschel's eyes as he thought of the others in the movement who had been dragged away and either tortured or murdered because of Ivan Nicolas Ilevich. The emptiness in Herschel's heart had filled with the bitter weight of betrayal as he'd waited stoically to be butchered like his comrades. But no one came for him in the middle of the night. He remained free and unharmed.

After many years Ivan had finally been spotted. Herschel had been asked to finish off the miserable weasel. He'd agreed, but held back—a ticketing agent was a valuable asset. Now he was glad he hadn't killed the bastard; he would use Ivan the way he and his dead comrades had been used.

"*Yop tvayu mat.* Thought you got away clean after all those years, didn't you, Ivan?" Herschel stamped out his cigarette, watched Ivan exit the ticket office and hurry down the street. Vaulting from the doorway, he caught up within a block, placing a hand on Ivan's shoulder. The traitor spun around, his fists raised.

"Comrade. It's me, Heshie Goldmich."

Ivan's eyes first widened with recognition, then his face turned a bright red. Both smiled and after a moment gave each other a tight bear hug, pounding hard on each other's back. "You red fart, what are you doing in Germany?"

Herschel nodded at a bar down the street. "Let's talk about old times with a glass of schnapps to stir our memories." He took Ivan's arm in his and led the way. "Seems to me, I owe you a drink from the last time we got drunk together."

A set of lines creased Ivan's forehead and his eyes had a wary look, but he went willingly.

They pushed into the crowded bar and took a seat at a small table. Herschel held up two fingers, then pointed to a bottle of schnapps. After the bartender brought the bottle and a couple of smudged glasses, Herschel poured them each a drink.

"*Na Strovye!*" they said, downing their drinks with one quick movement.

Ivan's eyes narrowed into hooded slits. "So they sent *you.*"

Herschel nodded, refilled their glasses. When he finally spoke, he barely recognized his own voice. "Why, Ivan?"

"You mean, why give up our comrades to the enemy?" He downed his drink. "Or why I let *you* get away?"

Herschel sipped his schnapps, studied Ivan for a moment. He

hadn't really changed very much—lean, rugged, hawk-like eyes. But he no longer looked like a peasant in his wool suit and dark tie. "You're a rotten traitor and a spy. You only did what that kind of miserable creature does." Another sip. "My friends and comrades are dead because of who and what you are. The first question requires no answer." He hunched over his drink. "But why am I still alive? *That* I would like to know."

Ivan shrugged. "Hah! If I hadn't given in to bourgeois sentimentality, you would not be the problem you are right now."

Herschel rubbed his neck, refusing to touch his head where the pain still throbbed.

"Sooo." Herschel drew out the word so that it ended on a note of sarcasm. "It was all about sentimentality."

Ivan tossed back another drink, his eyes starting to glaze. "Don't be a fool."

"Tell me, Ivan."

"You want to hear that I loved you, could no more be responsible for your death than I could be for my own? We were brothers, you fool." Ivan shrugged. "That's not what you want to hear, is it?"

"I want the truth."

"The truth, eh?" He filled his glass again. "There's your truth … and my truth." He loosened his tie as his forehead beaded with perspiration. "My truth is that my family is all dead … butchered. I was heartsick. Too much blood … too many screams from the dying." His voice was old and tired. "I did what I did because it was the only way out of Russia. I could not spend one more day there. Not one more day in Minsk."

"But didn't you understand? When the revolution—"

"Spare me your idealism, Heshie Goldmich. Do you think the Reds will love the Jews any better than the royals? And do you really think that when Lenin or Marx have what they want, you will still be a hero?" He leaned back into his chair. "No. *Then* they will remember who you really are … nothing but a dirty Jew. And *then*, they will do to you what they have always done to the Jews—make you a scapegoat and murder you."

Herschel refilled both their glasses. They sat in silence.

"What do you want, Heshie?"

"Why do you think I want something from a snake like you?"

"Please don't lecture me." Ivan's speech slurred. "I'd be dead already if you wanted me dead. Besides, I know when you're working up to something. Spit it out."

Herschel ran a finger across the lip of his glass. "I need immediate passage for my niece to America."

"You and every Jew from Germany to Russia … and back to Germany again." Ivan laughed, a harsh bark. "You know as well as I, that sitting right here, right now, could put us in the middle of a war. A war that could start any moment."

"Now who is lecturing?" Herschel said.

Ivan ignored him. "And did you see those miserable peasants, your very own comrades, outside my office?" He stabbed Herschel with his piercing brown eyes. "Of course you did." He tapped the table to underline each word. "Many of them have been waiting a year, some even two years for a space, *any* space on a ship bound for America. Why should I do *anything* more for you, you who fills me with schnapps but talks to me like a piece of shit?"

"Make no mistake, Ivan Nicolas. I will kill you if she is not on the *Deutschland* when she leaves in two days." Heshie began to hack, then fell into a spasm of a coughing. When he spoke again, his voice was shaky. He didn't even sound convincing to himself. "I will kill you."

"Maybe you'd be doing me a favor, little brother." He reached

58

into his pocket and brought out a crumpled cigarette, placed it carefully between his lips. As he lit it, Herschel shifted in his seat and stared into his eyes. "So, Heshie, even you will betray Lenin to get what you want?"

"I will do what I must to save my niece."

Ivan stood, unsteady on his feet. Herschel looked up at him, not sure he would be able to rise if he had to. "I will do this for you, Heshie," Ivan said, his cheeks wet with tears. "Not to save my miserable ass, but because you ask me."

Herschel nodded. "Thank you, Comrade."

Ivan turned to walk away but Heshie called his name softly. He turned.

"It would have been difficult to kill you," Herschel whispered.

Ivan broke into a wide smile. "Take care of yourself, my old friend ... I'll take care of your niece." He waved and headed for the door.

• • •

Herschel and Minna arrived at the docks hours before the ship was to leave. As they walked along the pier they came to a sparkling white ramp that led up to the huge passenger ship. No one was around. The brightly colored awning over the walkway flapped in the wind. Minna studied the steep runway.

"No, child. That's for the rich. For those with money, who travel for pleasure. You will be with the proletariat—proud that you are a peasant and a future worker."

Minna said nothing, clutched her belongings closer to her chest. She had changed to fresh clothes for the first time in almost two weeks. This skirt held the extra money her mother had given her. She tugged hard at her blouse, which was too tight across her breasts.

They walked almost the entire length of the pier. "Your gangway will be on the aft part of the ship."

"Aft?"

"The back part where they load the supplies and luggage." He pointed to large slings lifting huge crates aboard the ship.

Minna heard the frightened clucking of chickens as they were raised into the air. She had never seen a ship, never imagined it would be so large. The aromas from the sea were strong, different. At the aft gangway, people were pushing and shoving to join the single line that moved up the open slatted ramp.

Most were adults, but there were some babies, held close. Many of the older children appeared to be traveling alone, like her.

Heshie checked the ticket pinned to her blouse to make certain it was securely fastened. He tightened her babushka and gently touched her cheek. "Promise you'll think of your old uncle every now and then."

Minna dropped her bundle of clothes and wrapped her arms around him. "I don't want to go, Uncle Heshie. Can't I please go home with you?"

His voice was rough, raspy. "This is just one of the many times in your long life where there'll be no going back. Remember I told you that on the day you became a grownup."

Minna felt a strange sensation hugging her uncle. Although it was summer, he was as cold as winter's first snowfall. She knew then she would never see her uncle again. He started to cough and she heard that evil rattle in his chest. She tried very hard to hug warmth into his body, but when she closed her eyes, instead of a golden light, there was a cold blackness.

Blink, blink. She held the moment.

Waves of sadness swept across her shoulders, down her spine. She stepped back, picked up her belongings, and looked at her uncle with his large sad eyes. He smiled widely at her.

"*Da Svidaniya*, Uncle Heshie. I'll miss you forever." She turned into the crowd, her throat tight and painful.

She never looked back.

Chapter 10

Albuquerque

Aaron Lubin plopped into the seat of his baby blue Seville. The mid day sun, a blinding white light, glared through the tinted windshield, burning his eyes. He grabbed for his sunglasses and slipped them on, but the hot metal frame sent distress signals to his agitated brain.

"Damn!" The car was like an oven.

He left the door open, touched the steering wheel, then jerked his hands away. In one quick motion he jammed the key into the ignition and started the engine.

"Come on, come on." Each stab at the accelerator only brought a fresh blast of hot air from the vents.

"Shit!" He pulled an already wet handkerchief from his back pocket and mopped away the sweat that started at the top of his head and trickled in salty rivulets down his cheeks and neck. Slamming repeatedly at the pedal, he nodded when the blower put out a stream of frosty air. He shut the door and let the iciness wash over and around him.

He sighed, upped the radio volume when the ding-dong music that announced the latest newscast rang out:

WELL HIYAH FOLKS, TEMPERATURES HAVE HIT A RECORD HIGH OF ONE HUNDRED AND FIFTEEN DEGREE FOR THE THIRD DAY IN A ROW. WHOO-EE CAN YOU BELIEVE IT? AND JUST TO MAKE THINGS SCOOBI-DO, POWER OUTAGES ARE SOARING WITH OUR COOLING SYSTEMS PUSHED TO THE MAX. AND DON'TCHA KNOW SOME DUDE IS OUT THERE FRYING AN EGG ON THE SIDEWALK. YIKES!

"Fucking jerk!" That phony down-home chatter made him want to puke. He leaned back onto the headrest and tried to visualize ice cubes melting all over his body, but all he got were wisps of extraneous thoughts that irritated him even more. His blood pressure was probably soaring toward the smog-filled stratosphere.

His watch said he'd only been in the car for five minutes, but it felt like an eternity.

The Sandia Mountains, etched against a startling blue sky, stared back at him. Several vaporous jet streams bisected the air high above the peak's jagged outline.

He should get moving.

Aaron reached for a cigarette and lit up. When he opened the ashtray it was jammed with butts. He eased the tray out of its slot and tossed the contents out the window, swore when some of the ashes flew back in his face.

Time to get moving, he told himself again, but he still couldn't seem to spin into action.

His mother couldn't have picked a worse time for one of her sporadic disappearances. His ass was about as close to bankruptcy as it'd ever been and he didn't have time for distractions.

What the hell was he going to do without money? He wasn't about to live in some tiny shack on the mesa, and he'd be damned if he would give up his club membership—if he couldn't play golf at least once a week, he'd go completely nuts.

Hell, there's always the shysters.

But he'd used them in the past—not worth the intimidation or the death threats.

"Fuck." There was no turning back. The shopping mall would have to proceed—all his resources were sunk in that money pit. He fingered the rolled-up project plans next to him while his stomach rumbled. "Some architectural gem. Fucking strip mall."

He thought about his mother's nest egg. Basically, there wasn't much wiggle room—the interest barely paid for her upkeep and if he messed with the principle, his sister Frieda would find out sooner or later.

But if she died now?

Despite pangs of guilt, he allowed himself to examine the death scenario: His inheritance wouldn't get him completely out of the hole, but he would be able to see daylight for the first time since his father died and he and Frieda had shared a good-sized inheritance.

He jumped as his cell phone rang. Grabbing for it, he pushed the "on" button.

"Dad! It's me, Leah."

"Anything the matter, sweetie?"

"How can you ask such a dumb question," his daughter sobbed. "Mom told me about Grandma."

"I know, I know, baby. But we're looking for her. She'll turn up soon."

"But, Daddy. It's so hot. I don't want her to die. Please don't let her die."

"Come on, Leah. Let's not talk about dying. Your Grandma's a tough old nut and she's pulled these stunts lots of times. When we found her before, she was just fine. I think she laughs at the commotion she causes."

"Dad, it's a hundred and fifteen degrees. I can barely stand the heat. How's Grandma going to take it?"

"You let me worry about it. Okay?"

"I'm sixteen, Dad. Stop talking to me like some five-year-old idiot."

Aaron listened, but his mind was fuzzy. It took him a moment to realize the line was empty. Leah had hung up.

He stubbed out a cigarette, popped another, and slowly rolled it between his lips.

His father always said his mother spoiled him. It was true. Her money had sure-as-hell saved his ass more times than he liked to remember. But still, the two of them never bonded in any meaningful way. It was the kind of mother and son by-play that translated mostly into obligation.

He breathed in the cool air and wondered whether he and his parents had ever connected?

C-O-N-N-E-C-T-E-D. Some mickey-mouse, New Age catchall word. He couldn't believe he was using a dumb expression his daughter would likely toss at him with disdain as though he were some kind of Neanderthal.

He reached for the car lighter and watched the tobacco sizzle green, then bright orange. He inhaled deeply, filled his lungs to the limit. As he exhaled, he coughed. Puffs of smoke thickened the air in the car. Years ago he'd considered giving up smoking; now he avoided the thought and sweated through yearly, sometimes even panicky six-month chest x-rays. Cancer flashed through his mind and he immediately put out his cigarette. "Shit. It would just be my luck."

He clicked on the telephone and quickly dialed Carlos Ramirez.

"This is Aaron Lubin," he said to the receptionist at the police station. "Put me through to the chief, honey." He sat up straighter, stretched his arm across the top of the car seat, and took several deep breaths. To his relief he didn't cough again.

"Hey, Aaron! When are you going to learn you can't call every woman 'honey'? It takes away their sense of dignity."

"Fuck that women's lib crap. A broad's a broad. Would she be happier if I called her asshole?"

Carlos roared with laughter. "Christ, it's hell being saddled with a politically incorrect golfing buddy."

66

"Yeah, and police chief or not, you wouldn't be playing golf in that fancy club if I didn't put you up for membership."

"Interesting how you never let me forget that."

There was a long pause. "Sorry, Carlos. I'm a little stressed out. Mom's gone AWOL again."

"I know that, buddy. Knew about it right from the get-go. Hard on you, I know, but we're doing the best we can."

"That old bird may have flown the coop for the last time."

"Can the negativity, Aaron. The helicopters are gridding the area. I'll bet we have her in hand in another hour or two, at most."

"It's hot out there, Carlos."

"Damn hot."

"No water, no shelter. An old lady ... a person could die in that kind of heat."

"We're doing our best."

Aaron could feel the tension tearing at his throat. He knew what he wanted to say but he couldn't chance it.

"I'll call you later."

If only he could have found a way to tell Carlos not to search *too* hard. But the chutzpah evaded him.

Did he really want his mother to die?

No. He just didn't want to be penniless.

"Penniless." Even the sound of the word threw him into despair.

The car was filled with the cool air from the air-conditioning, but the thought of being broke made him break out in a fresh sweat. If Cynthia ever found out, she'd be out the door, taking Leah and his remaining assets with her. His heart skipped a few beats and he was suddenly close to tears.

• • •

Back and forth, back and forth. First one street, then the cross street. Aaron had covered most of the areas around the nursing home several times and still had seen nothing. He forced himself to keep searching. He had to at least try.

All the roads were strangely deserted for this time of day. The unbearable sun reflecting off glittering desert gardens in the upscale development made him want to crawl into a cool, dark hole and never come out.

His mother always complained about her legs. They ached, they were numb, they were swollen, they were ugly. So how far could she possibly have wandered off?

He stopped at an overpass, parked the car and peered down into an arroyo. The brief departure from the car, with its cool air, left him panting. When had the sun ever been this hot?

He stared into the river wash. A flash of his mother sitting and teaching him chess caught him off guard.

"You can't use the horse like that, sweetheart. Here, let me show you. Two boxes this way and a third to turn a corner. Do it the right way."

"It's just a game, Ma."

"Cheating is cheating. If you cheat here, what will you do with more important things?"

As a twelve-year-old he hadn't liked the answer to that question and he didn't like thinking about it now.

Hard to remember himself at twelve. Just a scruffy kid running around with a bunch of boys in the dirty streets of the Bronx. But there was more to it than that. He'd had dreams. Someday his designs would make Frank Lloyd Wright look like a second-rate amateur.

"Big dreams. Kid dreams," he whispered.

He lit a cigarette, stared into scrub brush that had rushed downriver in some past violent storm.

. . .

"Aunt Frieda, Grandma's run away again."

"Oh, Leah! Not again."

"I'm worried about her. It's so hot and she's out there without any water or anyone to care for her."

Frieda Lubin-Kahn tried to soothe her niece, Leah. When she hung up the phone, she reached for a picture of her mother with her grandmother—her namesake. The tiny snapshot was crowded among many photos of family and friends displayed on the piano. Instead of picking it up, her fingers lightly caressed the frame, then moved to rest on her daughter Sophie's picture. At twenty-five, Sophie looked like Minna when she was young: blue eyes, a shock of bright red hair. Except that Sophie had a wide, open smile that invited you into her life. Her mother kept everyone at arm's length, except for Aaron, of course.

When was the last time she'd seen her mother? Two, three years ago?

Frieda sat down at the baby grand piano and hammered out a discordant song. Should she leave California and fly down to New Mexico? Or should she sit tight and wait to see what happens, as she always had in the past?

She stopped playing and covered her eyes. She hated this inertia. Hated not having the rush of fiery emotion that usually pushed her into the right or the wrong direction without thinking about it. Why didn't she just jump up and pack her bags and fly to New Mexico, business or no business? Sophie could cover the Victor's wedding. No, no! It was too big—the logistics of getting all that food together might overwhelm her daughter. This was an important client.

She raced through a C major scale, her fingers moving faster and faster across the four octaves.

69

Who was she kidding? Sophie could take over the catering business without skipping a beat. Frieda's hands paused high above the piano.

"Why don't I want to go?" she asked the pictures on the piano? They stared back vacantly at her.

Why had Minna Lubin been so cold and indifferent to her? Her own daughter. Her own flesh and blood? And why even now, after all this time, did Frieda never want to see her mother again? Even her ex-husband used to snicker that Minna treated him better.

Questions and more questions.

She banged the piano keys. Tears flooded her face.

• • •

A glimmer of light caught Minna's eye. She bent and picked up a Coke can almost hidden in the shadow of a rock. She held it to her ear and listened, gently shook it. Lifting the punctured can to her lips, she waited for a few drops of liquid to fall onto her tongue. When they trickled out, there was not enough moisture to even wet her lips. She tossed the can, covered her head with the newspaper she'd been carrying, and started walking again.

"*Temnaia noch. Tolko puli svistiat po stepi.*"

The Russian song comforted her but seemed out of place with the mountains and burning desert listening.

What was it her son had said? If you get lost, walk toward the mountains? Or was it the other way—walk away from the mountains? "Eh, what does a *pisher* like him know anyway?" She smiled, thinking about his brown, baby eyes that would follow her every move. Oh, how she'd wanted that baby boy, her boy.

She suddenly laughed, a hoarse, dry bark. She bent over and stared into the steely eyes of a gray lizard. When she reached out

70

to touch it, it skittered away, disappearing into a crack in the ground next to a stringy, leafless bush. Her legs suddenly collapsed beneath her and she fell, rasping her skin on the sand.

She ignored the pain and poked a finger into the crack where the lizard had disappeared, but soon lost interest. She lay with the tented paper over her head, her tongue hanging from her mouth, tasting the dry hot air. She began to sing again.

"Temnaia noch. Tolko puli svistiat po stepi."

Her mother used to sing that song to her when she was a little girl. She couldn't remember the rest of the words. She reached for her Star of David, but when she fingered the folds of skin around her neck, she realized it was gone.

"Hungry!" she yelled at the sky. "Thirsty!"

Why was she here? What was she looking for in this lonely place?

"Mommmy!" She screamed. "Mommy!"

She sat up and the world spun like a yellow *dreidal*. A large black crack ripped the blue sky from the searing desert. Through the tatter, a golden sea spewed from mountain to mesa.

"M-O-M-M-Y!"

The crack gaped wider like the yawning mouth of a hungry dragon—its fiery tongue lapped out for her.

Chapter 11

At Sea

1914

Sounds of the raging storm were smothered by the constant hum of prayers deep in the steerage compartment of the *Deutschland*. The ship climbed, then crashed with a shudder into the sea again and again. Most people were vomiting, the reek of it filled every breath as they elbowed each other in a rush to toilets already overflowing onto the metal floor. Minna was shoved back and forth against clots of groaning people like a rolling sack of potatoes.

An old man dug his nails into Minna's arm. "Have you seen my granddaughter? Have you seen my Rebecca?"

"No! I don't know any Rebecca." Minna yanked her arm away. "Leave me alone, old man."

The man looked stunned, stared at her with glassy eyes. "You should be more respectful to your elders. God will punish you for your cruelty."

Her head spun with rage. "God rewards the cruel," she yelled. "*God* is cruel."

Her shouts silenced the noisy area, then a swell of anger roared in her ears—people shoved, shouted.

"God, help us!"

"God will strike you dead ... strike *us* all dead."

"Rotten child!"

"Disgusting animal!"

They beat at her arms, pushed at her head until it was bowed. "Pray for forgiveness, you ungrateful dog. Pray, pray! PRAY!"

"Forgive me, God," she said between clenched teeth. "Forgive me."

She was thrown to the deck as the ship groaned, then listed and rolled. The others forgot about her and started their frantic praying again. Minna crawled away on the slimy floor until she reached her cot. She clutched a pile of straw and vomited until only dry heaves shook her.

• • •

The first night had been the worst, crammed in the midst of hundreds of men, women, and children. How could her mother, her Uncle Heshie have betrayed her, have sent her here? How could her own family have done this to her? She'd cried herself to sleep, bitter with the pain of loneliness and self-pity.

She'd awakened with a start, caught in a nightmare of Cossacks tearing off her clothes and stabbing her breasts. Her heart pounded in her ears. She stared at the wicker lamps that cast a dreary light. Except for the constant hacking, which sounded like her Uncle Heshie, and the whimpering of little children, all was still. She'd climbed out of her bunk and crept up a long flight of stairs. At the top, a fresh ocean breeze washed over her. At last she could breathe again.

Lanterns lit the sleek wooden deck but no one seemed to be around. She climbed over a chain barrier and tried to read a boldly lettered sign next to the stairs—it was written in words she didn't understand. She tiptoed silently to the railing. The moon shone on the sea; its emptiness, its vastness, made her feel small, so unimportant. She turned away and fingered a round, white life preserver. *Deutschland*, was written across the top. It must be the name of the ship: Yiddish for Fatherland.

Someone was coming. She rushed to the shadows of a lifeboat

and squeezed herself into a ball. She was shaking so hard she thought the sailor, who passed no more than two feet from her, would find her. The sound of his footsteps faded, replaced with violins muffled by the steel walls of the steamship, joyful music, dancing music.

The orchestra had to be playing for the first-class passengers her uncle had talked about. They must be laughing, happy, grateful to be safe inside. She thought of all the beautiful, rich women she'd seen since she'd left home. Uncle Heshie called them "useless," and although she couldn't imagine how they lived, she couldn't help wondering what their lives were like on this huge boat, wearing fine clothes and eating at a real table. She knew they didn't dip their dinner from barrels of watery soup covered by dead bugs.

She edged her way to one of the round glass windows. Inside, men were sitting at tables, smoking cigars and drinking what looked like schnapps. The glint of jewelry, the fine suits they wore, and a haze of smoke made the room seem unreal. These men were so serene. That's what it must be like to be rich—content and secure. She tried to imagine those good feelings, but all she sensed was her stomach twisted in knots.

Minna watched as the men drank from squat glasses, only instead of tossing the drink down their throats as her father and uncle did, they sipped slowly, twirling cigars back and forth between their fingers. She turned away, gulped in the sea air again, and stared at the stars. She remembered her mother telling her about the different stars. "Just like diamonds." Minna squeezed her mother's Jewish star in her fist. Tears filled her eyes.

How could she have thought her mother had betrayed her? She was sent away to be protected, saved. A pain knifed through her body and try as she might, she couldn't swallow down the ache of separation from her mother. Her banishment would be forever—punishment for taking a human life.

"Juden, schwein!" Angry sounds exploded in her head. A shouting sailor appeared from nowhere. Grabbing her by the neck, he knocked her down and booted her back to the staircase and into the black steerage hole. She remained flat and motionless at the bottom of the stairs for a long time, wishing she were dead. But the throbbing prickles that tortured her told her that dying would be too easy.

That day, black and blue, filled with despair, she'd sworn never to pray to God again. And today they'd forced her to beg God's forgiveness. Well, she hadn't meant it.

• • •

She finally stopped heaving, but her stomach was empty and her mouth so dry she could barely swallow. She closed her eyes and tried to picture her mother, her peach tree, her farm. All she saw was darkness, and she knew if she opened her eyes she would see only unfriendly strangers.

They had been at sea for five days.

Five days since she left her Uncle Heshie.

Five days since she'd been sucked into a devil's pit where everyone fought over food, water, and a small space to breathe.

Five days of people trying to steal her belongings, her bed, her soul.

She'd fought them off, biting, kicking, screaming, nails raking enough blood for them to finally leave her alone. Now she carried everything with her: her dresses, her sweaters, her shoes, her underwear, all tightly wrapped in a sheet. And she spoke to no one.

Minna started to doze, then jumped as a cool cloth covered her forehead. Her hands formed two solid fists, her eyes snapped open.

"What do you want?" she growled at a girl who stared back at her with frightened eyes.

The girl was very slender, seemed younger than Minna. "You looked so sick. I only wanted you to feel better." She held out a cup of water and turned to walk away.

"No. Don't go. I'm sorry if I scared you." Minna patted a spot on the bed and the girl sat, pulling her bundle of clothes and her dirty dress tightly around her. Minna sipped the water slowly. "Thank you."

The girl still looked uneasy, but nodded and said, "My name is Gittel. Gittel Velick from Borisov." Her tight blond curls were mostly hidden in her babushka; her green eyes were large and solemn in her dirt-smeared face. She spoke Russian with the same accent as Minna's.

"Minna Goldmich from Bobruysk."

They both fell silent.

Finally, Minna asked, "Are you here with your parents?"

Gittel shook her head. "No. My parents only had enough money to buy one ticket. The rest of my family … my brothers and sisters … are … are gone. Murdered by drunken Cossacks."

Gittel's voice was soft and she spoke calmly. But her eyes were filled with the terror of her memories, the same terror Minna carried in her heart. She squeezed Gittel's shoulder. "You and I will be sisters in this horrible place." She pointed to Gittel's sheet-filled things. "How have you kept them away from you?" Her hand indicated the crowd around them.

Gittel's face flushed as she whispered, "I've been sleeping under different beds every night and getting my food with the same family. They take some of mine but they leave me alone and have said nothing to the others." She covered her eyes. "I've been so frightened."

Minna took her hand. "You can stay with me. We'll take care of each other."

Gittel pulled a small chunk of bread from her pocket, tore it, giving the larger piece to Minna. "Are you going to New York, too?" She pointed to the tag pinned to her coat. "I'm going to a cousin there."

Minna dug her teeth into the stale bread and chewed for a few moments, hoping she wouldn't vomit again. "Not to New York. I'm going to Birmingham. A city in a place called Alabama. My brother is there. He'll take care of me."

"Where is that?"

"I don't know."

"How will you get there?"

"I don't know. I don't know anything." Minna bowed her head and thought about the empty ocean. Maybe that's where she belonged.

Gittel touched her arm. "Don't worry. Everything will be as it should be. God will help you."

"God only cares about the strong and the rich. Why would God waste any time on a peasant girl?"

Gittel studied Minna for a moment, put her arm around her. "My God cares. My God will help you."

Minna smiled and soon was laughing.

• • •

The days became bearable with Gittel to talk to. At night they hugged each other for warmth and comfort on the tiny cot they shared, creating a private world filled with stories, some real, some imagined. Minna found out they were both fourteen, even though Gittel was half Minna's size. Gittel talked about her father, a baker who had recently lost an arm, how he didn't seem to care anymore, growing old overnight after her brothers and sisters were killed. Her mother was too old to have any more children so there would be no more sons. She was all they had now and she was only a girl.

When they had been at sea ten days, a sailor stood halfway down the steerage stairway and screamed to the crowd in German and Russian.

"Tomorrow we arrive in America."

There was a collective sigh of relief before cheers broke out—people crowded up around the sailor tugging at his clothes.

"First, you will all have to go through Ellis Island to make sure you are healthy. Then we will help you find your way in America."

Cries of joy turned into whispers. Then came the buzzing of frightening stories that made Minna's skin crawl: The Isle of Tears—that's what they called Ellis Island. If you were sick, or they thought you were going to be sick, they threw you into a dungeon like an animal and let you rot. If they ran out of space, they tossed you back into the sea as fish bait.

Gittel had been in bed all day, barely eating. When Minna tried to tell her what she'd heard, Gittel only clutched harder at a large clear marble she often played with, rubbing it furiously against her chest.

"Gittel. What's the matter?"

Gittel curled tighter into a ball, her breathing heavy and labored. Minna touched her forehead, her fingers burned from the fire of a high fever. She tried to coax Gittel to drink sips of water, covered her head with compresses. Nothing helped.

Minna soothed Gittel's forehead as she mumbled words, words that had no meaning. Suddenly, Gittel clutched Minna's hand and placed the marble in her palm, closing her fingers tightly around it. "For you, Minna. Thank you for being my sister. Now I won't have to die alone."

"No, Gittel. No! You're not going to die. I won't let you." But Gittel's body went limp. When Minna put her head on her chest, there was barely a beat.

Words like a buzz of bees flew around her.

" … girl is dead."

" … out of here before *we* get sick."

" … they'll send us away … never get to stay in America."

Minna grabbed Gittel—her arms flopped uselessly toward the floor. Under her breath, Minna crooned, "Nooo Nooo, Gittel. Nooo."

She closed her eyes and squeezed her friend to her, but Gittel's essence was drifting away, resisting. Minna squeezed tighter, enwrapping, merging.

Floating together, they soared through a velvety blackness. Minna willed them higher until the blackness melded into a golden globe of brilliance.

"Breathe the golden light, Gittel … feel it in your body … feel it take the fever." Minna's hands raked Gittel's essence; it made her own skin tingle, and soon her fingers were directing the eternal glow. Minna was filled with joy. The healing light—the one her mother had taught her to find when she was just seven years old—was with her again.

Gittel squirmed in her arms. "Minna. Minna! Let go! You're hurting me."

Minna opened her eyes. The room was deadly silent— people surrounded the cot, their eyes bewildered and fearful.

But her friend Gittel was alive.

Chapter 12

Minna and Gittel squeezed their bundles to their chests as they crowded toward the stairs. Surrounded by frantic shouts of "Amerika," they were flung into a mindless surge of arms, elbows, and shoulders that flowed to the open deck like a gigantic wave.

"Don't leave me!" Gittel screamed. But they were torn from each other. Minna's legs pumped harder and harder so she wouldn't fall and be crushed. When she reached the deck, she gulped down the sweet taste of summer, shut her eyes to the piercing light, and let the warmth of the sun soak her skin.

Ten days in darkness. Ten days of isolation from a world of freedom and movement.

She squinted. Green dots bounced across her field of vision. With them came the blur of a monstrous figure. Minna rubbed at her eyes again and again until she was finally able to see.

A magnificent statue of a woman was rising up from the sea. Not *just* a woman, puny and helpless as she was, but a powerful person, one who could stand against anything the world might throw at her, a woman like her mother, only with a flaming torch that reached for the sky.

Silence swept across the crowd, interrupted with occasional whispers of "Ahs" and "Ohs." Everyone stared at the huge figure. The stillness blossomed into a roar of shouts, screams of joy as everyone talked at once.

"The Statue of Liberty!"

"See the torch … she lights the way to the new world … welcomes strangers like us."

Minna listened to the excitement of the Russian immigrants talking about the green giant which was nothing like the statues of the Czars in Minsk, or the many figures of metal soldiers she'd seen in Germany.

For the first time since she left her home, joy filled her heart. Could Amerika possibly be as wonderful as she had heard? Could any place be that wonderful?

She tore her eyes away from the Statue of Liberty and studied the deck full of people. Everyone was smiling, but her happiness evaporated when she realized her mother and uncle were an ocean behind. She had not only come to a strange land, but she was going to live with a brother she didn't remember. Here, she only knew Gittel, a friend who brought back the golden light. Minna searched the crowds anxiously for her.

Everyone from steerage had been rushed to the top deck while sailors with buckets and mops hurried below to clean the compartments where they had been imprisoned. Minna could tell from the disgust on their faces that they had only contempt for people like her, blamed them for the horrible smells, the filthy quarters.

She looked down at her dress with its greasy spots and stains. They were right. She smelled and she *was* filthy. Why hadn't she changed clothes like Gittel? Minna studied her friend from a distance as she edged through the crowd. She seemed weak and moved awkwardly but she was wearing a flowered babushka, and a wrinkled but fresh dress. She watched and wished she could be as pretty, as tiny. Gittel's eyes lit up when she saw her.

"Look, Minna! Look at the statue!"

Minna nodded, wondering again about this strange land that honored a woman.

Gittel tugged at her sleeve. She held her marble out to Minna.

"Please don't give it back again. I want you to have this for saving my life … to remember me."

"Gittel, I'll never forget you … and that's your good luck piece."

Gittel grasped Minna's hand, placed the marble in her palm and closed her fingers around it. "It would mean so much to me if you would keep it. How else could I ever thank you for being my friend?"

They hugged for a long time. Minna felt Gittel's strength swelling with their embrace. She had healed her friend. Gittel would get well. And they would always be friends—even if they never saw each other again.

Tears stung Minna's eyes. Everyone and everything she cared about always slipped away from her. She took a deliberate step back from Gittel and thanked her for the crystal-like marble that glinted with the sunlight. Still, coldness spread through Minna's chest, and in that moment, she decided it was safer not to love anyone too much.

They were separated while climbing into a small boat that was to take them to Ellis Island. Minna tried to grab Gittel's hand, but one of the sailors pushed her friend away. Minna stood on the dock, watched the boat until it was only a distant blur.

• • •

After leaving the boat, Minna was herded into a large brick building where everyone was forced into different groups. Minna was sent to an area where there were young girls without family.

"You there!" A soldier with piercing eyes pointed at her. She stood close to him as he read the identity card pinned to her clothes. As his hand fell from the tag, his fingers dragged across her breast. He licked his lips and smiled. A knot of fear made her sick to her stomach as she hurried away through a maze of gangways dividing the huge entry room.

She searched for Gittel. But all she saw were strangers who looked as frightened as she was. They mostly talked with their hands, many in languages she didn't understand. Their words were a constant buzz around her.

She was directed to another line, which barely moved. When she got to the front, she clutched at the metal gangway to keep her legs from caving. A girl behind her pushed her toward a uniformed man who was motioning. He towered over Minna as he reached out and studied her ticket. He added the numbers from her tag to a long list. Finally, he spoke in Russian while a skinny woman standing next to him stared at Minna examining every part of her body.

The uniformed man said, "I'm one of the inspectors. One of the doctors. I will need to examine your eyes." He reached out and roughly pulled at her lids with a buttonhook, yanking hard. She bit her lip in pain. It was a long time before he removed the hook and jammed a flat stick in her mouth.

"Stick out your tongue!" He studied the inside of her mouth and pulled up her lips to examine her teeth. At the same time, the woman tugged at Minna's dress and felt her belly. She nodded to the doctor who asked her in a stern voice, "Do you have a baby in you?"

Minna was puzzled. When she understood, her face turned hot and sweaty. She shook her head.

As he poked fingers around the flesh of her neck, he asked, "Have you been with a man?"

"No! But the Spenovich boy forced himself ... I ... I ... mean"

The doctor marked her dress with yellow chalk, then waved her away. The woman pointed to another line. She joined a different group of young girls who were all crying.

"Going to send us away, going to kill us," one of the girls cried out.

Minna shook her head. Had she come all this way just to be murdered? Her heart hammered in her chest as she wondered how she could have thought, even for a moment, that Amerika was wonderful. This was a cruel place.

Sent to a new location, where sheets covered a metal grating, she could see a girl lying down on a table, her eyes wide with fear. A man with a white jacket was putting on rubber gloves while a woman held the girl's legs apart. She whimpered, then cried out as the man roughly thrust his hands between her legs.

"The doctor only wants to make sure there's no baby in there. If you are pregnant, you will be sent back. Do you understand?" The girl shook her head back and forth and bit down on her own arm. Minna could see blood on the sheet as the crying girl was finally led from the area. The doctor looked with disgust at the soiled linen and folded it over to a different spot. He turned and pointed to Minna.

She shrank back, holding her clothes over her face, but the woman took her arm and yanked her to the table.

"What is your name?" the doctor asked in Russian after reading her tag. "What nationality are you?"

"Minna Golmich. From Bobruysk."

"Do you understand what I'm asking you? What nationality?"

"Minna Golmich from Bobr—"

"Are you feeble-minded? Do I have to send you back to the ship? What country?

"Ru ... Russia."

"Aha. Maybe you aren't feeble-minded after all. How much money do you have?"

Minna shook her head, terrified to tell him about the gold sewn in her dress.

85

"Where are you going to live? Who are you going to live with? Where are your relatives? Your papers say you are fourteen. You look older."

"My brother. With my brother in Alabama."

He glanced at another paper. "I don't see your name on the list. Who paid for your ticket?"

"My mother—"

"But where is she now?"

Minna was getting confused. The doctor was asking questions so rapidly, she couldn't think of the answers. She stood mute, her body shaking.

The doctor stared at her for a long moment. Looked again at the tag on her dress, then ran his finger down many sheets of paper before stopping in the middle of a page.

"Yes, I do see your name here. Moishe Goldmich from Birmingham is listed as your sponsor."

"My brother."

"The money for your trip to Alabama has not come yet. If it's not here in five days, you will go back to Germany. If you are pregnant, you will go back today. Do you understand?"

Minna stared at him.

"I said, do you understand?"

Minna nodded.

The woman pointed to the table. "Take your underwear off … if you have any. Get up there!"

Minna drew back, looked around. There was no place to run or hide. The woman roughly grabbed her arm. "Do you think we can wait all day? Get up on that table!"

Limp with fear, Minna's mind clicked to emptiness. She knew she was walking to the table, but her feet barely touched the ground. The doctor said something to her but she only heard a jumble of harsh sounds when she lay back and closed her eyes. A sudden sharp pain stabbed inside and her mind swam in bloody images. The gurgling in her throat exploded into a shrieking scream.

• • •

She floated on a sea of distant sounds—voices became a sharp rumble and she forced her eyes open. Gittel stared back at her.

"Minna. Can you hear me?"

She nodded and looked around. They were on a bed of straw on the floor of a large windowless room. It smelled moldy and damp. Her bottom felt torn, her mouth tasted metallic. When she tried to talk, her tongue stuck to the roof of her mouth.

"Where are we?"

Gittel wrapped her arms around Minna's shoulders and hugged her tightly. "You've come back to me. I've been trying to wake you for such a long time. What happened?"

Minna stared at her friend, wiped away the tears that stung her eyes. "Nothing, Gittel. I just got sick."

"But something must have happened. Your dress is covered in blood. Did they beat you? Did they hurt you?"

Minna yanked harshly at her dress. She untied her bundle and reached for her clothes, pulling out a white cotton dress. "Hold the sheet up for me while I change, Gittel." Minna's teeth clamped down hard, she swallowed again and again to hold back the screams that kept bubbling up in her throat. Finally, she ripped the cloth from her body. A white light of anger made her shred the bloody material into small pieces before slipping into the clean dress. The gold coins were safe in the hem; she could feel them banging against her leg.

Exhausted, she lay back and looked around the room. It was

like being back in steerage. Angry men, screaming women, and whining children were jammed together in a tiny, airless prison.

. . .

It was after the third day that Minna realized she was crawling with lice. She spent most of her time talking to Gittel and picking out the bugs that wandered through her clothes and hair. Morning, afternoon, nighttime all blended into a seamless block of time.

On the fourth day, a soldier elbowed his way through the room calling: "Gittel Velick!"

Minna and Gittel stood. "I'm here, sir."

"Your cousin is here to pick you up. Come with me."

A smile lit Gittel's face as she brushed the straw from her dress and straightened the babushka on her blond hair.

The girls hugged each other good-bye. Gittel clutched her bundle and moved through the crowd with the soldier, but at the doorway, she turned. She gave Minna a final wave and a sad smile. Then she was gone.

Minna reached for the marble Gittel had given her, clutched it in her hand, and slid to the floor. She refused to cry even though her heart was burning with pain.

An old woman reached for her hand and squeezed it. "Don't you worry. Your time will come, too, *maideleh.*"

Minna looked at the woman. Her skin was wrinkled, her hands rough, but her arms were soft and warm as she drew Minna to her. And then there was no end to the rush of tears.

Chapter 13

Albuquerque

The colors floated into Sophie's life one night when she was eight years old. The moon's eerie presence shimmered through her window, awakened her from a deep sleep. Crystalline droplets materialized around her in circles of purple, gold, blue, and green; liquid prisms melted over her body and dripped from her fingers like bleeding rainbows. She wanted to call out, but the luminescent tones shifted into an enfolding presence so comforting she glowed not only with a blissful airiness, but with sensations of being spun into someone different.

Was it a dream?

She stood among the rainbows and watched them dance around her like a free-flowing cape. At first there were only prickles of pleasure, but soon they were replaced by a great calmness. After that moon-filled night, her life seemed changed.

She tried to tell her parents about the colors, about their alien radiance, but her father wouldn't discuss it, and her mother's eyes seemed lost and remote in a way that puzzled Sophie.

But Grandma Minna's face lit up when Sophie described that strange night to her. "Search for the golden light," she said in a soft and dreamy voice.

Sophie couldn't understand what her grandmother meant. "What golden light?"

Her grandma had taken her hand. "Close your eyes. What do you see?"

"I see colors ... floating rainbows."

Grandma kissed her on the cheek and gave her a special smile.

"Take the golden ribbon from the rainbow and carry it in your heart. Some day you'll know what to do with it."

• • •

Sophie stood at the door of her mother's bedroom and listened to her sob. If only she could run, hide from all the unhappiness around her, just like she had when she was a little girl. But now she was an adult and her mother needed her.

She tapped lightly. "Mom, it's me. May I come in?"

No answer. She knocked harder.

"Please, Mom. Let me help."

Frieda Lubin-Kahn finally opened the door partway. Her eyes were red and swollen, her blouse wrinkled and tear-stained. "It's okay sweetheart. I'm just upset over Grandma."

Sophie knuckled the door fully open and entered the room. "I knew something was wrong when you walked out and left the Victor's Bat Mitzvah in my hands. That's a big party they're throwing."

"I had to get out of there." Her mother went back to her bed. Her voice was lifeless. It always was when she talked about Grandma Minna. That, or hot with anger.

Sophie had such happy memories of Minna and she would do anything for her mother. For her, loving both women was as natural as breathing, and she couldn't understand why they didn't love each other.

She lay down next to her mother—it had been a long time since she crawled into this bed. Sometimes, alone in her apartment, even at twenty-five, she admitted missing the security of her childhood home.

She particularly loved this large room where paintings she had created over the years were beautifully displayed. Most had been created during her Loony-Tunes period. Bold, harsh primary colors splashed on rough cotton canvas—a digital salute to a fucked-up world. Those teen years had been rough on her parents. They'd put up with a lot of rebellion, especially after her father moved out.

But time had smoothed out most of Sophie's anger. All that remained from her teens now were the colors and her paintings, which matched visions from everywhere and nowhere.

Sophie studied her mother's face. Even unhappy and tired she looked younger than forty-six. Her smooth fair skin, long brown hair, and tall slender body seemed to attract almost every man. Yet her mother rarely dated, and Sophie knew her father was still the only man her mother ever wanted.

She sniffed the air, searching for the particular aroma that used to permeate this room when her father lived at home. Then, there would be piles of expensive Oriental carpets and stunning antiques he brought back from business trips. Though the room was smartly decorated now, it had a detached, professional touch. That "Daddy" odor, that "Daddy" feeling, was ten years gone.

Ten years since her father left.

Ten years since her Grandpa Saul died.

Was there a connection between the two events? Theirs was a small family; Saul's death had been a powerful blow.

In her childhood she'd seen her mother and Grandma Minna sitting on the edge of this bed, tight-lipped and hostile, while her father and grandfather talked about antiques with an excitement that shut everyone out. Minna's blue eyes would flash anger because Saul was addicted to estate auctions where he bought "useless" items with *her* money. Her mother would sit mute, eyes ablaze, angry, always angry at Grandma Minna.

"Talk to me, Mom. Why are you crying?" She reached over and

gently soothed her hair. "This isn't the first time Grandma's run away. They'll find her."

"For God's sakes, you sound like your Uncle Aaron." Her mother dabbed at her eyes, then hugged herself as if she were chilled. "I don't think they'll find her. Not this time. Don't ask me why ... whether it's because of the weather in that sand-filled New Mexican oven, or pure intuition ... but this time I know she's gone."

Sophie shook her head. "What is it about you and Grandma?"

Her mother blew her nose, confusion clouded her hazel eyes. "What is it? What isn't it! I wish there was some simple answer."

"You never want to talk about her."

"What do you want me to say? She loves your Uncle Aaron better than me? Pretty childish, don't you think?"

"Minna loves you."

"How do you know that? I don't."

Sophie rubbed her mother's neck, then massaged her back. Frieda continued talking about Minna and Aaron. With closed eyes Sophie blocked out syllables, blocked out sounds; began to sense the colors.

Waves of black and red with bright orange dots collided erratically. Her mother's colors were green and blue when she was calm—Sophie had secretly painted her countless times. "Portraits" masked by formless slashes of vibrant paint flung across the canvas—a safe way to express her feelings.

"I know Grandma's run away, but what's being done about it?"

"What's the difference? She's gone."

"What does Uncle Aaron say?"

"Can you believe it, he wasn't even going to call me. If it wasn't for Leah, I probably still wouldn't know she was missing."

"Leah must be miserable. She's very close to Grandma."

Her mother nodded. "I've been wrestling with the guilt of staying here and the uselessness of being there."

"Would you like me to go for you?"

Frieda studied Sophie, finally said, "I'm not sure there's anything either of us can do. I only know I don't want to spend any more time with your uncle ... it's hard to believe he's the older one ... I feel like an old woman dealing with a mean-tempered brat. Besides, with my asthma it takes me weeks to recover from those stinking cigarettes he smokes."

"Why don't I go? I haven't seen Grandma for a year. I've been so wrapped up in the business and my painting. I really want to see her."

"Don't blame yourself. It's hard to visit someone who only talks to herself and barely knows you're there."

Sophie, who had been calm, her emotions tightly in hand, was suddenly overcome with hot red visions of her grandmother dying alone in a burning desert. "She must be terrified," Sophie said, fighting back tears. "I wish Grandpa was still alive." She buried her head in the pillow and sobbed.

Her mother gathered her in her arms. "Me too, sweetheart. Me too."

• • •

Frieda tried to remember a time when she and her mother had any kind of happy relationship. But the necessities of life were what they shared. Happiness never was a part of the picture.

From the time that Frieda was small, her mother showed little interest in her, yet she was passionate about anything that had to do with Aaron. If he acted up, there was always a good reason: "He's a growing boy ... he won't do it again." Yet when Frieda

93

dared to rebel, tried to claim her attention, shrieks and screams of a wounded mother nearly shattered glass.

When Aaron was sick, her mother never left his side. When Frieda was feverish, sicker than a dog, it was her Dad who nursed her back to health. Dad was the one who cuddled her, who taught her how to bathe, how to take care of herself. *He* even taught her about her period after her mother's only explanation was to humorously slap Frieda across the mouth and tell her not to get pregnant. Her Dad tried to smooth Frieda's feelings, explained it away as a European tradition, but she felt humiliated and worthless.

"Stop babying her, Saul. She has to learn to stand on her own two feet," her mother would scold.

"Minna, stop it! Friedaleh is a child, your child, for God's sake."

Frieda wasn't supposed to hear those fights about her, even though any other disagreement was fair game for a shouting match.

Yet, it was her mother who pushed her into standing up for herself. Her father encouraged her to remain a soft and sweet little girl while her mother prodded her into grownup independence, challenged her to be forceful and strong. Well, she'd become strong all right. Tossed the love of her life out on his *tuches* when it became obvious most of his urgent out-of-town business was really monkey business.

Poor Sophie. Even though her daughter saw her dad most every week, sadness drifted into her life the day he left. Worst of all, Frieda missed him, still cried herself to sleep when he tried to come back into her life.

Ten years since she'd thrown him out. Ten years of pining for him. Ten years!

Like it or not, she was her mother's daughter. There would be no turning back.

Frieda closed her eyes, allowed a shaky barrier of memories to crumble out into the open.

• • •

It was only a two-bedroom apartment. Frieda spent many hours daydreaming on a fire escape bordering an old deserted film studio. It was a nice apartment, even if it was in a decaying part of the Bronx. Aaron and her parents slept in their own rooms, while she, like an outsider, slept on a lumpy convertible sofa in the living room.

Minna Goldmich-Lubin owned a small nursing home two blocks away from their apartment. Frieda would run to see her mother after school, hoping she could go home with her. But she was mostly sent off alone. Minna and Saul rarely arrived home before eight.

Frieda's only safety was in her building, the apartment door double-locked behind her. Daily, as regularly as brushing her teeth, she ran from roving gangs of boys who wanted to beat or rape her. Many of the older boys were even friends of her brother, a connection that brought her extra vicious taunts. One time when they almost caught her, she slid through the fence of the deserted film studio where rumors of rats and ghosts kept the pursuing boys from following. Even now she only had to close her eyes to relive the old terror: crunching glass, racing feet, screaming to a setting sun to ward off the shadow-covered demons. "Help me, God! Somebody help me!"

Frieda rubbed at her eyes and stared at the family picture on the bedside table: Mom, Dad, Leon, Sophie and Frieda. Sophie was only a little girl. She'd never wanted to admit how much

95

her daughter looked like her mother, but it was inescapable. Red hair, blue eyes, snowy white skin. She held the picture closer and studied her mother's face. She was barely wrinkled, and her chin was held high, an arm flung around Frieda. She could still feel her mother squeezing her shoulder. But the expression on Minna's face made Frieda uneasy. It gave her a glimpse of a time, almost out of memory's reach, when her mother would crawl into bed with her and sing. In those days, Minna even talked about the little village she grew up in. She would describe the farm in loving detail, but mostly, she talked about her mother, Grandma Frieda. So many stories about Grandma Frieda and Uncle Heshie.

Frieda always envisioned a miniature paradise Disney might have created: a thatched or sod roof perched on a white cottage surrounded by bunches of flowering primroses. When Frieda asked why Minna came to America, there never was an answer.

Why did her mother leave?

Frieda could feel the soft silkiness of Sophie's hair as her daughter continued to cry in her arms.

God, how much Frieda wanted her mother to love her. How badly she craved her attention, the kind of attention her grandmother showered on her mother. Instead, Frieda was left like a lone seedling reaching for a faraway sun.

The telephone's ring jarred her. Sophie started to reach for it but Frieda shook her head and lifted the receiver.

"Frieda?"

"Yes, Aaron, it's me." Her heart pounded wildly.

"Some kid showed up in a pawn shop with Mom's Star of David."

Chapter 14

Aaron sat in a hard plastic seat, stashed away in a small room at the downtown police station. He was so uncomfortable in his sweaty underwear, he constantly shifted back and forth—his underpants hadn't been dry since this miserable heat wave started and he was fed up with it.

Concealed behind two-way glass, he stared into a small windowless interrogation room. A fan of fingerprints on the glass distracted him from concentrating on Carlos Ramirez and another man seated at a table with a *mestizo* kid who couldn't have been more than thirteen.

Damn. It was suffocating. He flicked away a bead of moisture from his eyebrow and tried to ignore the rank smell of the cubicle. A red plastic ribbon hung limply from a filthy vent on the wall. He popped a cigarette into his mouth, lit up, and tried to calculate how long he could stand to be in this hot, tiny hole in the wall without screaming. He knew he would have to leave soon.

"Aw right, Jose. Lay it on me again."

Carlos made a show of looking at his watch and frowning as though he was only going to allow another moment or two before he got up and left.

The kid's face was a glare of perspiration.

"Tom here from Juvie sez ya know him. Sez you're a good boy. Helped him out before. So far ya haven't given me squat." His voice was sharp but the back-hills twang softened the words. "Fact is, kid, you're a piss-poor example of anything, much less a 'good boy.' Kinda messes up my opinion of Tom there, who by the way, used to be a sniveling punk like you back when."

Tom hoisted a two-finger salute, letting one finger dip.

Carlos stood over the boy in a short-sleeved shirt that was heavily mapped in perspiration. "It's damn hot in here. Gonna leave ya here with Tommy for a few minutes. Get us some cold drinks. When I come back … well, I hope you'll be ready to tell me somethin'." Instead of turning away, Carlos squatted down next to the boy until there was barely breathing space between them. "Gonna need somethin', Jose." He reached out and gently turned the boy's chin until they were staring at each other. "Ya get my meanin'?"

Jose's eyes flashed but he nodded.

Carlos left the room and in a few minutes he slipped into a seat next to Aaron.

"Where'd a *summa cum laude* like you get that dumb-ass accent?" Aaron said. "You sound like the dorks on the radio."

"Same place you got that stinking butt hanging from your mouth, wise guy. Out of my pocket."

"He looks like a hard case." Aaron turned and smiled at Carlos. "Cool as a cucumber."

"Yeah. Kids are tough today."

"Hell, I wasn't talking about the punk. It's you. You're the same whether you're playing golf or grilling some hard-nose."

Carlos laughed. "I keep telling you, getting all worked up over everything just shortens your life. When are you going to start listening to me, *gringo*?"

Aaron mopped his forehead and waved his soggy handkerchief in surrender. "Yeah, yeah, yeah." He sucked hard on his cigarette and let the smoke roll in his lungs a long moment before he exhaled. "You're not doing much good sitting here with me. When are you going back in?"

Carlos winked at Aaron and gave him a humorless smile. "When I'm goddam ready. Let the punk wait."

Aaron looked through the glass and studied the boy again. His skin was cocoa brown and he had wavy black hair that shone from the overhead light. Eyes were probably Mayan black, but he couldn't be sure since the boy never focused on any one spot long enough.

Tom said to Jose, "You know, kid, I wouldn't mess with the Chief of Police if I were you. He's pretty tough and he doesn't like teenagers."

"What do you want me to do, lie?" Jose's lip curled into snarl. It made him look like a grinning hyena.

"No, I don't want you to lie but you seem to forget *you* had that hunk of junk. *You* pawned the gold star."

"How you know it was me? You guys just like to hassle me every chance you get."

"Fact is, man, that pawn broker said you're in and out of there all the time. Had no trouble fingering you."

"You believe that faggot?"

"Where'd you see the old lady, Jose? No one gives a rat's ass about that junk you cashed in on. Hell, I'll bet you didn't even get five bucks."

"Shows what you know. That old geezer gave me a tenner."

"Where'd you get it?"

Jose shifted in his seat. "Christ's sake, I found that piece of shit."

"Where?"

"How'm I supposed to remember that crap?" He shrugged. "Some sidewalk, some street."

Carlos said to Aaron: "Ten years from now that little prick will be doing hard time. The system will chew him up and spit him out. A big time loser. He'll be lucky to live to twenty-five."

"Not always right, are you? That juvie officer in there seems to have beat the system."

99

"You talking about Tommy?" Carlos barked a laugh. "Nah. Tommy didn't beat anything. Just latched on to the wrong set of *companeros* and needed someone in his corner. Sure as hell wasn't going to be his drunken mother and father."

"And I suppose that someone was you," Aaron said.

"Like I said, Tommy was soft, not like that brick-shit in there."

"Do you think he knows something?"

"Punk's done something. That's for sure. Does he know anything about your mother?" Carlos shrugged. "Don't know and may never know." Carlos gently patted Aaron on the back. "This must be tough for you, man." Aaron could feel Carlos's eyes studying him. "Are you close to her? Your mom? Can't remember your saying much about her."

Aaron thought about what he should say but ended up only shaking his head. How do you tell someone you didn't know how you felt about your own mother? While he was worrying the right words, Carlos slipped out of the room and returned to interrogation.

"Awright Jose," Carlos said, hands flat on the table, leaning hard into the kid's face. "Where in hell did you get the jewelry?"

Instead of backing off, Jose leaned in even closer to Carlos. "I found the fuckin' Jew thing."

"Yeah? That so? But did you find it on the fuckin' Jewish woman wearing it?"

"I don't know what the hell you're mouthing about, Mr. Policeman. Lemme alone!"

Carlos straightened slowly, walked up to Tom. "Sorry, Tommy. This one's gonna spend a long time in juvie while I get his papers together."

"Yeah! And how long's that gonna be?" Jose snapped.

"Don't know, *niño*. It takes what it takes … if you get my

100

meanin'. Tom, get this piece of shit outta here before I crack open his empty skull."

As Carlos turned away, Jose yelled, "Hey cop! Where the hell is my fuckin' drink?"

Carlos turned back to Jose and smiled widely. "Plumb forgot, *cabron.*"

• • •

Cynthia and Leah were sitting at the kitchen table eating dinner when Aaron walked in and pulled up a chair. He held out his arms and raised his eyes toward the ceiling.

"My God! It's good to be home! Besides the car, this is the only time I've felt cool air all day."

"You pay a fortune for that office and that overblown staff," Cynthia said. "They could at least keep the air conditioning working."

"It's not their fault. It's just frustrating. What do you expect me to do? Fire them?"

"That isn't what I was going to say. Why do you always think the worst of me?"

"Daddy, can't you and mom just not fight for one day?" Leah said, getting up to give Aaron a hug and kiss.

"Hi, baby. How's my girl?"

"I'm worried about Grandma out in this horrible weather. Can't we go and look for her?"

"Honey, I've been doing that all day. So have the police. Besides it's getting late."

"But why can't they find her?"

"Because your grandma doesn't live in the same world we do. That, or she's a crafty old woman who doesn't want to be found," Cynthia said. She filled her fork and took a big bite of her salad.

Aaron separated some of the tomatoes from the serving bowl and shook salt on them before popping a few into his mouth. "You know, I can't understand how one little old lady in a bright pink robe and slippers can hide from the entire police department in broad daylight." He got up, walked to a cabinet and pulled out a cut crystal glass and poured four fingers of bourbon.

"Damn it, Aaron, can't you get through a day without sucking up a bottle of booze or stinking up my home with your cigarettes?"

"As a matter of fact, I can't." He pulled a Camel from his shirt pocket and lit up. "This is also *my* goddam house and I'll do any fucking thing I please."

"Daddy! Stop it!" Leah gently took the cigarette from him and doused it in the sink. "Mom, can't you leave him alone? Grandma is missing and the two of you only make it worse."

Cynthia stood abruptly. "Why don't I just leave? I'm sure you'll never notice I'm gone anyway." Her voice quavered, but she walked out with her head held high. She looked cool and composed, her white shorts and blouse barely creased. "Get your own damn dinner, Aaron."

Leah cut a large slab of prime rib and set it on a dinner plate, then scooped out a generous portion of salad and carefully placed it alongside the meat.

"Sit down, Dad. You look so tired."

He gulped down half of his drink and eased into a chair, heart racing. "Thanks, Leah."

"I remember having so much fun with Grandma. What happened to her? The last few times I went to see her, she didn't even know me."

Aaron twirled the bourbon in his glass, studied his daughter. Sometimes when she looked intently at him, it was like staring into his mother's blue eyes. How strange that Sophie and Leah resembled their grandmother so much while he and Frieda didn't look like any family member he knew.

"After Grandpa Saul died," Aaron finally said, "she slowly went downhill. The last couple of years have been impossible. She'd leave her apartment and couldn't find her way back. Stuff like that."

Leah picked up a glass of milk and took a sip. "But what was she like when you were growing up?"

Aaron picked at his food and wondered why everyone wanted to probe his fifty-year-old mind about things he could barely remember. As far as he was concerned, the highlight of life in the Bronx was running away when he was eighteen.

"When I was a kid, your grandparents were always working. If I saw them an hour a day, that was a lot." He took a sip of his drink and stared out the window at the setting sun glowing on the mesa. "Minna was my mother and I grew up," he mumbled. "What else is there to say?"

"You must have spent some time with them. What about weekends?"

"What about them?" His stomach churned, an unexplainable anger made his drink gurgle in his throat. "My mom and dad worked seven days a week, honey … winter, summer, spring, and fall. They had no time for me or your Aunt Frieda."

"But they were still your mother and father," Leah said.

Aaron stared hard into those earnest blue eyes. "The streets of the Bronx were my mother and father."

• • •

Minna's mouth was gritty, filled with sand from the dust devils that jumped up from the desert floor and disappeared into

103

nothingness. She stared up at the globe of sun hanging over the horizon like a suspended orange squirting color across the darkening sky.

She stumbled on, rubbing at the mass of blisters riding her arms and face like hot coals. She stopped again and looked around her.

Emptiness.

Silence.

One minute she was standing, the next her legs refused to move. She crumpled down hard, crying out as skin tore open across the scraping sand. She hardly noticed the splintering sound of sagebrush or rattles like a shake of a baby's toy.

"Mommy, Mommy, Mommy," she cried out. "Help me!"

When she looked up, beady eyes stared back. Waves of pain rode the length of her body with only the snake's eyes to keep her afloat.

"Help me," she whispered.

The creature lowered its head and silently slid away.

Chapter 15

Train to Alabama
Early 1914

The fat man in the dark uniform had a red, devil face. Old and mean, he sniffed at Minna and made a sour grin. He yanked at her dress until she was pulled up close to him. A strong smell of schnapps blasted her face. She tried to shrink away, but he reached out and tugged at the tag hanging from her blouse.

Minna couldn't understand what the man was saying, but she could tell he was angry with her for some reason. She clutched her bundles and bag of food tighter to her chest as he grabbed her by the arm and shoved her into a seat like a bag of dirty clothes.

What could she have done to make him so angry? He frowned and pointed for her to stay, then walked away, still muttering under his breath.

Everyone seemed so mean. The conductor was nasty and the woman who brought her to the train from Ellis Island had barely spoken a word during the ferry ride or the walk to the station. At least the few words tossed at Minna were in Russian, but when Minna tried to talk to her, or ask questions, they went unanswered. Around her was a blur of sounds and new things to see, but Minna kept her eyes pinned on the woman, afraid she would vanish, deserting her to the swirling crowds.

Amerikans moved with an energetic ebb and flow of jerky rhythms that almost made the air sparkle around them. She sensed the strangeness between herself and them, knew she was the one out of step.

At the train, her escort spoke briefly, told her about the conductor, an official who would watch over her during the journey. After handing Minna a bag of food and some coins, she left without saying good-bye or even looking back.

The conductor grabbed her hand and yanked her up the train steps, then shoved her into a seat next to a young woman. She had kind eyes and a nice smile, but Minna felt trapped and helpless as the woman continued to stare at her, her clothes, her bundles. Minna Goldmich was being studied and it made her feel naked. She jerked at her skirt several times, tucking it tightly around her legs.

"My name is Annie Langtree."

Minna wondered what she was saying.

The woman pointed a finger to herself. "Annie Langtree."

"Minna Goldmich." She put down her bundles, protected them by planting her feet on top. The woman nodded toward the rack over the seat but Minna shook her head.

The whistle blew and soon they were moving in fits and starts. Minna looked around to see if there were any others from Ellis Island, but saw no one else wearing an identification tag, no one else dressed in peasant clothes.

She settled down into the seat. This train was bigger, roomier than the ones she'd been on in Russia and Germany. She missed having the huddled mothers, fathers, and screaming children jammed in next to her. Their bodies pressed against her had brought comfort and safety, like when she slept at home with her brother and sister.

In this train, everyone was distant and silent. There would be no comfort, not from these people or anyone until she met her brother Moishe in Birmingham.

How would she know him? He'd left home before she was born. While her mother had tried to describe him, in her mind's eye he was a fuzzy outline of a man. Would he like her? What if he didn't? Where would she go? Or what would she do if he were like her father? She longed for her mother—an ocean, a lifetime away.

"Where are you going?" Annie Langtree asked, interrupting her thoughts. At Ellis Island officials had questioned her about where she was going and then they ignored her answer and read her tag hanging from her blouse, repeating the name of the city again and again, like she was some kind of idiot. Now she knew the question and the answer.

"Birmingham."

Annie smiled at her. "Your English is good." When the woman didn't look at her tag, Minna knew she was finally saying it right. "I'm going to Atlanta. It's not too far away."

Minna nodded politely, not understanding, although she noticed Annie spoke English with a musical singsong kind of sound.

As the train moved along, Annie Langtree pointed out different things using the strange new language of Amerika. When Minna repeated a word or phrase, she would pat her lightly on the shoulder and say, "Good." Minna liked the Amerikan woman; she seemed really interested in her.

Throughout the day she watched the cities fly by the windows. A new universe, yet a world the same as the old—big cities, where clean clothes hung limply from tall buildings and women beat mattresses and blankets full of dust while others hung out of windows, waving to neighbors or children down below.

And the streets: dusty, filled with horses and carriages carrying food or passengers. She even saw an automobile now and then—sitting high up in the train, they seemed less frightening.

She tried to think of this place as her new home, but Amerika remained *their* world, not hers. And they could keep it—she hadn't asked or wanted to come here.

She sneaked a sidelong glance at Annie. Would Minna ever have clothes like hers? She tried not to stare, but every now and then when Annie's long silky dress brushed against her hand, the softness sent a pleasant shiver racing up her arm.

Mostly, it was a long and boring trip. Between cities there were many stretches of farmlands with cows and sheep and large orchards. But what were the giant machines that raced across the land, plowing without horses to pull them?

Every few hours, Annie pulled down a sack from the overhead storage and took out some strange-smelling meat which she called "ham." She delicately laid it across a piece of bread and took a small bite. She offered to share, but Minna shook her head.

Late in the day Minna opened her own bag of food for the first time. Inside was a large chunk of bread, a heavy slab of cheese, and a spotted yellow something that she held up to her nose. She turned it over and over in her hand before taking a large bite, chewing it, then spitting it back into the paper bag almost in one breath.

Annie Langtree laughed until tears flowed from her eyes. Every time she started to speak, she would break out into laughter, holding her stomach in pain.

"It's a banana. Take the peel off first."

When Minna just stared at her, Annie took the thing and stripped away the yellow part, which released a sweet, oily smell unlike anything Minna had ever known. Annie gave it back for her to eat. Minna suspiciously put the tiniest piece in her mouth. She ran her tongue over the slick surface and smiled. It was strange, but sweet and delicious.

The first night on the train Minna refused to sleep. How could she be sure no one would grab her bundles or steal her hidden gold coins? By the second night, exhausted, she fell asleep anyway.

Floating, floating, floating among the stars. Enclosed in a

golden light, she bathed her body in the warmth of surrender until a far-off voice called out. She couldn't understand the words. She tried harder to listen but everything turned black. She started to cry, then there was a whisper: "Stay with the golden light."

"Wake up!"

Minna was confused as she straightened. The train was almost stopped. Annie Langtree was trying to hand her a piece of paper. "This is my address. If you ever come to Atlanta, I want you to come and see me." She pointed at the paper and then to herself. Annie hugged her, then left.

Minna watched her from the train window until she was gone, swallowed by the shifting crowds.

• • •

The conductor yanked her by the sleeve and pulled her to her feet. Her heart was racing, and her breath came in short puffs. He pulled her along until she was off the train, standing on the platform.

He looked around, checked his pocket watch two or three times, sighed with relief when a tall, redheaded man walked up to them. The conductor was now very polite, spoke to the man for several moments. Then the man took some coins from his pocket and gave it to the conductor, who quickly walked away and got back on the train.

"Minna? It's me, Moishe."

She noticed his Russian had a strangeness about it, as though he hadn't spoken it for a long time.

"Hello, Moishe." Her heart was racing, she wanted to run, but she stood her ground and smiled shyly. The man nodded, but he was stiff and uncomfortable as he took her hand.

Then she knew—he didn't want her.

Lost, afraid, all she wanted to do was get back on the train and ride away, but he tossed her belongings onto the seat of a beautiful carriage and helped her inside. The horse was sleek and shiny, nothing like Uncle Heshie's scruffy Alexdrova.

She wanted to ask her brother so many questions but even in the warm summer air, she had to hold herself to keep from shaking.

He remained silent and separate.

"Where are we going, Moishe?" she finally asked.

"I've recently been appointed Medical Director of Birmingham General."

"What does that mean?"

"It means I have two rooms to live in at the hospital. He tightened his hands on the reins. "It's a very small space but it will have to do for now." He turned to look directly at her. "School is out in the summer months, but it will give you time to learn English. After today, we will only speak English."

Now that he was finally talking to her she had to know more. "Do you work in the hospital every day?" Minna asked, not really understanding what a hospital could be.

"I'm a doctor, Minna."

"I know. Mommy told me."

He smiled for the first time. "I miss Mother."

Minna sighed. "I miss her, too." She tried to hold back, but the words flew in the air before she could stop them. "I don't miss Father. I hope I never see him again."

The silence between them grew even longer. When he reached out, she flinched, afraid he would beat her. But he only rested a hand on her shoulder. "Me too."

For the first time since she left home, she sucked in the warm summer air in contentment. She immediately nodded off to sleep until Moishe woke her by gently shaking her arm.

"You wanted to know what a hospital is? This is Birmingham General. This is where I work. Where we will live."

Minna rubbed hard at her eyes, saliva stuck in her throat. She looked at the huge brick building with six floors of gloomy windows; many had bars like a jailhouse she'd seen in Minsk. She was ready to run again.

But to where?

Chapter 16

Every day Minna began her patient care with Amber.

Amber's knees were drawn to her chin and her knobby arms hugged her legs so tightly Minna cringed with imaginary pain. It was hard to get started. She would stare at the small woman a long time before sighing and stepping up to the bed repeating the same Russian words each time. "I'm so sorry, little colored girl. So sorry."

Amber was twenty, they said, but she looked like a juiceless old woman: Head flung back like an invisible hand yanked at the nappy strands of hair, neck veins bulging like blue rubber tubes ready to pop. If she opened her eyes in that position, flaking plaster from the ceiling would be the first thing she saw. Scattered pieces were always flung across her bed and white flakes spotted her dark skin.

Minna had never seen Amber's eyes open.

Stalling, she flattened her white starched apron that rustled with every step and refused to lie flat against the blue dress underneath it. She noticed she had a hole in her black cotton stocking and her anklebone poked through like a huge white polka dot. She tried pulling her dress down so it would cover the tear, but she barely fit into the uniform. It wrinkled and climbed up her hips, uncovering the torn stocking again.

She turned from the patient and stared at the ward—fifty beds squeezed together, each occupied by old and young colored women, most with horrible diseases that kept them moaning in constant pain.

Minna had never seen coloreds until she came to America. At first they frightened her with their wide eyes and thick features, and those with purple-black skin and cottony hair used to make her want to run the other way. Moishe said most of them were poor and lazy but she noticed that when there was work to be done, it was the coloreds who did it while the whites sat on their verandahs fanning themselves and drinking lemonade or mint tea.

She turned her attention back to the patient. Minna imagined what it would be like living inside the colored woman's body. Could she bear to be helpless like this, so helpless that all she could do was breathe? What would it feel like to die alone with no one she loved nearby to care for her?

No one ever came to see Amber Bout.

In the last few days Minna had sensed a cold blackness close in and curl around the bed. She knew Amber would die very soon from the horrible wound under the weeping dressing that traveled from the top of her ear and across her forehead. Under the gauze was a mutilated face that looked as though a dog had taken a hungry bite.

Miss Barron's voice boomed. Minna jumped.

"Miz Goldmich, y'all just standing there when there's work to be done? And ... I see your stockings are torn again. I do declare, you must be the sloppiest white person I ever had work for me."

"I was just get—

"Don't think because your brother is in charge, that will cut the mustard."

"No, Miz Barrons."

"Y'all been here for four months now, and you're not only lazy but you still can hardly speak a decent sentence in English. WE—DO—NOT—SPEAK—RUSSIAN—HERE."

"No, Miz Barrons."

"Might as well be one of these Nigras—useless as a pot of turnip water. Lord only knows why a body is burdened with them *and* you." She pointed a finger at Amber. "Best be doing your job now, Minna Goldmich. Someone has to clean up this mess." She whipped around and marched away.

Minna watched her supervisor move down the aisle, her hair in a tight bun tented by a large white cap as stiffly starched as the uniform that rustled with every step.

She wondered why Miss Barrons and Moishe didn't like colored people. Once she got used to them, they weren't much different from anyone else—funny looking, but their eyes held the same pain as the whites.

Minna stepped up to Amber's bed and lifted the sheet. There would be no saving this sheet; Amber's diaper might as well not have been there. Well, at least she could use the pillowcase as a washcloth. She loosened the sheets and saw that the top sheet, although grubby, was almost unspotted. It would have to become the bottom sheet since they were almost out of linen.

She walked to the closest sink and filled a basin with warm water, threw in a thin slice of soap. She waved to the other nurses' aide, Ginny, who was just arriving. Late as usual.

Although she gave Minna a sour smile, Ginny waved back. Before the day was over, the two of them would have taken care of all fifty patients as well as scrubbed the floors and helped out in the laundry, if there was time.

Rich folks didn't come to Birmingham General; most wards were for the colored. Minna couldn't help but notice that the few white patients they had were treated much better than the coloreds. At least the whites had clean sheets most days and the doctors visited them more often.

As she removed the pillowcase from under Amber's head, she thought about Miss Barrons. The head nurse didn't need to tell Minna how long she'd been there or that her English was bad. Moishe already spent most of his free time yelling English words at her. Whenever she tried to speak Russian, he would scream in frustration, "English, you will speak only English."

She tried, but it was such a difficult language—the same words sometimes meant different things. There were some advantages though; when others were around they spoke as if she didn't exist, but she understood a lot more than they would have liked.

She learned that most of the staff didn't like her brother very much. They thought he was strict and unfriendly. They also talked about his being one of the head medical doctors working in the jungles to build a canal. When she asked Moishe about it, he told her of the hardships and disease they had fought every day as the Army cut through the jungles so ships could sail through Panama from one ocean to another. Moishe had been discharged early from the Army because of a disease called malaria—although living in the jungles sounded horrible, he spoke about it as though it was just another way of life. One that he missed.

It was as if seeing Minna made the staff immediately think of her brother and they talked about the way he treated them—like soldiers on a battlefield. That's where they thought Moishe belonged—in the war in Europe, or in any war for that matter, ordering people about. But that wasn't all of it. They especially laughed about how he slept with every woman he could lay his hands on, white or colored.

Could that be right? Maybe she only thought she understood them.

She turned back to Amber and for the first time saw her straighten her neck, open her eyes—they pierced hers with a black bolt of anger.

"Amber. I'm ... I'm Minna ... here to bathe you, change your dressing." She stumbled over the words while Amber's eyes never left her. "Can you talk to me?"

"Ain't wasting ... my breath ... on some fool ... white woman." Her words were spaced funny.

Minna stared, tugging at her apron.

"Get on ... with it!"

Minna jumped and immediately arranged the sheets so she could bathe Amber, who watched her every move. When she'd finished the bath and changed the linen, she went to work on the bandage. Minna swallowed hard as gray-green pus bubbled from the wound and pulled away in clumps with the old dressing. A sharp, rotting odor filled her nose and she could barely breathe as she carefully poured peroxide into the wound. Amber jumped.

"Damn you, girl! You been hurtin' me for weeks doin' that."

Minna's neck was stiff as a board as she watched the wound fizz from the peroxide. She wondered again why they didn't use the leeches she'd seen used on other infections like this. Those horrible creatures could suck away all this awful stuff until everything was pink and clean. Maybe it was because Amber's sickness was too deep or gone too far.

Amber's death was near, that was for sure. Minna noticed her brown skin had turned a pasty yellow in the last few days, and her eyes had a yellow tinge, too.

"What your name, white girl?"

"Minna Goldmich."

She finished with the dressing, making the bed in silence.

"Crazy ... trust some white woman."

Minna stared at Amber.

"Big brother Sam ... only kin."

Minna nodded.

"Got to see him 'fore I die." She stared hard at Minna. "Unnastand?"

Minna nodded.

• • •

"But Moishe, she just wants to see her brother. She's not going to live much longer. He's the only family she has."

"You're not going into that part of town, I don't care what reason you think you have." His red hair was wild. He looked like their father: mean and hard.

"I thought maybe you'd go with me." She was so scared she barely could get the words out.

"I'm not an errand boy, especially for some colored trash." He shook his head in disgust. "You are a stupid girl. I wish I could send you back to all the other ignorant peasants in Russia. That's why I left them behind and never looked back."

"I wish you could send me back, too."

Moishe ignored her and paced back and forth near the kitchen table. When he spoke again his voice was low and scary. "Why have you stopped going to school?"

Minna knew her face was red, heat seared her ears and within she could hear her heart pounding wildly. "They put me with the youngest children. Everyone laughs at me. I couldn't stay."

"So they laughed at you, huh?" He grimaced and kicked at the kitchen chair. "Tomorrow you will go back to school and work on the ward afterward."

"I'm never going back!" Once she said the words, she realized that had been her plan right along.

Moishe paced around the table. Minna felt him studying her and she was embarrassed. It seemed like forever before he spoke. When he did, there was finality in his tone:

"You look like a grown woman, Minna ... not a fifteen-year-old child. So I will have you placed in the nursing program where you will learn not only how to take care of others, but yourself as well." He sat down at the table and rubbed his fingers back and forth on the flowered oilcloth.

"This is America, little sister. There are many opportunities here, but it's a hard world. You will have to learn to stand on your own two feet. Do you hear me? Your own two feet!"

. . .

They were mostly wooden shacks with little or no paint on the outside, lined up in a crooked row on either side of a dirt street. She walked down the middle kicking up dust that landed on her new blue dress, and her hat tied under her chin was choking her. Every now and then she noticed a little flower garden in the front of a house, but most times space was taken up by colored people standing around or sitting on steps. Some peeked out of windows, but she sensed that all their eyes were on her.

It wasn't until she spoke to one of the colored aides at the hospital that she had been able to find directions to Amber Bout's house. She'd been afraid to ask any of the whites for fear they would tell her brother. When she explained about Amber, the woman gave her the directions, but looked at her as though she were crazy.

Maybe I am.

But Minna couldn't ignore Amber's request. The dying woman had a right to see her brother, even if no one else seemed to think it was important.

It had been a long, hot walk from the hospital and Minna was now so scared, perspiration ran down the length of her arms and legs. She bit into her lip to keep her teeth from chattering even in the summer heat. She pushed away any thoughts of Moishe finding out what she was doing, as though not thinking about it would keep him from knowing.

She clutched a soggy piece of paper in her hand, and was sure she had followed the drawing the woman at the hospital had given her. The lines were like chicken scratches, but they were supposed to take her to Sam Bout.

Over the last mile she'd seen no women on the streets and the sun was now very low in the sky. Minna stopped several men and showed them the paper with the address. Some walked away without a word, some pointed straight ahead. Three or four little children followed her and occasionally pulled on the hem of her dress, then scampered away when she turned to them. They laughed out loud, white teeth bright against their dark faces, and teased her some more before finally running away.

Just as she was beginning to think of turning back, a large group of men approached, then encircled her. One of them grabbed her arm and spun her around. She screamed but the group closed in until she was smothered in the heat of their sweat.

"What you want wit' Sam?"

She swallowed her words in a clutch of fear.

"White bitch ain't gonna bring nuttin' but grief down on us. What she want? Get rid of her."

"I ... I work at hospital," Minna said, gulping back her fear.

"Wha you say, white woman?"

Minna tried to speak up but their hot breath on her face made her feel faint.

"Sam, you best go in the house while I take care of this."

Minna reached out. "You ... you Sam Bout?"

Finally her voice had returned. She screamed, "I help your sister in hospital. She send me."

There was a low murmur in the crowd of men. Women suddenly began elbowing their way through the gathering, pushing the men away.

"Lord a'mighty. Leave that girl alone," said a fat colored woman who was strong enough to push her way to the front of the crowd. "Can't ya hear? She here 'cause of Amber."

When she reached Minna, the woman's dark arm engulfed her shoulders. Minna's world took a quick spin before she sank to the ground.

When she opened her eyes, she was lying across an old torn sofa in one of the houses. The room was very clean, furnished mostly with wooden chairs and a large cross that took up most of the wall. The woman who'd helped her was smiling down at her and holding a drink of some sort in her hand.

"You drink this. Make you feel strong ag'in."

Minna sat up slowly and reached for the cup. "Thank you."

"Now you tell Elsie what you doin' walkin' around these here parts."

Minna looked at a sea of dark faces staring in the windows. The doorway was packed with men and women whispering to each other. Sam Bout was just inside the room.

"Amber is dying," she said softly to Sam.

"Now, how you know that?" he answered, his voice cracking with anger.

Elsie gently took Minna's hand. "Sam here raised little Amber when they mama died." Elsie shook her head; her eyes seemed to be filled with a bottomless sadness that reminded Minna of her own mother. "Amber was only two years old. Sam and Amber only have each other."

Elsie said softly, "Why Amber send *you?*"

"There was no one else." Minna looked at Sam. "There isn't much time left."

"How you know that?" he asked again.

Minna couldn't answer. Instead, she turned away from the pain in Sam's eyes.

• • •

"I'm ashamed to call you my sister, Minna Golmich. I told you not to go to that nigger town. But no, you had to go looking for trouble, just like you did back home."

"Why do you hate those people? They were kind to me. Sam Bout loved his sister … she died in his arms."

"Two steps before the police came looking to take him back to prison."

"But he never hurt anybody. They locked him up for stealing food."

"I suppose stealing food makes it right. He's a thief, Minna. Don't you understand?"

Any English she might have learned disappeared. She yelled at him in Russian. "All I know is that you are as cruel and as selfish as our father. I am your sister and you treat me like an unwelcome stranger."

He slapped her hard across the mouth. "And what made you think you could talk to me like that?" He took her by the shoulders and shook her hard. "Or do just anything you please? Or go anyplace you want? I said you couldn't go to that nigger town!"

Minna shoved his hand away, rubbed a spot on her face that stung like a bee bite. In that instant, any love she might have had for him disappeared. She stood tall, thrust out her chin and stepped closer to him. There was only a breath between them when she spat out the words.

"I'm glad I did it and I would do it again. I never want to be cruel or heartless like you."

"Better to be cruel than stupid."

"I don't care what you say anymore, Moishe."

"You'd better listen to me, Minna."

"I did listen to you. You told me to stand on my own two feet. That's what I did."

Chapter 17

Albuquerque

The 747 floated through layers of clouds on its sweeping descent into the Albuquerque airport. A constant hum from the jet engines was hypnotic. Sophie put her book on her lap and let her mind sift through stratospheres of thoughts and ideas about herself and her family.

After Minna and Saul, there was only her mother, her uncle, and Leah—all so unlike, they might have been randomly tossed onto the planet.

Uncle Aaron was a mystery. Any impressions she had were based on her mother's emotional outbursts of anger and disappointment. He was like a stranger; he never came to California to see them and her visits with him or his family had been short and rare when her mother took her along to visit New Mexico.

In the last two years she'd yearned to know more about her cousin Leah. At first, she only wrote to her. Now, they talked on the telephone at least once a month. Although Leah was a teenager, their conversations made Sophie feel close to her cousin.

She turned to the window as the plane floated toward the Sandia Mountains with such ease it could have been a kite guided by a thread of string. They seem to hover above the desert—the sand looked soft and gentle with the pink hues of the setting sun creating a deceptive, benign patina. The mountains were beautiful but eerie as they spread across the skyline like a giant saw with jagged granite teeth biting into the horizon. Below lay the sprawl of Albuquerque. In the dying light, from mesa to mountain, the city was surrounded by an ugly thick cover of smog.

Was Grandma Minna out there?

Sophie abruptly turned from the window.

A faraway look is what she remembered most about her grandmother. Grandpa Saul had been animated, filled with questions, answers. But Minna always seemed lost in the in-between—a place where dreams and secrets mingled in wary silence.

When her grandparents lived in New York City, she would stay with them during the summer months. It was there that she became interested in painting. Northern California offered beautiful tree-studded hills, but New York, with its multiple museums, opened her mind to a different kind of beauty. She discovered the complexities of art with its world of color: a place where symmetry and chaos co-exist—functional, imaginative, fantastic, somber. In New York she surrounded herself with art, delved into the expressions of joy, despair, curiosity, love, hatred. The entire amazing spectrum lay exposed for her to study.

She would sit in front of a painting and pretend she was the artist, explain to herself why she created it that way and what she was trying to reveal, or maybe hide from the world.

Her secret quest was to locate every depiction of Christ and study it. She was sure one of them would have an answer as to why humanity tortured those who separated themselves from the crowd. As a Jew, she wondered what her family would think if she told them about her research. She never did.

Not even her Grandpa Saul.

Instead, it was to him she confided how her colors were a secret code of thought. He would try to explain beauty to her: its sheerness, its rapture, the folding, the unfolding, the singularity, the duality. What she didn't grasp then, she better understood now. With pangs of disappointment, she realized that she could never talk to Grandpa Saul again.

The captain's modulated voice informed them they would be at the terminal in ten minutes. As the plane dipped toward the runway, she put her book away and speculated on what she could do or expect to find in New Mexico. She'd mainly come to support her mother, but there were things she wanted to know about her grandmother, and the rest of her family.

Sophie closed her eyes, visualized Minna:

What were you trying to tell me, Grandma, when you lay next to me, hugging me in the darkness? Tales about Russia, the earth, the animals, the steppes, great-grandmother Frieda. "Frieda the healer, the keeper of the flame." What had it all meant?

How much easier it was to grasp meaning in something tangible like paintings and sculptures. They existed in a three-dimensional world and allowed her to reach out, to touch something solid. What Minna described was a wisp of air, a scent of mystery, strange talk of a golden light, of connecting within a cosmic realm where healing and God were one. Sometimes Sophie thought she knew what her grandmother meant without really knowing why, yet if she had been asked to explain any of it, her mind would have grasped only soft nothingness.

• • •

Leah flung her arms around Sophie while Cynthia stood on the sidelines.

"Was it a good flight? I couldn't believe you were actually coming. How is Aunt Frieda? Is she going to fly down, too?"

"Leah, let her catch her breath," Cynthia said. "The poor girl has hardly touched the ground and you're off and running with a million questions."

"I'm sorry, Sophie. I'm just so happy to see you. You look just like your pictures."

127

"I couldn't wait to see you, either," Sophie said, hugging Leah tightly.

"Before we get cozy let's go pick up your luggage." Cynthia smiled, offered a hand to Sophie. "Nice to see you again. You were quite young the last time we were together."

Sophie realized her aunt was undecided about Sophie's visit. But when she stared into Leah's blue eyes, Sophie saw excitement. It was almost like staring into a mirror. Both of them had bright red hair and their rounded bodies had the same tall, strong frame that belonged on a farm. Definitely unfashionable in a Barbie culture.

The airport, with its southwestern Native American theme, was captivating. Warm terra cotta colors seemed out of place in the artificial air-conditioning.

"Any news about Grandma Minna?" Sophie asked.

"Here we are babbling on and haven't said a word about Grandma," Leah said. Her blue eyes became melancholy; her whole body seemed to droop.

"Don't be silly, honey," Cynthia said. "Nothing we say is going to change anything. People are out there searching for your grandmother. Please try to be grown up about these things."

After they collected the luggage and left the terminal, the air hit Sophie like a slap of hot putty. It was difficult to breathe. Even though it was dusk, the sun might as well have been high in the sky. Cynthia opened the trunk of a silver-blue BMW and tossed Sophie's things inside.

"Your uncle should be home by the time we get back. He's looking forward to seeing you."

The minute they were on the way, the air conditioner blasted away the heaviness of the heat. A cool breeze flowed through Sophie's hair, bringing an immediate sense of relief.

• • •

Aaron gathered Sophie in his arms as soon as she entered the house. For the first time, she understood what her mother had been trying to tell her about her uncle—when he focused his attention on you, you were caught up in a strange sense of security and love, but when that attention drifted, you were left stranded on the top of a mountain.

"I thought Frieda was coming. This is a big surprise."

"Too many banquets right now. Mom said you told her there wasn't much she could do." Sophie shrugged. "So here I am."

She allowed herself to sink into a large leather sofa. Leah immediately plopped down beside her. Cynthia brought in a tray of hors d'oeuvres and iced tea. Sophie knew the miniature quiches had come out of a box in the freezer—Cynthia didn't seem the kind of person to slave over food. "You know, Uncle Aaron, I've been wondering if we could go to the nursing home where Grandma lives?"

"I don't see why not. We'll go first thing in the morning."

"Well, actually, I was hoping we could go now."

Cynthia's eyes widened. "You must be kidding." She wrinkled her face into tight frown lines. "It's eight o'clock."

"I don't know, Sophie. They don't allow visitors after six. The nursing home might refuse," Aaron said, his voice cracking.

Leah squeezed Sophie's hand and remained silent.

"It seems to me they're directly responsible for this whole mess," Sophie said. "You did say this was a high security facility, didn't you? They might at least make some concessions under the circumstances. And since Grandma had her own room ..." She let the words trail off while she studied her uncle.

He broke into a sweat even though the room was cool and comfortable. Cynthia bit her lip, remained silent while Leah held

129

her breath. Moments passed. A clock chimed somewhere in the house. Sophie waited.

"Why do you want to go there?" her uncle finally asked. "It's just a small room with a barred window. There's absolutely nothing to see."

"Maybe. But I still want to go." Sophie scooted to the edge of her seat. "Maybe there'll be something … anything that could help us find her."

"That's ludicrous," Cynthia said. "What do you think she'd do … leave a map? She's totally loopy. Doesn't have a marble in her head that doesn't rattle."

"I'll call," Aaron said quickly, moving toward a telephone. When someone answered he made his request in a gruff voice, then seemed surprised.

· · ·

The sound of canned laughter could be heard in the distance as they moved single file down the corridor of the nursing home—the administrator, followed by Aaron, Sophie, and, finally, Leah. Cynthia refused to come.

Most of the lights in the individual rooms were out, but occasionally they saw the glow of a television as they walked by. The smell of disinfectant seared Sophie's nostrils as she wondered about these people's lives, wondered what they thought about from day to day. Did they still dream? Did they still hope?

The first thing she saw as they entered Minna's room was a six-inch wide golden-yellow ribbon that hung from the window to the floor. Sophie stared at it for a long time, could see it had been fingered repeatedly. Smudges of grime streaked the ribbon but it was still bright as the lamplight reflected off the satin.

"There's really not much to see," the administrator said in a soft, wary voice.

"It's hard to imagine someone's life crammed into one small room," Sophie said.

"Maybe. But she doesn't have much in the way of belongings … and she doesn't seem to want anything," Aaron said. "Well," he added, pointing, "except for that ribbon. It's been replaced over and over and she's fussy about the color."

Sophie wondered why her uncle continued to be so uncomfortable. "When was the last time you saw Minna?"

Leah turned away from the both of them.

"It's been a long time," he said softly. "Leah's the faithful one … comes to see her at least once a week."

Sophie felt a flash of anger, but who was she to judge? Her own mother hadn't seen Minna for a long time and Sophie last saw her in New York three years ago.

The administrator shifted from foot to foot before finally saying, "I'll wait for you in the front office."

Sophie moved to the dresser. She ran her fingers through the small selection of clothes in each of the three drawers. There were no clues about Minna here. She walked to the closet— five dresses and two pairs of shoes plus a long Persian lamb coat hung neatly. As she looked closer, moth holes scattered between the black curls of fur seemed to jump out at her. Except for the yellow ribbon, everything was impersonal and empty. The room of a mannequin—no past, no present, no future.

All three sat on the small bed, stared at the yellow ribbon.

• • •

The air was cooler now that the sun had disappeared. Minna tried to gather some spit in her mouth but her sand-coated tongue

131

stuck to her cheek. The lights of the town seemed very far away and she was too tired to move toward them.

The moon was perfectly round as it hung in its nothingness. She stared at it for a while until her eyes drooped. She laid her head on the sand—the diminishing heat still radiated to the raw skin of her face, but she couldn't find the energy to sit up again.

Stars dipped onto the horizon.

So close.

She reached for their brightness, but Orion and the Seven Sisters eluded her, as they always had. Why was something so beautiful always out of reach?

No one could answer that except her mother. A question within a question: "Would they be more beautiful if you could touch them?"

"Mommy?"

Her mother's face, round as the moon, hung suspended in the night sky. "Time to go to bed, Minna."

"So hot."

"I know, little girl, but you need to rest."

Minna looked around at the shadowy sagebrush—in the diminished light, the bushes looked like splintered beds. She tried to imagine herself in bed, her mother hovering over her.

A flash of shooting stars scattered across the sky and in a rush fell to earth.

Chapter 18

Spanish Flu Pandemic
1918

Minna fingered the wrist of the dying child, groping for some sign of life.

"Don't die, little boy! Please don't die."

As she prodded his neck, the faintest string of beats blossomed under her fingers, then disappeared into nothingness.

"Get up!"

Trembling, she shook the ten-year-old hard by the shoulders. His limp head jerked violently back and forth.

Oh my God!

She had barely examined the boy, barely touched his skin, and now, staring at her fingers, she realized they had no memory of him.

Such a short train of events: Carried in, hacking, coughing, gasping for air. No more than five minutes had passed since he was dumped on one of the few empty cots by a silent, overworked orderly. Minna had called out for the orderly to stay, but he turned and left, slowly pushing his gurney now loaded with a dead woman.

One dead woman. Just one of many who had died and accumulated in the ward in the last hour—the flu was sucking the life out of everyone in its path.

Her eyes blurred as she looked around the packed ward. She wanted to scream for help, but who could she call? There were no others standing in this sea of misery; doctors and nurses were sick or dead along with everyone else.

Her eyes felt full and strange as she gazed at the wall-to-wall patients. Most were feverish, tending to themselves, while the dying closed their eyes with no one to hold their hands.

For a moment she listened to the screeching of those calling out in a delirium of spiking fever. The words swirled around her: Mommy … Papa … Etta … Ruby. Names whispered or screamed in desperation or resignation. Some stared vacantly at the ceiling, others pointed into the empty air moments before death overtook them. All of them polluted the air with a rank smell of urine, feces, vomit, and worst, the reek of helplessness.

Runawayrunaway.

It was all she thought about while tending patients or curled up in her own bed. But could she run from this cruel God? Could she outrun His judgment of mankind? Of herself?

A letter from home said her mother, brother, and sister were still alive, but the disease had swallowed up her father. Four years since she'd left Russia and still her hatred for him remained an ugly stain corrupting her soul. At first there was grim satisfaction when she heard of his death, but then guilt settled in and she was haunted in her dreams by his screaming, and by the kind face of her Uncle Heshie who also had died in the past year.

Minna edged closer to the dead boy. There was barely room to stand in the spaces between the clog of bodies. She caught a whiff of death. It mingled, then overrode the stink of her body odor. It had been days since she had taken a bath, and over forty-eight hours since she'd slept.

She allowed herself a moment to finger a loose strand of the child's kinky hair. The rest was sweat-plastered to his small skull.

How many times since coming to the hospital had she stood over beds and watched children like this die? Diphtheria, measles, small pox, pneumonia, malnutrition.

Now influenza.

Creeping signs of death settled like a heavy blanket over the child. She removed a tiny mirror from her pocket and positioned it under his mouth and nostrils: no sign of breath, black skin now a pasty gray, pupils fixed and dilated. She gently closed his vacant eyes.

"Poor li'l child."

She didn't need a doctor to pronounce this boy dead. He was gone. Not wanting to let go, she stared at the muscles of the young face, frozen in a grimace of desperation, hands in tight little fists.

Minna straightened, tried to pull herself together. "Who are you, little boy? Where is your family?"

She gently unclenched his hands and placed his arms at his side. Emptiness from his body filtered into her bones, settling heavily with a coldness that took her breath away.

Three years as a probie, one year as a trained nurse, and she still cried about every dying person as though their death was her personal failure.

Today, death left her dry-eyed and exhausted.

Without warning, a wave of heat swept over her. Her legs gave way and she fell to the floor. She laid on her back, puzzled by the piles of dust and dirt, papers, old dressings, bits of food, all scattered on the grimy tiles around her. Something was wrong. Hadn't she scrubbed these floors almost daily for the last four years? Hadn't she spent hours rolling bandages? Hadn't she fed patient after patient and cleaned every mess they made? She stared up at the cots hovering above her like distorted umbrellas at the seashore. What were they doing up there while she lay wasted and still? Then darkness closed in, telescoped around her until there was only one bright spot of light, and soon it blinked out.

The Russian Girl

• • •

"Stupid child! ... Why can't you learn anything? ... Can't get along ... Speak English, you idiot! Forget Yiddish! Forget Russian! How will you ever be an American? Take you out of school ... Big ... Stupid .... Old looking .... Put you into nurses' training .... Can't be smart .... Be useful .... Serve! Serve! Serve!"

Minna's eyes drifted open. For a moment Moishe's face floated by, then returned.

"Minna, Minna! Wake up!"

Always yelling at her, always angry.

"Minna, do you hear me?"

He made her feel lonely; he made her sad. He made her wish she'd died in Russia. Her tongue was sluggish, a fat and sloppy foreign object. "Mommy, forgive me. I tried to save them all."

Moishe's hovering face was pale and worried. She tried to speak again, but instead she drifted away.

• • •

The Desert

Tem-na-ia noch, tol'-ko pu-li svi-stiat po ste-pi, tol'-ko ve-ter gu-dit vprovo dakh, tusk-lo zvez-dy mer-sa-iut.

Minna sang, stared at the stars. Pinpoints of wavering lights blinked back at her among the softness of the Milky Way. She felt safe in their company, knew there was an endlessness that she was a part of. She didn't belong here. She belonged out there in the heavens. Out there she would find the golden light she'd lost so long ago.

The blisters on her mouth burned. The same kind that covered her mouth when she almost died from the flu.

136

Blink. Blink. The stars froze. The sky opened up. Her brother's face appeared, hovering over her.

"Stupid child! Stupid!"

She raised her fist and laughed at his face. "Did you think I would be your slave forever? Clean the rooms, your clothes, your dishes. Never a thank you. Never a smile."

Why couldn't she have something to drink? She sucked harder on a stone she had found, which only reminded her that her lucky marble and her Star of David were gone.

What had happened to them? She wept, sobbing until an animal-like groan filled the air. She looked around in surprise, wondering where the noise had come from. Forgot what she was crying about.

Shadowy sagebrush was highlighted by moonbeams dancing in the softness of the night. How lovely. Almost like her golden light.

Where had it gone?

The buzz of a radio across the desert interrupted her thoughts:

HOTTEST DAY OF THE YEAR … HEAT WAVE PREDICTED TO GO ON WITHOUT RELIEF FOR THE NEXT TWO DAYS.

She was so tired. The sound was comforting even though the words were meaningless.

Voices came closer. She curled up tightly under the scraggly limbs of a sagebrush. Blasting music filled the air, made the sparks of moonlight dance faster.

Her mouth was too dry to sing anymore. She whispered:

Dark is the night, only bullets whine over the field.

Then she turned toward the bright globe in the sky, the side of her face resting lightly on the sand. She stared at the Milky Way and remembered her mother singing:

Tem-na-ia noch, tol'-ko pu-li svi-stiat po ste-pi

137

Chapter 19

Birmingham to New York City

Minna couldn't breathe—her lungs were filled with so much fluid she drowned with each ragged breath. Fiery hallucinations surrounded her, tossed her into a pit of belching flames. She drifted high above, watched Moishe fight hard to yank her from death's jaws. Finally, the golden light surrounded her and she settled back into her body and slept.

When the infection passed, Moishe seemed grateful she was still alive. She recovered slowly, and during that time, he was tender and caring and swore he would be the considerate brother she needed. But once she was well, he was barking orders again. Everything was the same—never spoke to her as a person, never questioned how she felt about anything.

Often she thought she would be better off dead, or at least housed in the isolation wards where it would be worth risking disease if it meant having someone to speak with. She pined for her lost homeland, worried about her mommy so far away, and feared that she would never see her again.

Her decision to leave Birmingham came after receiving a letter from her mother—she, Sarah, and David, were coming to America in six months.

When Minna told Moishe she was leaving, he promised again that if she stayed things would be better. When she refused, he'd turned nasty.

"I'm not giving you one single penny," he said. "You'll stay right here where I can watch over you, you silly child."

"I'm eighteen, not a silly child. I don't need your money to go anywhere. I have my own money."

He sneered. "Where will you go?"

"Mommy, David, and Sarah will be coming in six months." Just the sound of the words made her happy. "I want to be ready for them. I'm going to New York and find a job."

He stared at her with piercing eyes. For a moment she was stunned, turned into a small, very backward child.

"Mommy? Did you say Mommy? This from the grownup going off to the big city?" He moved in closer, and with every finger-poke on her arm she flinched, sank deeper into humiliation. "Isn't it time you called her 'Mother' like the adult you claim to be? And what makes you think she'll stay in New York? I've made arrangements for her to come to Birmingham."

"I want to be there. I don't want her to be alone in a new country, the way I was." Minna hadn't cared what she said after that. "Where were you? Where have you been all these horrible years of being a stranger in this new world? You think I don't know about the women whose bodies you used for pleasure? Think I don't know about time you had for everyone but your sister? My big brother Moishe was supposed to be my lifeline. That's what Mommy promised."

His face flushed a rosy red. "What the hell are you talking about? What horrible years? I saved your miserable neck bringing you here to America. I gave you a chance to become a nurse, an independent woman. Paid good money to have you tutored in English, even lied about your age after you dropped out of school so I could get you into nursing school. This is how you repay me?"

"Am I to have no life of my own? Am I to wash your clothes, feed you forever like some slave?"

"I'm a doctor. I couldn't drop everything to run off to New York because you came to America ... or sit by your side gossiping like a useless little girl. I have to tell you this? Can't you see for yourself?"

"Well, I've been busy for the last four years, too, or doesn't what *I* do count?"

For the first time she was telling Moishe exactly what she thought and although her heart was racing in terror, there was something else—a sense of control, a sense of power.

"And what do you care what I call Mommy? I'll call her what I like and I'll go wherever I please."

Minna realized her brother was now worried. If he wondered where she was getting her money, he said nothing. The gold she had brought with her from Russia had remained her best-kept secret. Whenever she'd become panicky she would feel the hem of her peasant dress where the coins were hidden, tell herself that someday she would be free.

Today was that day.

. . .

The train jolted, pulled slowly away from the station. Minna leaned out the window and waved at the rigid figure of her brother until he was only a black speck in the distance. A sigh escaped her lips, an unbearable weight lifted from her chest.

She took a deep breath, leaned back in her window seat and let the rhythm of the train loll her into remembering the first time she came to Birmingham.

She wasn't the frightened girl she'd been then. Well, yes, she was scared, but in a different way. Then, all she'd heard was babble, strange sounds that made her feel helpless and alone. Now she understood the voices and they understood her, even though when she spoke she still had a heavy accent and people often asked her to repeat what she said.

She toyed with her hatpin, reset it in her new brown hat with its spray of flowers across the brim—a farewell present from three of the nurses on the day shift—then pulled at the collar of the long brown dress that she'd bought especially for the trip. It had taken her a long time to save the money from her salary, and even though the dress was plain, she liked the cut—it made her look thinner. She felt very grown-up.

An elegant man dressed in a dark wool suit sat down next to her. He tipped his hat and she smiled at him.

"Where are you going today, young lady?"

Minna studied the handsome man, guessed he was somewhere in his forties. "I'm going to New York, sir."

"Have you ever been there?"

"Yes, sir, I have. A long time ago when I first came to America."

He nodded as though she'd said something very important. "Where did you come from?

Minna realized she was confiding in a stranger, yet she could feel his genuine interest. Besides, he had kind eyes and a warm smile.

"I'm from overseas ... Russia. I left four years ago."

He nodded again, waiting. Soon she was telling him all about her life. Everything that had happened since she left her home spilled out like spring water in a rush for freedom. And then she was crying and laughing at the same time.

The man reached for her hand and gently squeezed it. "So you're beginning a new life?"

She smiled.

"And you've been a nurse for four years?"

"Actually a real nurse for only a year." She dabbed at her eyes with a handkerchief.

He held out a hand. "My name is Pincus Levine."

She shook his hand. "Minna Goldmich."

"You know, I've been looking for someone like you."

Minna could feel herself flush, feel her breath catch in her throat. "I don't understand, Mr. Levine."

"I own a brownstone in Manhattan near one of the hospitals. One of the apartments just became vacant this week. You'll need somewhere to live and I think you'll love this place."

"I don't know. Can I afford it?"

"I'll charge you ten dollars a month and you don't have to pay me until you have your first check from the hospital."

At first she was excited, then she became suspicious. Ten dollars was a lot of money. "Why would you do this? You don't even know me."

"I want a good tenant." He rubbed his chin thoughtfully. "Let's just say, you remind me of my little sister who died last year." His face became troubled, his eyes sad as though he would cry at any moment.

• • •

The buildings were tall, some ten stories or more. Pincus pointed out a strange-looking one he called the Flatiron. She smiled when she saw it—it looked as though someone had plopped hard on it, squashing it into its comical shape.

Minna had thought she would remember New York City. Yet, none of it looked familiar—all she really remembered was following the quick steps of the matron from Ellis Island to the train station, and even the station didn't match any of her memories. Still, instead of being frightened, she was filled with sunlight. In six months she would finally see her mother again.

They moved past rooming houses, places where she had planned to live before she met Pincus Levine. All along the street were little shops selling food, clothes, and shoes. Finally, they stood and waited next to metal tracks buried in the rough cobblestone street.

"A trolley will be along soon."

She set down the small, worn cardboard suitcase she had bought from a street vendor in Birmingham.

When the trolley finally came, Pincus paid her fare, which made her uncomfortable although he said it was a city custom to welcome a newcomer. As they rode, he pointed out and described some of the sights.

The city was bigger than Birmingham and much, much noisier. Everybody moved at a rapid pace, while in Alabama people took their own sweet time getting from one place to another: In the summer heat they barely moved at all, their voices slow and syrupy. She listened for a moment to others sitting in the streetcar; their accents told her most of them came from other countries, too.

"We'll get off at the Sixty-Fourth Street stop," Pincus said, tugging at a cord above the window. They stepped down from the car and walked for a couple of blocks, Pincus carrying her suitcase which she'd finally allowed him take.

"Most of the places in this area are brownstones," he said.

She noticed that although the buildings looked alike, some were three stories and occasionally there was a four-story building. All had different designs carved into the cocoa brown stones and many had flower boxes with gay red, yellow, and white tulips swaying with the gentle breeze of the spring day.

"It's so beautiful here."

"Wait until you see your place." They climbed up two flights. Pincus unlocked an apartment door. Sunlight cascaded across the wooden floors of the two rooms that were actually going to be hers.

"But there's no furniture," she said, rushing to look into a closet and pull open another door. "My own bathroom?"

He nodded and smiled. "I have an extra mattress you can use. It won't be long before you'll be able to buy things of your own."

Minna walked to the window. This was like a whole new planet. She could see the trees of a park in the distance and best of all, everything smelled fresh without even the hint of the disinfectants that had followed her to the nurses' dorms in Birmingham.

"How can I ever thank you enough?"

Pincus seemed flustered, but recovered in an instant.

"It'll be nice to have my very own nurse in our building."

• • •

Miss Elliott, the nursing supervisor of St. Helena's Hospital, adjusted her wire spectacles carefully on the bridge of her nose. "I see you received your training at … a hospital in Birmingham, Alabama?"

"Yes, ma'am."

"How old are you?"

Minna hesitated for only an instant. "Twenty-one."

The supervisor nodded. "That accent. Where do you come from?"

"I'm from Bobruysk."

Miss Elliott's thin lips barely spread into a tight smile. "Yes, my dear. But *where* is that?"

"In Russia."

Minna could see Miss Elliott was staring at the Star of David in the folds of her blouse—it had slipped from behind the soft material into view. Just a touch of a frown creased Miss Elliott's forehead.

"Mmmm. I've had Southern nurses work for me before. Take

no offense when I say most of them were very poorly trained and quite lazy."

Minna bit her lip. The supervisor was treating her as if she were not only dumb, but like a badly mannered child. "I can't speak for the others, but I think I'm a good nurse."

"Good is one thing. Lazy is another." Miss Elliott wrote some notes on the paper that reviewed Minna's history and training. "I guess my biggest question about that … hospital you trained in is whether they gave the proper basic nursing education—sweeping, wiping the floors, dusting, taking care of plants and flowers. Nothing makes me more unhappy than to see a beautiful plant wither and die."

Minna stared into the women's disapproving eyes. Her starched and pleated nursing cap—like an upside-down cupcake holder—didn't seem to belong with the granite eyes. The tilt of her head and the folds of her stiff, laundered uniform spoke of a steel-willed woman who would criticize often, smile rarely.

"Miss Goldmich, one of the marks of a good nurse is her ability to see things."

"I think—"

"Please do not interrupt me, Miss Goldmich. I was not finished."

"I'm sorry."

"As I was saying. One of the marks of a good nurse is her ability to see things. From the moment you walk into this hospital, you should be able to spot from far across the room a dirty spill on a table or a disordered bedspread. If you can't, you'll hardly be able to recognize the fine points of change in a patient's condition, which are often important danger signals."

"Yes, ma'am."

"I want you to understand that this hospital only gives the very best of care." Miss Elliott removed her metal glasses and sat back in her seat. "Do you think you can do that in the fine tradition of St. Helena?"

"Yes, ma'am. I think I can."

"You will be on probation for ninety days. Then we will review your salary again, if we choose to keep you."

Chapter 20

April 15, 1919

New York City

Dear Mommy,

I was so upset to hear your trip to America is delayed six more months because of Sarah's health. She has always been the strongest in our family, so it's hard to think of her sick for even a day, much less a whole year. Yet in Birmingham during the influenza epidemic, even strong-looking men collapsed at my feet only to die in minutes from pneumonia, prostration, or high fevers. So, we can only be grateful she's still alive.

I wish I could answer your questions but I don't know why she's been sick for so long or why she continues to shake, to be so nervous. Maybe Moishe would know if you could get him to write to you. He doesn't answer my letters.

You never talk about yourself. How are you doing, especially now that Father and Uncle Heshie are gone? I know you think David can protect you, but I still worry about you in the middle of all the changes that the war and revolution have caused. The newspapers are filled with horrible stories of people being butchered on the streets. It sounds even worse than the pogroms ever were. Of course, nothing could be worse than that.

Nightmares continue to plague me and I worry that I will never see you again. Between the newspapers and my experiences, I continue to be lost in constant confusion. I have so many questions. What is the truth?

149

The Russian Girl

I would feel so much better if you moved into the shtetl. At least there's some safety in numbers and the other Jews will help you. Please think about it.

It's been five years since I left Russia. When I think of home, it makes me sad. Memories of our wonderful farm are fading and it grows harder and harder to picture my beautiful peach tree anymore.

But I like living in New York. It's such an interesting city even though the work at the hospital is very tiring. Most often we work twelve-hour shifts and there's barely time to do anything else except eat and get some sleep.

New York people are so full of fire and energy. Sometimes it takes my breath away just to walk down the street. Alabama was so different. Although people moved slowly and talked sweetly, they did terrible things. They hate Negroes even more than our people.

I volunteered to work in the colored quarter during the influenza epidemic, and although the coloreds live squashed in shacks with barely room to breathe, no bathroom to relieve themselves, or sometimes not even outhouses like we had, they seemed like such kindly people. Moishe looks down on them and calls them terrible names, thinks it's right to hang them, kill them for the smallest of crimes. I've even heard of gangs of white boys just grabbing a colored boy and lynching him on the spot for no reason at all. When I used to ask Moishe why this wasn't wrong, he never had an answer that made any sense.

All of this is so difficult to understand. There's so much I don't know.

Pincus is such a kind landlord, and now he is becoming a close friend. We have gone on long walks together and he helped me celebrate my nineteenth birthday. He took me to such an elegant restaurant in the Waldorf Astoria—a very fancy hotel. I felt out of place even though I wore a beautiful dress Ellen O'Hare helped me buy. (Do you remember, she's one of the nurses I work with?) She took me to a pushcart where this wonderful tailor had piles of the most beautiful clothes you have ever seen. The dress I bought is a deep wine-colored material with red velvet piping. Ellen insisted I buy a pair of bright red shoes to go with the dress, and even though it seemed so loud, I couldn't resist. Sometimes I just sit and stare at the dress, touching the lovely material. I still can't believe it belongs to me.

I feel so much closer to you when I write, but the moment I stop, you seem to vanish along with our wonderful life together so long ago.

Please take care of yourself. I don't know what I'd do if anything happened to you.

Come soon, Mommy. I miss you so much.

Love,

Your daughter, Minna

. . .

"Morning."

Minna curtsied, smiled at Miss Elliott.

The stern-faced supervisor made a deliberate point of stopping to watch her tend to her patients every day during AM Rounds. Her hard critical stares followed Minna's every move until she was visibly shaking. Today Minna was with a septic woman with childbed fever. Emma had delivered several days ago and her

151

breasts were engorged and sore. She moaned in pain, called out for her baby. If her fever didn't break soon, her newborn would be motherless.

"It's all right. Shhhhh," Minna said. She wiped Emma's sweaty hair away from her brow and put a cool cloth on her forehead. She turned her back to Miss Elliott and bit her lip to keep from screaming for her to go away.

Minna pretended to straighten the bed, turned Emma carefully, held her shoulders, and whispered, "You'll be fine. You'll have your baby with you very soon."

Minna's fingers jerked as a raw surge of energy flew from her—a shaft of golden light melted into the skin of the infected woman.

She squinted against the glaring light and allowed her fingers to clutch harder at Emma's shoulders. Minna broke out in a bubbling sweat from the intense heat radiating from the sick woman. One moment Minna was breathless, burning up, then she quickly cooled as if she had been plunged into a snow bank.

Emma's fever had broken.

Miss Elliott watched her closely. Minna felt her eyes boring into her shoulders, but she knew the supervisor would see nothing unusual—she had done this before with crowds of people surrounding her. No one other than her mother ever saw anything. Today would be no exception. Only Minna would know what happened.

She couldn't understand why her powers worked with some and not with others. She wanted to help them all.

Emma stared up at Minna with eyes that reflected the golden light. "I feel so much better."

"I told you would have your baby again soon."

Emma clutched Minna's arm. "Thank you, nurse. Thank you for helping me."

Miss Elliott finally stepped away, tossing over her shoulder: "If you want to keep working here, Miss Goldmich, do something with that mop of red hair. It looks sloppy and it's spreading more germs than it's worth."

Ellen O'Hare muttered, "Grrrr. In God's name, what did you ever do to her?" The petite Irish nurse was a feisty bundle of energy who made Minna smile even though she knew her face was wet with salty tears.

"I don't know why she doesn't like me."

"Oh, stop the belly-achin'! And for all the saints, stop the cryin'. Can't let an old hag push you under. Only picks on you because you're a sweet, quiet, and tidy girl. Learn to be more of a hellion, like me. Punch the old fart a good one right in the eye. See how her majesty's dignity fares prancing around with a big shiner."

"Maybe I will one day."

"Yeah! And maybe you won't." Ellen gave her a knowing smile. "Wake up, Minna! You haven't traveled halfway 'round the world to let some old harpy beat you down."

"But she seems so scary."

"Don't scare that easily with that sweetheart of yours, do you now?"

"Pincus is not my sweetheart!" Minna knew she'd turned a bright red.

"Like to be. Noticed the way the lad looks at you?"

"You always talk about him that way. He's just a friend." But Minna couldn't ignore the heat in the pit of her stomach when she looked at Pincus. The mere mention of his name was enough to make her breath catch.

"Just a friend?" Ellen mimicked, moving onto the next patient, giving her a look.

Minna smiled. Ellen always made her feel better no matter how tired or upset she was.

The nursing duties at the hospital were hard, backbreaking

labors. Miss Elliott's marvelous St. Helena wasn't much different than Birmingham General—scrubbing floors, walls, giving personal care to patients, feeding, changing dressings, assisting doctors with procedures—it was difficult work, and many nights Minna cried herself to sleep from exhaustion. But Ellen made everything brighter. Most of the other nurses were helpful, even friendly, when they had time, but they not only moved at a faster pace than Minna, they seemed to think faster. The doctors remained the same—cold and demanding like her brother, Moishe. She finally decided it must be a requirement for becoming a physician.

That and feeling up the nurses whenever they could get away with it, which was most of the time.

Pasty-skinned Dr. Winston rubbed his hands against her buttocks every time he was close to her. The first time it happened, she let out a piercing scream. He told her to be more professional if she wanted to keep her job.

Yes, she wanted to keep her job. How else would her mother have a home waiting for her when she arrived? But she could smell Winston before she even saw him and winced every time he approached her. One day, Ellen punched him in the gut after he'd cornered Minna in the Nurses' Station.

"Touch her again and I'll pop you in the eye."

"Who the hell do you think you are, Mick?"

Ellen smiled sweetly at him. "Me? I'm the lass who could sully your miserable life. Imagine, waking up one morning with your bloody balls dangling in your miserable hands, screaming in high C. That's who I am."

Flustered, he stubbornly stuck his chin out and asked, "You and what army?"

"I have four big brothers who aren't as sweet and cuddly as I am, Doctor. They especially don't like that word 'Mick.' Mannering you could be very interesting." With that she'd tilted her head and bounced away.

Although there were others to replace him, Dr. Winston had been the worst. He never touched Minna again.

• • •

"Really I should do the cooking for you, Pincus," Minna said as they sat at his dining room table.

He smiled kindly, but he studied her until she wanted to squirm.

"Minna, wake up. Women will be getting the vote almost any time now. You can be one of a new generation of women—women who can sit still while their sweethearts fix dinner."

She squeezed her hands into a fist while her heart skipped several beats. Minna stared in disbelief at Pincus. "Did you say sweetheart?"

"Aren't I your sweetheart? You must know by now that I love you."

Minna jumped up from the table and rushed into the living room. Her head was exploding as she collapsed onto the sofa. Pincus came up behind her, ran his fingers through her hair.

"Don't you love me, Minna?"

"With all my heart." She turned and stared into his eyes. "I'll never love anyone else but you."

He wrapped his arms around her shoulders. "Don't run away from me ... don't run from the person you *can* be ... you must learn to believe in your future."

"I'm just a woman. I'm doing the best I can."

"Minna. Open your eyes. Look around you. This is an important time in your life. You're a nurse, an independent person who has so much to offer."

155

"I'm not sure what you mean ... I don't know—"

"How could you not know?" He sat down next to her and gently took her hand. "Didn't they teach you anything in that nursing school? Teach you about the power you have as a woman?"

"My brother says women are meant to serve. Isn't that my future?"

"During the great war, almost twenty-three thousand nurses served in the Army and Navy—more than ten thousand went overseas. Those were powerful women."

Minna nodded, but she didn't fully believe him.

He lifted her chin. "Many nurses, women, just like you, died in the war, died because of the influenza epidemic. The world needs strong women willing to risk themselves for an idea."

"It frightens me when you talk to me this way. I don't feel strong. I feel small and weak."

He pulled her away from the sofa until they stood in front of a large oval mirror in the hallway. "Look at yourself. What do you see?"

Minna stared, embarrassed. "I see a fat nurse with a pile of red hair." She looked away. "So?"

He turned her head back to the mirror. "What I see is a beautiful young woman with hair the color of a robin's breast, eyes bluer than the sky on a crisp winter day, and a smile that melts my heart."

"Pincus, *you* make me feel important, but inside I know I'm small and weak."

"When are you going to understand the power we have as individuals? The power *you* have as a woman?" He took her in his arms and buried his face in her hair. "You are not weak."

Minna felt her heart pounding against her chest. *Could he be right?*

Chapter 21

Frieda Goldmich gritted her teeth, held onto the sides of her bunk. Waves of nausea doubled her over. She had not kept any food down for days and every lurch and jolt of the ship had her dry heaving. Her insides were like a huge, empty cavern. She moaned, turned from side to side to escape the pain that rippled across her stomach and chest, but nothing brought relief. A deep breath of the dank air in the steerage compartment only made her feel as though someone was crushing down on her ribs. She closed her throat against screams struggling to escape, clamped her nostrils to ward off offensive smells.

The worst were her hallucinations. Others: men, women, children were oozing, spreading their arms and legs like immense blobs of fat spilling over into her tiny space. Even when she closed her eyes she was still breathless with the feel of their suffocating sponginess.

What was she doing here?

Here there was no sky with dots of faraway stars to make her wonder.

Here there was no fresh soil with its special aroma of freedom to make her want to dance barefoot in the moonlight.

Here there were no cows to speak of their pain in their own strange language, to lick her face in gratitude when she healed them. Oh, how she missed their sweetness, their soft breath on her cheek.

Most of all, here there was no Russia, her homeland, her

Motherland, a world where her family had been rooted since the beginning of time.

David was excited and kept sneaking to the top deck to stare at the sky and the waves, but Sarah was frightened and sat quietly holding Frieda's hands.

"Mama, why couldn't we stay?"

"Sshh. Calm yourself." Frieda sat up, took hold of Sarah's shaking hands. "You know they stole our farm. It was not safe."

"But I'm so scared."

Frieda looked at her daughter. Her large brown eyes were soft and trusting like a beautiful cow, but her limbs were wasted and bony since her illness. The Milovich boy had backed out of his marriage commitment when Sarah became ill, leaving her rootless, with a mind that, if not simple, was more childlike with every passing day. The matchmaker had declared Sarah unfit. No one from the village would want her now.

Poor girl. She looks so much like her dead father, a stranger Frieda had lived with for forty-five years. She'd worked, slaved for the man to make him happy, yet the only time he showed any interest in her was when he was rutting like a pig in a pen on the *goyishe* farms.

She tried to think back to the time when his very breath brought her joy. She was sad for a moment. Those memories were only whispers in the dark.

Now, each day that passed, she thanked God for her freedom.

Now, she answered to no one but herself.

Guilt stemmed the rush of thoughts. She hugged Sarah to her breast, forcing herself to overcome the revulsion of her daughter's pressing body. All the pressing, crushing bodies.

Frieda closed her eyes to the waves of nausea that started again.

• • •

The burly sailor reeked of liquor. Every word delivered his foul breath as an assault to Frieda's senses. He held David by the neck of his sweater, shook him back and forth, shrieking in German, "Is this your son?"

Frieda swallowed hard and nodded.

"Next time I'll chain this miserable turd in the brig. You understand, you fat old Rusky piece of shit?"

Frieda nodded again, sorry her Yiddish allowed her to understand the German crewman. The sailor spat in David's face before pushing him to the floor. He stared at her and Sarah as though they were "things," and branded his own putrid smells into their tiny space before he turned, kicked, and elbowed his way to the stairwell.

When he was gone, the others encircled the three of them, an army of rats closing in on its prey. Screams like darting whips lashed hard at the Goldmichs. Spittle slimed their faces.

"Troublemakers! Take their food, throw them overboard!"

"Idiots."

Fists threatened them from every direction.

The crowd froze as a piercing whistle cut through the furor. David stood on his bunk bed, blowing one of the crew's whistles.

"You stupid cowards. *You* will throw us off the ship? *You* will take our food?" He pulled a dagger from a scabbard hidden in his clothes and ran the point of the blade across his dirty palm. In the dim light it left a trail of black blood.

There was a collective intake of breath, then the area became so silent, the only sounds heard were people retching.

David swung the knife in a perfect arc, forcing those closest to him to fall back against the tightly packed crowd. One man's coat was slashed, but he remained silent and wary.

161

"Get out of here. Mind your own fucking business before I plant this into one of your necks."

Frieda stared at her son. He looked like a dirty tramp: clothes torn, sweater unraveling. But what alarmed her the most was the murderous glare in his eyes. Everyone turned away, their anger dissolving like a pinch of salt tossed in boiling water.

Frieda said, "So this is what you have become, hanging out with those Bolshevik killers."

The knife went back in its leather sheath, disappeared, swallowed up by his baggy clothes. "Did you expect me to let them murder us?"

Frieda bit her lip to keep from screaming at him and began picking lice from Sarah's hair. Her fingers rummaged for the bugs; she crushed them with her broken nails, shuddering. "If you would stop running away, none of this would happen."

"You expect me to stay down here and puke my guts out like the rest of you? No, thank you!"

"Do you want to be thrown off the ship, be branded as a troublemaker? Maybe they won't let you stay in America." She glared at him. "Do you want to be sent back?"

"At least I will be with the heroes who rid our country of those stinking, blood-sucking Royalists."

Frieda shook a fist at him. Sarah seemed to shrivel into nothingness. "Those 'heroes' won't even remember you. Do they think of your Uncle Heshie? He was going to change the world, too. Instead, he just died."

"Uncle Heshie was just a cog in a large wheel. The wheel keeps turning without him."

"What have the Reds accomplished by getting rid of the Romanoffs? Nothing, I tell you!"

"What have those parasites ever done for you that you give

them your blessings?" David said, his eyes blazing. "The Reds at least promise a world forged by your fellow workers.

"Rednicks, shmednicks. They are no different than the Royalists. They're all the same. They hate Jews with equal venom."

Sarah's eyes were like twin moons, wide and fearful. She covered her ears and shook her head back and forth.

Frieda thrust her chin at her son. "You think you're so smart. Look at you. Blind to what stares you right in the face." She clutched her belly and rocked before staring hard at her son. "You can't build a new world without better people."

David looked puzzled. "What better people?"

Frieda spit out the words. "People who do not hate."

"You talk like an ignorant peasant woman."

She'd always loved her twenty-five-year old son for his curiosity, his strength, but disgust now shone from every pore, every line of his face, and it made him a stranger.

"And *you* talk like an ignorant child. Am I not the one the Bolsheviks praise? Am I not the worker of a new world order? Isn't the peasant at the heart of your revolution?"

"You're just a woman. What do you know?"

"I'm your mother and I expect more respect from my son. Or are the Bolsheviks against mothers now?"

David sank down on his bunk and turned his back to her and Sarah. "I'm sorry, Mama."

Frieda knew better.

Chapter 22

The shouts and curses of the passengers clawing their way up from the bowels of the ship made Sarah's skin crawl. It was as though a bolt of lightning sizzled her body—she became a dangling puppet controlled by some faraway master.

The noise crushed her concentration, her composure: shoulders, hands trembled out of control. No matter how hard she tried to force herself to stop, winter's ice had settled within.

She knew she didn't look normal shaking like a dervish, and her mother and brother's stares made her feel vile and unclean.

David was one of the first to climb his way up and out of steerage. Others around him held back, their bundles pressed to their chests, giving him plenty of elbowroom. No one wanted to be slashed by the knife they all knew he had hidden in his clothing.

David made her feel sad. He was really a nice person and she knew he loved her, but Sarah hated when he acted like such a bully. Worst of all, she didn't know what to do when he and mother fought. All she could do was shrink up and crawl into a tiny hole where it was quiet—a place where no one could ever hurt her.

"Isn't it time for us to go, Mother?" Her own voice sounded far, far away.

"Soon, *maideleh*, soon." Her mother had always been so strong. Now she looked old and defeated, speaking in a whisper with a rasps that made the hair on Sarah's neck prickle.

Sarah had watched her brother race up the stairs until he was out of sight, but she stayed dutifully next to her mother, who was so sick she could not bring herself to stand.

What was to become of them if they didn't go soon? The

compartment had emptied out except for those who never seemed to adjust to the swaying movement of the ocean. Even now, many of them continued to vomit. At least her mother had stopped. Sarah wrapped her arms around her. Both were exhausted and the silence was a relief. She dozed off until someone poked hard at her arm.

"Get outta here!" It was the same sailor who had brought David down from the top deck. "Did ya think we would feed the pack of you forever? Foreigners! All alike. Drop 'em into a spot ... they think they'll be taken care of. Outta here now, you clumps of shit!"

Sarah's mind's eye shrank until there was only a pinpoint of light. She shook so hard her teeth chattered. Clutching an arm, she helped her mother up. Frieda swayed back and forth until Sarah thought she would fall, but smiling weakly, her mother remained standing.

"The poor woman who gave birth to you must have died of fright the day you were born," her mother said in Russian to the man.

Sarah could see that the crude sailor didn't understand or care what her mother said. He moved away to prod others left behind.

"Come, *maideleh*. Can you carry the bundles?"

Sarah nodded, but she wasn't sure whether she could. Everything floated in near darkness.

. . .

Frieda became stronger with every step. When they reached the main deck, fresh air whipped her hair across her face. She started to tighten her babushka, but impulsively let it slide to her shoulders. She looked up at the skies, closing her eyes to the bright sun.

"Sarah, do you feel that? How warm and sweet the air is?"

"Yes, Mama."

Frieda didn't need to open her eyes to know her daughter was frightened. "Sarah, don't be afraid. We've made it to America."

"Yes, Mother. I'm trying, but … but it's so loud, so noisy."

Frieda searched for David, spotted him at the rail, talking and laughing with the people around him, friends with everyone now. As Frieda watched, she felt the same joy. She wanted to wave her arms, dance, jump with excitement.

She looked from her son to her daughter. He was strong, so strong he never got sick, never got the flu like the rest of the family. But now his father was dead and poor Sarah, although recovered, was drained of vitality and courage. More of her brain ebbed away with each passing day.

At that moment, when the world seemed the brightest it had been for so long, she sent a prayer to the heavens.

Dear God. Please give my daughter back her health, her mind. Please let her thrive in this new place.

David came running up to her like a little child, interrupting her thoughts, flinging his arms around her and Sarah.

"Mama! Sarah! Look! The Statue of Liberty."

• • •

They were shoved into a large building after the boat docked. Sarah clutched her mother's arm and shuffled as quickly as she could. Once her mother was torn from her, pushed ahead by the surging masses. Sarah screamed and everything turned black again.

"Mama! Come back!" She covered her ears and shrieked her mother's name again and again. "Frieda, Frieda Goldmich!"

A man in uniform grabbed Sarah's hair and yanked her out of the flow of people. Everyone shrank back as though she was contaminated. He yelled at her, shook her hard until she thought her head would burst. He poked a finger into her face and screamed at her again.

Although Sarah didn't understand his words, she stopped screaming. Her tongue was caught in her throat, every part of her was shaking, and her eyes spun. Her legs turned to water, she started to collapse when her mother materialized out of the gawking crowd and pushed past the line of ropes to grab onto her.

"Maideleh. It's okay. Mama's here."

"Oh, Mama, what happened to you? I was so afraid. I was all alone without you."

Her mother smiled at the uniformed man and she gently removed his hand from Sarah's hair, then slipped an arm around her shoulder. The world became strangely silent and Sarah was whole again. She stared at her mother who was surrounded by a beautiful shining light. Everything glistened with her presence. Nothing to fear as long as Mama was there.

• • •

Frieda didn't like this Ellis Island. Minna had warned her about the place. She smelled fear in the air, hers mixed in with the others.

The guards wore dark uniforms and fierce expressions as they checked people through the gateways. She held on tightly to Sarah.

David had fallen back into their line until he was with them again.

"How is Sarah?"

"Don't talk as though she's not here. Ask her!"

But he didn't have to ask. Sarah had gone into her own world. She moved like a lost soul, her eyes unseeing, head shaking.

• • •

David was sad for his sister. He'd already heard about the check-in process, knew there would be trouble ahead.

How was she to answer questions without becoming terrified? It took so little to set her off. Would they let their mother stay with her during the questioning, or would she have to go by herself?

He stared at Sarah. She used to be such a beautiful girl. Men in the village had hounded the matchmaker to present them to her right up to the time she turned twenty-five and the Milovich boy came into her life. The family had felt such relief. She had turned down so many suitors, they thought she would never marry.

Then the influenza. The illness that killed their father and sickened their mother and Sarah.

His sister was never the same after that.

Her soft brown eyes and graceful movements, smooth complexion that made you think of thick milky cream, had changed. Her eyes became dull and uncomprehending, skin pasty white.

Maybe that would change now that they were here with Minna. Maybe now Sarah would find peace and security.

Chapter 23

Everyone was funneled into two lines. Frieda watched David for as long as she could, but soon he was swept away in the line for the males.

A throb of pain pierced her. She had relied on David for so long it was hard to imagine life without him.

What if they take him away and I never see him again?

"Where are they taking David?" Sarah asked in a voice Frieda hardly recognized.

"It's all right, *maideleh*." Frieda tucked an arm around Sarah to reassure her with hugs and pats, but nothing she said helped. Sarah shrank into herself and looked at Frieda with empty eyes.

Even though the area was packed with people, the room had a muffled sound. Everyone spoke in whispers, even the children.

Frieda and Sarah inched along with the rest of the women. When they approached the head of the line, Frieda's heart fell as she spotted a tall man in a white coat. She knew he was probably a doctor. He was examining a woman with a torn dress who was so weary she swayed back and forth and could barely stand. Frieda knew the man by his gruffness, his impatience, the way his hands jabbed like sticks, poking, prodding.

He pushed the woman's head back and looked into her eyes, turning the lids until she yelled, "What are you trying to do, blind me?"

The doctor nodded to a matron who moved in closely, tried to calm her speaking in very poor Russian. "Doctor is checking your eyes for disease."

"Tell him I'm not an animal! Tell him he's hurting me!" The woman was filled with rage and pushed at the doctor's arm.

171

"Cooperate, or go back to where you came from." He stepped away, loosened his tie, and stood with his arms folded while the matron translated.

She glared at the doctor, took a deep breath and tossed her head back again.

"That's better." He examined her eyes, this time with an instrument. After a few more minutes he unbuttoned the top of her dress—even though Frieda wanted to look away, she had to watch—and the woman's breasts popped out. He pushed at her roughly, placing an instrument to her chest. Perspiration blossomed, soaked through her clothes and ran down her face as he ran his hand down her belly.

The matron translated. "No baby in here?"

The woman shook her head violently.

He stared long and hard at her, then pointed to the next line. The woman quickly buttoned her blouse and moved away. "Motherfucker," she shouted back over her shoulder.

He nodded to Sarah to step up.

Sarah's face turned bright red and she clutched Frieda, her nails digging into her mother's arm. Frieda moved with her in front of the doctor.

He nodded to the matron. "Just the girl."

Frieda spoke rapidly, softly. "The doctor's just going to examine you. We have to let him if we are to stay in America." Frieda tried to move away from Sarah but her daughter clutched her dress.

The doctor watched for a moment, nodded to the matron to translate: "Well, what is it to be?"

"Can't I stay with her?" Frieda pleaded. "She's so frightened." The tendons on Sarah's neck stood out like ropes stretched to their limits, and her eyes were wild like a dying horse. "Please sir, please!"

The doctor shrugged, and tried to examine Sarah's eyes. She was like stone and would not budge.

"Sarah! *maideleh,* please!" Frieda closed her eyes, whispered in her ears. "Do this for me. Let the doctor examine you." Sarah stood rigidly. "If you don't they'll take you away from me."

Sarah allowed her head to fall back so the doctor could examine her eyes. He was impatient as he pulled and tugged at her lids, opened her mouth, took a flat stick and studied her teeth, her tongue.

Frieda spoke to the matron. "Tell him she has no baby inside." The matron nodded.

Maybe it was Sarah's face: eyes closed, lips stretched into a grimace. Or maybe the doctor was really a decent man, for he took pity on her frightened daughter. He quickly waved her on to the next line. Sarah refused to move, stood next to Frieda and waited until her mother's examination was completed.

The next line moved even more slowly. It seemed like hours before they reached a closed door.

"What are they doing in there, Mama?"

Frieda took her daughter by the shoulder. "Whatever it is, you will go and I'll be right here. I won't let anyone hurt you."

Sarah nodded but her brown eyes were twin puddles of mud.

• • •

Through the closed door Sarah's screams echoed in Frieda's head. "Mama! Mama!"

Frieda shoved away the man guarding the door and barged into the room. A matron on each side of Sarah clutched an arm. They tried to get her to sit in a chair at the table where a doctor sat shaking his head.

"Take your hands off her," Frieda screamed at the matrons as she ran to Sarah. "Do you hear me? Take your filthy hands off her."

The doctor stood. "Are you this girl's relative?" He spoke Russian with the smooth accent of the Ukraine. The softness of his voice stilled Frieda's hand. "How long has … " he leaned across the table so he could read Sarah's tag pinned to her dress, " … has this Sarah had these fits of tremors? How long has it been since her mind was … compromised?"

Sarah pulled away from the matrons, threw her arms around Frieda, and began to sob. "Mama, he asked me such hard questions." Her fingers dug into Frieda's flesh, tears poured down her cheeks. "I couldn't think how to answer. You weren't here. I was frightened."

"Shah, Shah. It's all right." Frieda smoothed Sarah's head, her fingers combed gently through her hair while she spoke to the doctor. "A robber put a gun to her head … tried to take our money."

"When did that happen?" the doctor asked softly.

"In the trains as we rode across Germany. Since then she has had some difficulty concentrating. She's very afraid."

As Frieda looked into the doctor's eyes, she knew he didn't believe the lie.

"Please, sir, she is a very smart girl but she's frightened."

"The rules are the rules. I don't make them but I can't ignore them." The doctor stamped a piece of paper and nodded at the matron. She marked an X on Sarah's ticket, and a yellow X on the arm of her sweater. Inside Frieda's head a blinding spray of red and blue exploded.

"Nooooo!"

174

• • •

Minna walked into the darkened area filled with happiness. She was finally going to see her mother after five long years. But the disgusting smells of unwashed bodies, old vomit, urine, and the reek of defeat made her want to turn and run. This was the Ellis Island she remembered.

She found David, Sarah, and her mother huddled together on a pile of straw.

"Mommy!" The three of them looked at her as though she were a stranger. She bent over her mother. "Mommy, it's me. Minna."

They stared.

"Sarah, David. Don't you remember me? I'm Minna, your sister."

"Oh, for God's sake. Of course we remember you," David said, his eyebrows set in a frown.

It was then Minna saw the X on Sarah's arm. Looking around, she saw that all the people in this room except for David and her mother wore Xs on their arms. Then she knew. These people were being returned to Europe for being ill, pregnant or mentally deficient.

"Oh, Mommy! What are we going to do?"

• • •

The guards came at the crack of dawn the next morning. Frieda had made up her mind. She could not let Sarah return to Germany by herself.

As everyone went through the door toward the ship, the guard stopped David, Frieda, and Minna.

"You cannot go any farther. These people will be leaving shortly."

"Tell him I want to go back with my daughter," she said to Minna.

The guard, about Sarah's age, said, "You will have to buy a ticket." He pointed at Sarah's arm where the X stood out as though she were a branded cow. "They go back for free."

"You don't understand. She can't go alone. She has no one on the other side to help her," Frieda said.

Sarah looked first at Frieda, then at the guard as they spoke. Frieda could see her mind shutting down—she no longer understood or cared what was going on. As they talked, people moved toward the ship, most of them dragging their feet to delay the inevitable.

David gently took his mother's arm. "Mama, you have to let her go."

Frieda turned to her son. His eyes were filled with tears. "How can I let her go? She's my child, my heart, my soul. Davidla, don't you understand? She's your sister."

"Mommy," Minna said, trying to speak between the sobs that choked her. "You have to let her go. We'll find her again. We'll do something."

Frieda hugged Sarah to her. "I can't let her go alone. I can't!" Sarah stood staring blankly, twirling a lock of her hair, humming softly to herself.

An old woman stopped and tugged gently at Frieda's arm. Her eyes were clouded and runny. "Let her come with me." She put an arm around Sarah and gave her a sweet, toothless smile. "I'll take good care of her."

Sarah looked at the woman. "Hello! What's your name?"

"Why, I'm Anya. You and I … we're going to take a long trip together." She gave Sarah a slight nudge and she stepped away from Frieda. "Come, little girl. We will have fine times together telling each other stories. Come along."

Frieda's heart tore at her chest as they walked away. Her arms reached out toward Sarah, empty fingers clutching the air. Minna and David wrapped their arms around her shoulders holding her back.

Sarah turned several times. She waved at them each time. But the old woman gently pulled her along and Sarah would skip every now and then.

As they were about to enter the ship, Sarah turned one final time and gave them a crooked smile.

Chapter 24

Albuquerque
The Desert

"Don't die. Don't die. Don't die. Don't die. Mommy, don't die!"

Minna was startled by the sound of the babbling that ended in an animal grunt. She tried to sit up, but fell, her spine crushing down hard on the packed sand. She groaned, looked at the stretch of desert around her, and couldn't remember where she was.

Waves of nausea, bolts of pain struck her from everywhere. Her feet throbbed, the beat of her heart was agonizing, and her face was raw from the sand blowing across her skin. She screamed at the moon. It stared benignly back from a sky that glowed like sapphire velvet.

Wishing she were dead, she inched farther under splintered sagebrush.

• • •

Leah awakened during the night, her face bathed in a strange golden light.

She lay still, listened. Sound was heightened and she could hear crickets chirping in the far distance while her breathing whistled back at her: wheezy, raspy. Instead of being frightened, she was calm.

The night with its black emptiness still frightened her even at fifteen. It was always then that her asthma slipped out from the shadows to smother her. But this was different—tonight she felt protected, she wasn't afraid.

She crept out of bed and walked through the house until she

stood outside Sophie's room. The eerie golden shimmer took on a life of its own as it followed her and hovered outside the door. Leah laid a palm on its softness reflected on the wall. Her fingers turned to inky filaments against the warm glow.

"What are you?" she whispered.

She knocked softly on Sophie's door. When there was no answer, she silently entered the room.

"Sophie! Are you awake? It's me, Leah."

The light trailed her, dragging her elongated shadow. Leah looked at the sleeping Sophie, then watched the beam spread to include her cousin, who was already covered in silver moonlight.

The luminescence and the golden sheen mingled, flared into a spray of glittering rainbows that flipped and swirled, reborn as prisms floating like wispy seeds in the breeze. She had never seen anything so beautiful.

"Strange, isn't it?" Sophie said, startling her.

"I should be afraid, but I'm not," Leah said. "What is it?"

"I don't know. That same light has been with me ever since I was a little girl. It seems to come when I'm stressed or worried …" Sophie patted the bed and Leah crawled under the sheet, "… or when I'm with Grandma Minna."

"Does Grandma know about it? Did she tell you what it is?"

"The light has been with her most of her life, too, since she was a little girl in Russia," Sophie said. "She called it a healing light."

"Healing light?"

"Grandma said it started with Great-Grandmother Frieda."

"She saw the light, too?" Leah said.

"Frieda healed the cows in their village."

Leah laughed. "Cows? What's so cool about healing cows?"

"The villagers would have starved to death in the winters if anything happened to their cows."

"Did they pay her?" Leah asked.

"Oh, yeah, they paid her all right. They hid our family during the pogroms so Frieda could take care of their cows. I guess that was payment enough."

"You mean you and I are here only because of the cows?"

"As far as I know, the cows are the only reason."

"Why didn't Grandma ever tell me?"

"I don't know … I think you were too young. She's been … out of things for a long time," Sophie said.

"You mean she couldn't remember."

"Couldn't, or wouldn't. She told me the light simply disappeared one day."

"It never came back?"

. . .

Cynthia sat up in bed and pointed a finger at Aaron. "Don't you talk to me like that. How many times do I have to tell you I'm not hired help that has to put up with your abuse?"

"For Christ's sake, lower your voice," Aaron hissed. "We don't need the girls hearing this. Isn't it bad enough their grandmother is lost?"

"I'll speak as I wish."

"Maybe I'd be more civil if you didn't treat me like an idiot. And right in front of Sophie. Hell, I haven't seen the kid in years."

"She's smart enough to know what's going on. Besides, she's not a kid."

"Well, hell's bells, she's a kid to me. My sister Frieda's kid."

"So now you're a loving uncle, a loving brother, too. You certainly have selective memory loss when it comes to your sister. You don't talk to her for months on end, Aaron. Why do you even care what her daughter thinks?"

Aaron moved in closer and glared at her. "One of these days

you're going to open that big critical mouth of yours once too often."

"Threatening me, Mister Lubin, or are you trying to get me all worked up over nothing?"

Aaron, who had been pacing around the bed, sat down heavily on his side of the bed. "Hell, Cynthia, I'm being an ass, aren't I?"

She remained silent.

"It's hard having Mom out there. Where the Christ is she? I can't believe an old lady like her could make it through the day in the worst heat wave we've had in years."

"She's a wily old woman. She's probably sitting on some verandah drinking iced mint tea, telling someone how badly she's treated."

"Very funny," Aaron said.

"I feel sorry for Minna, but I don't feel sorry for you, Aaron. How many times have you told me that you never even liked your mother?"

He stared at her for a long time. "You're a cold woman, Cynthia. I often wonder if anything touches you."

She was flustered for a moment, her eyes glistened with sudden tears. "Living with you has molded me into the wonderful person I am."

Aaron turned away, crawled back into bed. "My parents were always working. They never were around … for me."

"I know that story, Aaron."

He continued anyway. "I was a Depression baby. If it wasn't for Uncle Moishe, I guess we would have starved to death."

"Right! He put your mother to work in his nursing home and your father became his janitor. Do we have to go over this one more time?"

Aaron wondered again what he was doing in bed with this stranger. But he knew the answer. Knew why he'd married

Cynthia. She'd been young, beautiful, and very rich. He'd almost been rich, too, but that was all about to change … unless his mother—

Cynthia flipped over, her back to him. "I'm going to sleep." She clicked off the light on her side of the king-sized bed but he could hear her breathing: uneven and ragged.

Soon he turned off his bedside light, too, and watched the moon through the open window.

He must have dozed. When the phone rang he sat up with a jolt.

"Hello?" He took the walk-around and moved through the house until he was in the living room.

"Aaron, it's me, Carlos."

The hairs on his neck prickled. The chief of police wasn't calling at four in the morning about Aaron's pending bankruptcy. Aaron wanted to be polite but he blurted, "Have you found my mother, goddam it?"

There was an instant of silence. "Yeah. I think we have, I'm sorry to say."

Aaron could barely breathe. "Just lay it on me, Ramirez."

"We found an old lady at the foot of the Sandias. She's at the morgue … do you want to come down now to see if it's her?"

"The morgue? I … I … " One moment he was relieved, almost happy. The next he was remorseful, drowning in guilt.

"Take your time, Aaron. I know this is hard."

He moved to sit, ready to collapse. But in the moonlight he saw Leah and Sophie sitting on the sofa holding hands.

"I'll be down in ten minutes. Where is she?"

"County. I'm sorry, Aaron. We have to autopsy."

"Okay, Okay. I'll be there soon." He set the phone on the coffee table and stared at Leah and Sophie.

"Was he talking about Grandma?" Leah asked in a tremulous voice. Sophie wrapped a protective arm around her.

"I'm afraid so." He was going to be sick. If he didn't get to a john, he'd throw up all over everything. "I have to get dressed," he said, racing out of the room.

"I'm going too," Sophie said, standing.

"Me, too," Leah said, getting to her feet.

• • •

"We're going to the morgue. I think they've found Mom," Aaron said to Cynthia.

"I'm sorry, Aaron." There was a moment of silence. "We? Did you say 'we'? You're taking my daughter to a morgue?"

"If you can talk her and Sophie out of it, I'd be very grateful. This is going to be hard enough as it is."

"I don't see how we can allow either one of them to do this. I don't want our daughter to go."

"Fine," Aaron said. "You argue with her."

Cynthia scooted down in the bed, her eyes hard and angry. She finally turned away. "Go ahead, take them. Maybe they'll learn life isn't a bed of roses."

"That's a lesson we all could learn."

With her back to him, she said, "Soon this will all be over and we can get back to having a life."

"Yeah."

• • •

Even though he knew the temperature outside had dropped, the air in the garage was like an oven. They climbed into the car and in a moment Aaron had the air conditioner blasting away.

"I'm not happy with the two of you going."

"Uncle Aaron, we have a right to know what's happened to Grandma Minna."

"She is our Grandma, Dad. How could you think of not taking us?"

Aaron let the conversation lapse into silence.

In a few minutes they were parked outside the county hospital. They entered the building, a sheriff's deputy walked up to them.

"Are you Aaron Lubin?"

"I am." He pointed. "This is my daughter and this is my niece."

The deputy nodded. "The Chief said I should take you to the morgue."

The cousins held hands and followed. "This is spooky," Leah said as they took the elevator to the basement.

"It's just a building," Sophie said.

They walked through swinging glass doors. Carlos Ramirez was talking in a soft voice to a morgue tech behind the desk. He turned away when he heard them approach.

"Thanks, John," Carlos said to the deputy that escorted them. He shook Aaron's hand. "I'm really sorry." He raised an eyebrow in the direction of Leah and Sophie.

Aaron shrugged. "It's their grandmother. They have a right to know, I've been told."

"Still … it's going to be rough."

"Let's just get it over with," Aaron said, his voice cracking.

They walked through another set of doors into air heavy with the musty smell of mold and strong disinfectants. Aaron's eyes watered. They stopped in front of a panel of stainless steel compartments. The cousins squeezed each other's hand.

"I think you girls should wait outside," Carlos Ramirez said. "This is going to be difficult."

"We want to stay," Leah said. Sophie nodded.

The chief stared long and hard at them before nodding to the tech. He opened one of the bins to slide out a sheet-covered body.

"Aaron, the animals had gotten to her before we did. I'm sorry."

Aaron gulped and pulled the sheet back. "Oh, my God…" Half of the woman's face was shredded, an eye and ear was missing.

Leah and Sophie cried out, covered their eyes.

Aaron studied the mutilated corpse for a long time before finally croaking out the words, "Carlos, that's not my mother."

. . .

A fiery ball climbed up from the mountains, rising so quickly, prickles like hot pokers stabbed at Minna's flesh. She winced, her eyes slit to a crack. She examined the sun.

It glared back at her.

She tried to remember where she was but her head was filled with gauzy cotton. Her mind jumped from thought to thought: first it was her mother, then it was Pincus, then her brother, David.

Finally she rolled back and forth in the sand trying to find a way up. She settled on her knees, then grunted herself erect, each part of her screaming in agony.

"It's not your fault they sent Sarah away. You've got to eat, Mommy. Please eat or you'll die!"

Minna shook her head and walked in circles, held her arms up to the sky.

"David, Pincus, tell her she has to eat." She stomped her feet. "Don't tell me that. Make her do it."

She turned away from the sun and began to stumble ahead. Her feet scraped against shards of glass before she realized she was barefooted. She looked dumbly at the ground, saw where she had left her slippers. She shuffled back to them and jammed a foot into each.

"David, help me," she muttered. "Eat, she has to eat. Mommy, Mommy. My Mommy's wasting away."

Tears blinded her for a moment. She wiped them away with a sleeve. "All you had to do was eat, Mommy."

A soft breeze crossed the desert and a small dust devil rose and twirled in front of her. It lasted for a breath and was gone. For a moment, the confusion, the indecision, the emptiness drifted away. She looked around and saw the wasteland of desert, saw the broken bottles, realized she was alone in a landscape of heat and nothingness.

Wasn't there something she was supposed to remember?

She turned a full circle, almost fell in the spin.

"What am I doing here?" She looked toward the city. "Why, that's Albuquerque. Aaron must be there. My God, what am I doing out here?"

She shook her fist at the sun. "Is that you, God? Isn't it just like you to hide behind an unbearable brightness so no one can find you? Oh, yes. Hide from me. Hide after you've taken away everything that ever meant anything to me. My mother, my Sarah, David, Pincus. Now you've left me out here to die in this nothingness.

"Pincus!"

She screamed his name over and over. Not even his echo remained.

Her eyes closed against the sun. The color red spread everywhere, starting as wispy tentacles, spreading like a huge grasping hand. The sun burned her face, its heat turned her stomach, stewing her insides. She opened her eyes as another dust devil did a brief dance before returning to the desert floor.

White cotton spread through her brain again.

She started singing.

The Russian Girl

"Little curly hair in a highchair.
"What's your order for today?
"Little curly hair in a highchair.
"I'll do anything you say …"

Chapter 25

New York City
1927

His arms wrapped around her, lips trailed across her neck, eyes. Her fingers clutched, wound around black ringlets of hair. Heat rose between them, spread through her groin.

She had to say it, had to say it now. "Pincus, please, please, let's have a baby," Minna whispered.

His voice was breathless, words slurred. "We promised. No marriage ... no children." He squeezed tighter as he moved within her. "No innocent children ... in this world."

She forced herself to think. "But we've been together for eight years ... I love you so much. I want to have our baby. I don't care about anything else except us ... all that matters."

Her thoughts were scrambling as she rose to meet his thrusts. Ideas evaporated as she hungered for him. "More, more ... please more. Don't stop." Their bodies entwined in mindless rapture, words were silenced.

• • •

David's voice was getting louder. "Did you read the *Daily Worker* today?"

Minna watched her brother's grim expression. His face was framed by flying hair, and his hands emphasized every word. How many times had she listened to him lead these discussions around their small kitchen table?"

"After seven years they're finally going to do it. They're going to murder Sacco and Vanzetti."

189

"I know," Pincus said, his face a grim mask.

"Fry those poor men," David said. "My God, what a horrible death."

"It's a travesty," Pincus said.

"America, land of the free is not so different than the old country," David said. "Except *here*, capitalists are the mad dogs butchering radicals every chance they get. *There*," he pointed wildly toward the window, "they murdered the peasants."

Minna's stomach churned as she thought of Nicola Sacco and Bartolomo Vanzetti. "No one believes they were involved in the robbery or the deaths of that guard and paymaster," she said.

"'Two men who look like Italians.' That's all they ever got from some bigoted pig of a witness," Pincus said.

"A jailbird even admitted being involved in the robbery," David added. "Sacco and Vanzetti weren't there."

"We've gone over this at least a hundred times, David," Minna said. "The truth doesn't matter and it won't stop them from being executed. Now only the governor can spare their lives."

"Two communist lives in the hands of the richest man in Massachusetts," David snapped. "Hard-working comrades depending on some capitalist who has forty million dollars?"

"Think of the poor … think of how many we could feed with that kind of money," Minna said.

"That man is evil, evil like all capitalists," David said. "He won't lift a finger to save our comrades. What does he care about a working man like me who toils on the dirty, grubby docks every day of his life?" David held his hands out. "See that dirt under my nails? No matter how hard I scrub, they never come clean. Does that ass even know what it means to endure the pain that hard labor inflicts on your body?

"A shoemaker … a fish peddler," Pincus said, squeezing Minna's arm. "Could he know anything about people like that?"

Minna couldn't stop her mind from drifting even though she cared passionately about the fate of the two men. She still remembered the judge who tried their case: Judge Webster Thayer, who had promised to "get those guys hanged."

She tried not to think about Pincus and his continued refusal to have a baby, but lately when she looked at him it was the first thing she thought about. She would be thirty soon and she was still unmarried, still without children. She was supposed to be a progressive woman, look past bourgeois double standards. But she couldn't help it—she wanted children.

She stirred a spoon in the dregs of her vegetable soup, made designs on the oilcloth with the rings of moisture from her water glass. David and Pincus continued to rail against the injustices of the capitalists, as they always did, but their voices faded into the background.

Today was the anniversary of her mother's death. It was hard to believe she had been dead five years.

Minna fought hard against it, but the imprint of her past was disappearing along with important memories: her mother's fair skin, intense eyes; Uncle Heshie's crusty humor, his coarse, gentle hands; her little farm in Russia, her beautiful peach tree that she would climb into to be cradled, protected from the horrors in the world below.

Even her sister Sarah had vanished, not only into the crowds of deportees sent back to Germany, but from Minna's reality.

She had hired German lawyers to find Sarah, but so far there wasn't a single trace of her existence.

Was her sister destined to become an inconsequential notch in a wall of Minna's brain, merely planted next to all those other past faces? Was she to become only a faded image dangling in space out of the range of clarity? Was she to be a part of a random collection that grew fainter with every breath Minna took?

It puzzled her because in the years when her mother was in Russia, she could remember with perfect recall her mother's every feature, every gesture. Now, time and death were sweeping her mind clean until all she had left were snippets of visions and feelings about the woman who had given her life.

Minna was startled, realized Pincus was talking to her. "We follow the *Daily Worker* reports together every day when she gets back from the hospital, don't we, sweetheart?"

"Minna's a hard worker, not like those rich bitches who exist on the backs of the proletariat," David said. "She's a true communist."

Minna smiled, forced herself to stop thinking of the past. Today, she and Ellen were working the swing shift. Ellen would be here any moment to pick her up so they could walk to work together.

Minna knew Ellen only came to the apartment because she was crazy about David, even though she wouldn't admit it. Pushing herself from the table, Minna said, "Thanks, David, but this communist better move or lose her job. Miss Elliott would love to toss me out, even after all these years."

"A suffragette like you?" Pincus said proudly. "I don't think so. Without people like you, how would women ever have gotten the vote?"

"You'd be surprised how few care about that, particularly Miss Elliott. She's hard-headed, Pincus, and she'd love to toss my tush out the door." Minna chuckled. "But she has mellowed over the years. Maybe because my English is so good now, I don't stick out like a sore thumb." She ran a hand down Pincus' arm. "Thanks to you and all your tutoring."

"You're still afraid of her, aren't you?" David said.

"Yes, I guess I am. And if it wasn't for Ellen, I'm sure she'd have found a way to fire me a long time ago."

"Can't see how a little thing like Ellen could protect you from anyone," David laughed.

"Small, but powerful. Makes sure she's right there when the old witch does her rounds on our floor." Minna giggled. "Everyone's afraid of Ellen. She'd take on a lion if she had to."

"She's a lovely little lass," David said. "Why haven't you brought her to the meetings? We need more people like her ... fearless comrades ... especially beautiful fearless comrades."

Minna laughed. "I've asked her."

"So?"

"Ellen hates communists almost as much as she hates the English. And besides, she says we're boring."

"Boring?"

Minna nodded. "Seems all communists ever talk about twenty-four hours a day is the workers of the world." She pointed a finger at her brother. "But she thinks you're cute, David, communist or not."

"Now that you're living with Pincus, she can move right into my apartment. Well, *your* apartment ... but it's my apartment. Well, maybe it's still your apartment—"

"All right, already. She gets the point," Pincus said with a wide smile.

The doorbell rang; Minna stood. "David, you're a good-looking man and we all know women fall very hard for you ... but if you're interested in Ellen, she won't come running like the rest of them. You'll have to win her heart."

• • •

They took their time walking to the hospital. It was a lovely summer afternoon and Minna didn't feel like working.

"Don't you wish we could just sit on the bench in the park?" she asked Ellen.

"You are a foolish lass, Minna Goldmich. Of course, I'd give anything to have me a little picnic and lay back and read the clouds."

"What would happen if we didn't show up?"

"Ignorant child. You'd be canned and so would I."

They walked in silence for a few minutes. Finally, Ellen spoke. "What's really on your mind? Not this foolishness about not working."

Minna smoothed down her starched white uniform and played with the clasp of the pin that secured her summer cape.

"Now, Minna Goldmich, you stop stalling this instant. What's simmering in that wee head of yours?"

Minna looked at Ellen's curly hair and petite figure, wished again that she were dainty and small instead of big-boned with rolls of fat that clothes couldn't contain or hide. Now that dresses were shorter, her fat seemed to overflow everywhere. Pincus said she was beautiful, but she knew he was blind to the truth.

"Minna?"

"I want to get married, Ellen. I want to have a child."

"Well, that's an easy one," Ellen said, laughing. "Pincus adores you, he'd do anything you ask. Have you told him?"

"Yes. But he thinks the world is going to hell. Thinks all the progress we've made ... radios, flying machines, cars ... have nothing to do with making this a better world."

"Waiting for a better world, is he? If that's what the fool wants, you'll never have a baby."

"Pincus is a good communist. He thinks we can change everything. And maybe he's right. But I want a family."

"You could walk out on the man."

Minna turned to Ellen. "He's one of the few people other than my mother who has ever really loved me. The only one who can make me feel beautiful ... smart."

"I can see you've fooled the dear man."

"I've told him that and he tells me I don't know my own worth." She started walking again.

"Does he always talk like a commie, even in bed?"

"If only you understood, you wouldn't make fun of us."

"Silly lass, what are you talking about?"

"Who else cares about the nightmares of a working person, cares about the lower classes in this rich country? The communists worry about babies, children, the poor."

"Oh, do stop smothering me in that communist horse shit. Countless numbers of people care." She tugged at Minna's cape. "I care. I care about the wrongs that are done to the little souls like you and me. And there are others who care ... even if you refuse to see them."

"You know how people treat the Negroes in Alabama: lynching, murdering, turning them away from hospitals because of their color. Do you think that's right?"

"Lord in heaven, do I have to listen to this day after day?"

"You do if you're my friend."

"Oh balls! What makes you think the commies would do us any better?"

"I know."

"Sure you do, Minna."

"I know because they try to change things, change our world. Make it a better place for everyone. Not only the rich deserve a fair break. We deserve it, too."

"Oh, enough! I'm sorry I asked." Ellen hooted one of her loud laughs. "For pity's sake. Do all communists go over the same old hash hour after hour, day after day?"

"We talk about what's important."

"Well, I'd rather talk about playing hooky from work."

Chapter 26

Minna, Pincus, Ellen, and David were smashed against each other. They clenched hands, formed a tight circle as they tried to move to the edge of the crowd. It was useless. The relentless crush of trapped bodies kept them solidly in the center.

Someone said there were more than 10,000 protesters crammed into Union Square.

Minna believed it. There was no place to turn, and even with bright lights shining on them, Minna felt buried alive.

They had been warned there would be spies. Secret agents wearing crimson rosettes would be circulating among them posing as "Reds." At least no one had to wonder where the bluecoats were—their sawed-off shotguns were easy to spot.

But the most frightening were the mounted police. Their horses would suddenly crash through the crowd, trampling panic-stricken people. The horses terrified Minna. When she looked at them, her throat closed as an old terror pierced her heart: She was back in Russia, Cossacks were hunting them down with their deadly sabers, only here, the police swung their nightsticks, crushing skulls.

Amidst the noise and agitation, organizers used bullhorns to repeat the different bulletins released from the *Daily Worker:*

SACCO AND VANZETTI CALMLY AND HEROICALLY AWAIT END.
WITNESSES OF EXECUTION BEGIN TO ARRIVE.
ONLY WORKERS' COURTS CAN GIVE JUSTICE TO WORKERS.
STRENGTHEN YOUR UNIONS TO PROTECT OUR FUTURE CHAMPIONS.

As the clock moved toward midnight, the crowd became subdued. Screams and shouts subsided to murmurs and whispers.

David had an arm around Ellen's shoulder and Pincus squeezed Minna's hand. Tears kept filling Minna's eyes. She could barely stand the oppressive crush of fear and hopelessness.

Had she done all she could to save them? Had anyone done enough?

She had marched, rallied for seven years in both New York and Boston, and demonstrations had been staged all over the world—London, Paris, The Hague.

Massachusetts responded by calling the world "interfering outsiders."

Minna had followed all the news reports. Writers and intellectuals like John Galsworthy, H.G. Wells, Anatole France, Robert C. Benchley, Edna St. Vincent Millay and Albert Einstein joined the voices that cried out against executing the two men. Minna knew in her heart, they weren't being put to death for crimes they had committed—the execution was for their belief in communism.

Her Uncle Heshie, David, Pincus had given her the insight to understand, to believe in communism. That belief had given her a sense of power, a sense that she *could* change the world. This final treatment of Sacco and Vanzetti drained that power, left her feeling weak and useless.

Standing among the thousands in Union Square, Minna knew, along with everyone else, that this time there would be no reprieve. The shoe peddler and the fisherman would die. August twenty-third nineteen twenty-seven at midnight.

The organizers shouted the *Daily Worker* Bulletin:

THEY ENTER THE DEATH CHAMBER.
SACCO MURDERED!

Minna burst into tears. She and Pincus wrapped their arms around each other. Boos and catcalls vibrated in the air.

VANZETTI MURDERED!
DON'T FORGET OUR MARTYRED COMRADES.
JOIN THE WORKERS PARTY AND FIGHT ON.

Minna squeezed her eyes shut as she heard Ellen scream, "Rotten, no good, slaughtering bastards!"

• • •

People milled around arguing the various highlights of the seven-year Sacco and Vanzetti disaster. Most repeated the same points, the same issues. Everyone was stalling. No one wanted to leave or let go of the two dead men.

Minna, Pincus, David, and Ellen silently worked their way through the clusters of people. Occasionally there were muted voices singing the *International*, along with cries of **WORKERS OF THE WORLD UNITE!** To Minna it was an unreal buzzing.

She felt numb. Her legs were wooden, difficult to move. If only she could turn back the clock to one minute before midnight, keep it there for the rest of her life, find some way to keep the executed men alive until people finally did the right thing.

A powerful focus had been taken away from Minna—the sense that she could make a difference, change the world to something better. Pincus had promised it, her communist comrades had promised it, and she'd believed it. Maybe after tonight, nothing would ever again change for the better.

The four of them walked, each separated by their own thoughts.

There was a sudden clash of deafening noise: bullhorns, whistles, hoof beats, screams assaulted her ears, while body odors, heat, fear, and the heavy musk of horsehair singed her nostrils. The world became a blur of motion and colors. Pincus shoved hard. She stumbled into the street.

She quickly picked herself up, only to be staggered by a charging mounted policeman. He kicked out at her with his spurred boot.

Minna couldn't focus on any single part of the confusion: a horse's terrified neigh, a policeman's angry commands. Suddenly she heard Pincus cry out in pain.

Then the sickening sound of crunching bones above everything else.

"Pincus!"

His name echoed around her as she ran to his side. Pincus's skull had crashed against the building.

Eyes that should have been staring at her rolled up to the top of his head. As she grabbed for him, a glob of blood splattered down her face, into her mouth.

Ellen and David helped her lay him on the ground.

He was barely breathing. A strange pallor descended from his forehead down, as though someone had pulled a plug to drain the life from him.

Ellen pressed a handkerchief to his head to stop the bleeding. "The ambulance is coming. It's going to be all right, Minna."

"I can barely feel his pulse," Minna screamed. She started moaning. "Oh my God. He's dying."

Pincus's eyes fluttered open.

"Minna ... Minna ... D ... Don't cry."

• • •

Even though it was four in the morning, Pincus's mother and father were dressed as though they were arriving for a fancy dinner party. Mrs. Levine wore a dark blue velvet dress, decorated with four stands of pearls. Mr. Levine wore a dark wool suit; his gold tie clip caught a glint from the room's light.

"It is *you!*" Bella Levine cried. "You and your ignorant, foreign ways!" She shook an accusing finger at Minna. "You made this happen to my son."

Minna stood, her legs shaking. They had been in the hospital waiting room for three hours.

"Bella, how could you say that? You know I love Pincus, would give my life for him." Minna burst into tears. David reached out and hugged her to him.

"Love? Did you say love? Was there a marriage? Do I have grandchildren from my only son?" Her face had turned a bright red, her eyes bulged with hatred. "You only lived with my son because he's a rich man and gave you and your brother a free place to stay. That's all he ever meant to you."

"Bella! You don't know what you're saying," said her husband. "Calm down." He put an arm around her shoulder.

"Leave me alone, Max!" She shrugged his arm away.

Ellen stepped up to Pincus's mother, her chin thrust out, her eyes fiery. "Minna has lived with your son for eight years. No one could have loved him more ... not even you." Ellen's hair stood out in all directions, a mess of curls flopping everywhere. "And what kind of mother is it who hasn't even asked how her son is doing? What do you really care about?"

Bella looked at Ellen as though she was a noxious bug. "And what are you? Some trashy Irish street urchin?"

Ellen clenched her hands before she spoke. "You're a wicked woman, Mrs. Levine, looking to place the blame for this misfortune on the woman your son loves with all his heart."

The doctor entered the waiting room and stared at them with large sad eyes. "Who is Pincus Levine's wife?"

Minna started to answer but was stopped by Bella. "Pincus has no wife." She took Max's hand. "We are his parents."

David said, "We are his friends."

The doctor slowly shook his head. "I don't know how long he will linger, but he's in a coma and I think he will die soon. I'm sorry. We've done everything we can for him."

Minna was mute for a moment, then she stared at the doctor. As her legs gave way, she screamed.

"NOOOOOOO!"

• • •

For three days Minna sat by Pincus's bed. For three days she tried to surround him with the golden light. Bursts of it would come, then fade.

She kept murmuring to him, whispering in his ear—promising she would save him.

Ellen and David wandered in and out trying to get her to drink soup, nourish herself. She would speak to no one.

Pincus lay pale, struggling for air in his protective oxygen tent while Minna held onto his hand, afraid if she let go, he would die.

Bella and Max Levine drifted in and out, only speaking to Minna once.

"This will be very brief ... we have met with our lawyer," Bella Levine said, barely concealing a sneer. "Common-law wife or not. You will not get one penny. We'll see to that."

They turned to leave, but she whipped around and spoke in a voice that crawled up from her belly, "Oh, you go ahead, Minna Goldmich. I dare you to take us to court, you rotten piece of Red trash!"

"I don't want your money," Minna said. I don't want Pincus's money. All I've ever wanted was him." Her eyes bore into Bella. "Now get the hell away from me!"

. . .

Minna closed her eyes, squeezed her hands around Pincus's hand. She let her mind reach out. She had to find the place, that place her mother had shown her when she was a little girl. It was somewhere beyond the stars where everything and anything could happen. The place where the healing began:

She was at the top of a mountain under a purple sky.

Her feet were shoeless but she was firmly planted and she was unafraid. She looked around at the purple void.

She knew if she fell, it would be into the endless nothingness that was between heaven and hell.

She raised her arms high.

A huge golden egg undulated through the purple layers.

The light became brighter as she held out her arms, wanting it to surround her.

Here was the oneness of the universe, the totality of God.

This was the golden healing light that had always been a part of her mother's life.

This was what her mother meant when she told her that everyone had God's great power.

The egg dipped closer. Minna raised her arms higher.

Are you really there? Why don't I believe in you anymore?

Why do you mean nothing to me?

Why am I nothing?

The brightness of the egg hung above her, opened just a crack.

The golden light within flowed out onto her, then washed down the mountain.

When she looked around she was left alone with only the mountain and the purple sky.

The nurse was tapping her on the shoulder. Minna opened her eyes. She stared at the starched uniform, the organdy cap with its black RN strip. But it was the nurse's eyes, filled with pain and sorrow that made her look at Pincus.

The oxygen tent had been pulled back. Pincus's hand was no longer curled around hers.

The man with the big heart was dead.

Chapter 27

Row upon row of tombstones stretched across the Brooklyn horizon as their car entered the gates of the cemetery.

Ellen looked out the window and winced as she saw that each stone was almost straddling the one next to it. "Good Lord! Pincus is to be buried here?"

Both David and Minna nodded.

Ellen shook her head, bit back a response.

So this was Jewish holy ground—a vast sea of Star of David's etched into the tombstones of buried souls awaiting the Messiah. Ellen's mother would have sneered, called it a pauper's bone yard. One that would doom its occupants to a crowded eternity.

With a backdrop of rain clouds, the stark cement block building where the service was to be held stood forlorn and ugly next to the cemetery. Ellen wondered if the day could possibly be any drearier, only to be answered by the heavens opening up. Sheets of rain poured down and exaggerated an already God-awful stench of moldy soil.

As they stepped from the car, David cradled an arm around Minna. Her face was sheathed in a thick black veil that covered skin as chalky white as any corpse Ellen had ever seen. Ellen reached to tuck in tendrils of matted, dull hair that escaped from the back of Minna's hat. Minna gently pushed her hand away.

Ellen gathered their umbrellas, placed them dripping among the heap that lay in wet piles outside the main service room. The three of them went in and sat down.

The area was filled to overflowing. A small group of the Levine family sat up front, but all the others were friends of Minna and

Pincus. Most belonged to the unions and the Party, others they had met while attempting to save Sacco and Vanzetti.

Ellen still wasn't sure how it had happened, but she had been swept up into the idealism of these people trying to perform the humane act of saving two lives. For her, it wasn't politics—she'd become an active participant because she knew a bloody frame-up when she saw one. The fact that the condemned fish peddler and shoemaker were Italian was not lost on her—her Irish brothers could have easily changed places with the condemned men and been hated equally by a government that wasn't interested in justice.

Much to David's disappointment, she had remained firmly resistant to joining the party—she loved the man but she'd told him the comrades were too fanatical for her taste. But as she now looked around, she questioned her defiance—these communists were decent, caring men and women who were only trying to help their fellow workers, to help people like herself who were considered common and ordinary—slaves of the rich.

The words of the service penetrated her thoughts:

The Lord is my shepherd;

I shall not want.

He maketh me to lie down in

green pastures: he leadeth me

beside the still waters.

Ellen clutched Minna's hand while David held his sister's quivering shoulders.

He restoreth my soul.

He leadeth me in the paths of righteousness for his name's sake.

Ellen drifted, half-listened to the drone of words and looked around at the solemn audience, many of whom Pincus had taken in when they were broke, out of work, or thrown out of their apartments.

Yea, though I walk through
the valley of the shadow of death,
I will fear no evil: for thou art
with me; thy rod and thy staff
they comfort me.

A heavy sense of loss dragged Ellen down. Pincus had been such a generous person, with little use for money except to help others.

The many stories Minna had confided over the years left Ellen with respect for Pincus Levine. Even the way he'd met Minna eight years ago was through an act of generosity. And long before they'd become lovers, when Minna's English had been so poor, she could hardly make herself understood, Pincus had helped her. Helped her to understand the different meanings of a difficult language she might never have mastered without him.

Ellen turned toward Minna and sensed Pincus's presence within her, sensed the kindness and enthusiasm that had allowed the Russian waif to learn everything at break-neck speed.

When she first met Minna, all Ellen saw was a frightened creature that seemed to flounder at every challenge. Yet, when you scratched the surface, hardiness sprung out. It never allowed Minna to back away from anything.

Although no one was afraid of Minna, Ellen was branded a rebel who was left alone, not only by those who could cause her trouble, but by those who didn't want problems befriending her. She had been very lonely until Minna came into her life, who treated every patient as a somebody, not a custodial unit. Why wouldn't Ellen want to be her friend? Why wouldn't everyone?

Many of the mourners shifted in their seats, craning their necks to catch a glimpse of Minna, who continued to hide behind her dark veil.

Thou preparest a table before
me in the presence of mine enemies:

thou anointest my head with oil:

my cup runneth over.

How many times during the last three days had Ellen heard Minna cry, wishing her last moments with Pincus had been filled with happiness instead of wedged in a crowd awaiting the execution of two innocent men?

Now she grabbed Ellen's hand as she swayed in her seat. Ellen wondered when her friend had eaten last.

"Are you all right?"

Minna took a deep breath. "Yes," she said in a shaky voice.

"Do you want to leave?"

"I want to be with Pincus for as long as I can."

"Let me take you home," David whispered to Minna.

"I will not give his parents that satisfaction," Minna said, her voice catching.

Ellen studied Max and Bella Levine, seated in the front row next to a plain pine box that held Pincus Levine's remains. Bella, comforted by her husband, sobbed loudly.

Ellen stared at the Levines, wondering at the hypocrisy of the family. How could a fine man like Pincus come from such arrogant, selfish people? Minna had lived with their son for eight years and she was to be left out in the cold with nothing while they stole his wealth and his intentions.

Too much of a bloody communist to make a will. Oh, dear lad! There are limits.

Now she was angry, had to bite her tongue to keep from blurting out her feelings.

Why were the Jews in such a bloody hurry to plant a corpse? It didn't give a person time to absorb their loss. Black clothes, black hats, black grief, but not a flower in the room to bring a breath of life to those left behind to mourn.

The air was getting closer and the smell of sweat and other

sour odors surrounded her. Ellen's stomach turned queasy. She concentrated on the words of the psalm and it soon allowed the feeling to pass.

Surely goodness and mercy
shall follow me all the days of my
life; and I will dwell in the house
of the Lord forever.

. . .

In turn they had each thrown a handful of dirt on Pincus's coffin. Minna was the last. At the head of the coffin, she looked down into the place where Pincus would rest forever. She started to throw the dirt. Then she stopped. She couldn't let go of the fistful of wet earth. She couldn't be the one who would bury him for eternity.

David and Ellen stood on either side of her. "Minna, girl, throw the dirt. Let it be done."

Minna squeezed her fist tighter. Maybe she could keep them from burying him. Maybe she could stop them from taking him away forever.

"Please, Minna," David said softly.

"It's not fair," Minna said. "I need more time."

Through all the kindness surrounding her, it was the malevolence of Bella Levine that brought her back to the moment. Minna saw Pincus's mother glaring at her through the long sheets of rain.

"Good-bye, Pincus," she said, tossing the dirt down below. "I'll never stop loving you."

The three of them washed their hands in a basin next to the gravesite. Friends surrounded them, not wanting to let Minna go. But she nodded to David and they walked towards the car.

Bella broke free from her husband. She chased after Minna, screamed, "You are a whore! You hear me? A whore!"

Ellen stepped in front, shielding Minna. "And you're a witch of a crone. Christ in heaven, how can you be so full of hatred for someone your son loved so much?"

Bella grabbed Ellen and tried to shove her out of the way. There was a loud gasp from the crowd that encircled them.

Ellen punched Bella hard in the stomach. "It's the good Lord that'll lay a hand on me before you ever will again."

Max held onto his wife as she doubled over and sobbed.

When Bella finally caught her breath, she said, "Minna Goldmich, you will leave that flat tomorrow and you will never return or I will have you thrown in jail. Is that understood?" She pointed a finger at Ellen, then jabbed at the air. "And if I ever see you again …" She took a forward step. "I will make your life a living hell."

Ellen wrapped an arm around Minna, and with David they walked toward the car.

Bella shrieked at Minna. "Don't walk away from me, you tart! I haven't finished with you.

Minna stopped at the opened car door, and tore off her veil.

"But I'm finished with you, you miserable bitch!"

Chapter 28

Albuquerque

Golden, glittering, grasping goop.

It engulfed Sophie, sucked hard at her. She struggled to lift herself out, but no matter how hard she tried, she remained entrenched, caught in its golden clutch—the harder she fought, the deeper she sank.

Sophie stared hard at a benign yellow sky.

"Minnnaah! Where are you? Help me!"

She wanted to straighten, stand. But her legs were caught in the yellow muck. It was getting hotter, more molten, dragging her down.

"Granndmaaa! Where are you?"

In the bright light, a dark spot jumped out at her. A flaw? A mini fissure?

A tear in time and space?

She grabbed for it and like a crack in an eggshell, it branched out at her touch, spreading until it fractured the entire yellow world.

Golden heat rays sliced through, burning her skin. Hot air sucked at her body, dragging her through a opening. She was blasted onto burning sand, blinded by the sun. Covering her eyes, waves of heat, nausea washed over her.

"Minnnaah! I know you're here. Tell me where you are. I need you!"

She started to walk, the sand searing the bottoms of her feet. Her arms blossomed huge blisters, hair frizzled away leaving behind a scorched skull. An unbearable pounding filled the air—her own heartbeat gone wild with fear.

A faraway voice cut through the terror.

"Don't be afraid, Sophie."

"Grandma Minna! Help me!"

A woman in tattered pink floated toward her.

"Sophie. Don't be afraid. I'm coming."

"Help me. I'm on fire."

Her grandmother's face was a mask of scabs, her feet covered in blood. But her wavering golden arms reached out, encircled Sophie. Minna's arms puffed up with heat as Sophie's body cooled.

"Don't cry, little girl."

But Sophie couldn't stop crying. "Where are you Grandma?"

• • •

Sophie jolted to a sitting position, ran her hands over her body. There was no blistering, no pain. Tears flooded her face.

"She's in the desert."

She sprang out of bed, threw on some clothes and ran down the hallway. Everyone was gathered around the kitchen table.

Leah's eyes brightened the minute she saw Sophie. "Sit down and have breakfast. I made coffee cake just for you."

Aaron smiled at her while Cynthia watched her carefully.

"She's in the desert! Minna's in the desert!"

Cynthia turned her nose up. "Brilliant! We're surrounded by desert. This is New Mexico. Remember?"

"How do you know?" Leah said, ignoring her mother.

Sophie sat down. "It was in a dream. Grandma Minna came to me. I was dying from the heat. It was horrible ... she came, and she saved me."

"Oh, my God," Cynthia said, dramatically, then covered her eyes.

"You know," Sophie said to Cynthia, "I don't think you give a damn whether we find Minna or not. Less trouble if she died."

Cynthia looked thoughtfully at Sophie. "I've never wished Minna any harm."

"Why do you sound so cruel then?" Sophie spat the words out.

"Not all sweetness and light, are you? Cynthia said. There's a nasty side, too. Like your uncle after all."

"You bring out the best in us, Cynthia."

Aaron held up a hand. "Far be it from me to agree with my wife, but there *is* a lot of desert out there."

"Everybody, stop it." Leah said. "Why won't you listen to Sophie?"

Sophie smiled at Leah. At least she had one ally.

"She can't be too far from town. In my dream there were broken beer bottles everywhere. Oh, that bright golden light ... the heat was overwhelming. It was like being in hell." Sophie covered her eyes. "I wish I could remember more."

"I swear this is the craziest family. Golden lights, golden desert, golden this, golden that. I think you're out of your ever-loving minds, and I'm not exposing Leah to anymore of this." Cynthia pointed a finger at Leah. "*You're* coming with me. I have a luncheon in Santa Fe, and we may not come back until this is settled, one way or another."

Leah glared at her mother. "No! I'm not going with you. I want to help find my Grandma; I want to be with Sophie."

"Aaron, for God's sake, talk some sense into her," Cynthia said.

He turned to Leah and Sophie. "She's right. There's not much we can do for Grandma but wait."

"I'm not going with you, Mom."

Cynthia stood, threw a half-eaten slice of coffee cake at her plate, and turned to leave. "I've tried to understand this fuss over

Minna but I don't. Everything is being taken care of … the police are doing their job. I think we have to stand by that." Over her shoulder, she said to Leah, "Do what you want, but *I'm* staying in Santa Fe with or without you. I've had about all I can take of this family."

The three of them sat in silence after Cynthia left. Leah wiped at her eyes.

"You'll have to forgive her," Aaron finally said to Sophie. He squeezed Leah's shoulder. "She doesn't mean to be cruel to you. Only to me."

• • •

It was nine-thirty by the time he backed the car out of the garage and it would be about a ten-minute ride to the nursing home.

Aaron's crotch continued to burn where the sweat seemed to puddle even in the air-conditioned car. He hated leaving his comfortable home, and wondered again when the heat wave would finally break. When this whole damn thing with his mother would be over and settled. He needed some peace and quiet.

He needed that goddam money.

The girls sat in the back together, talking mostly about his sister Frieda. Aaron let his thoughts wander until their voices were just background noise.

Frieda. He hardly remembered her, except she always seemed to be in the way. Mainly, she blended in with Minna and Saul and their miserable home life. Even now he was reluctant to refer to his parents as Mom and Dad. After all these years it made him sick to think about his family.

It was the bickering that got to him. Actually, bickering would have been tolerable. It was more the screaming that made him swear he would leave home as soon as he could.

"Uncle Aaron. Uncle Aaron!"

He realized Sophie was calling out to him.

"Yeah, Sophie. I'm sorry. I was lost in my thoughts."

"What do you think if we fan out toward the desert from the perimeter of the nursing home?"

"That's sort of what I had in mind."

He looked in the rearview mirror—the girls were back to their own conversation.

God, he didn't want to do this. He wanted to be left alone and let everything happen around him—without him.

He grabbed his handkerchief and mopped up the perspiration running down his face, then adjusted the cool air to its highest level.

The smartest thing he'd ever done was join the Army, even if he was barely eighteen. It was his ticket out and he'd gotten away for good. But the best had been after the Army when he went to the University of New Mexico. It was there he'd fallen in love with Southwestern architecture.

God, those were good times. He was happy in school.

Damn it. Why did he ever toy with the ambition of becoming an architect? After he finished school, all he did was leave his dreams behind.

Money.

Always the chase for the greenback, the mighty dollar.

He'd stood at the crossroads and gone down the wrong pathway. Instead of following his dreams, he'd chosen a roller coaster ride of being rich and poor.

Life fucking sucks!

• • •

Minna reached out for the pain and cut her fingers on the shard of a beer bottle jammed into her arm.

"*Boshestva moi*," she screamed at the sun.

She yanked at the glass until it fell away. A rush of blood trickled down her arm, clotting almost instantly in the hot sun.

She looked around.

Studied the sand.

Glittering pieces of glass reflected the golden orb in the sky. It continued to sear her already burned skin. She fingered crusted blisters on her face and didn't recognize what she touched.

Whose face was this? Who was she?

Her pink robe, now a grimy tan, was ripped wide open. Pain forgotten, she played for a moment with the accumulated sand on her breasts and abdomen, wondering how the grit had gotten there. Then, she pressed the indentations on her robe where the buttons had fallen away—she studied her bright red skin exposed to the scorching rays of the sun. Something was wrong here.

She had almost figured it out when all at once pain struck from every part of her body—feet, legs, arms, and especially her head, which pounded like a loud drum.

Boom! Boom! Boom!

"Miss Elliott, I can't work here anymore," she screamed to the blue sky.

"No, no. Don't try to be nice to me. Not after all these years of treating me like dirt."

Minna walked in circles: round and round.

"Ellen, David, stop telling me what to do. I'll make my own decisions."

She looked off into the glaring horizon. The pain continued

to pull at her face. She carefully touched herself, and then forgot about it.

Why was her mouth so dry?

She sat down on the sand and looked at the mountains. They seemed so close, yet so far.

Chapter 29

New York City
Late 1920s

Minna criss-crossed a complex of municipal offices that seemed to follow no particular pattern. She took several wrong turns and became lost in a maze of corridors, and when she asked for help, people were brusque, sent her off in other wrong directions.

She had no time to be upset, she needed to hurry along or she would be late for her ten o'clock appointment. But her heart wasn't in it and it was all she could do to keep from turning around and running back to the apartment she shared with David and Ellen.

Why hadn't she stayed at St. Helena?

Maybe she wanted to run away.

Maybe she wanted to bury herself in something new.

Maybe she hated the feeling of helplessness that kept her up night after night.

Finally, she stood outside a glass-windowed door:

VISITING NURSING AGENCY FOR THE CITY OF NEW YORK was painted in dark bold letters. She reached out but when her hand clutched the doorknob, she was paralyzed.

A woman dressed in a dark blue uniform yanked open the door, pulling the handle from Minna's grasp. They grabbed at each other to keep from falling.

"Sorry! Did I hurt you?"

"No, no. I'm fine." Minna picked up the black leather doctor's bag the woman had dropped and handed it back to her.

She was about Minna's age: a spotless white cap on the top of her head was tipped off center, her black hair was pulled tightly into a bun, and wisps of stray hair had escaped the restraint of planted hairpins. Her eyes questioned Minna.

"Are you coming to work for us?"

Minna hesitated.

"Oh, don't be surprised. The only people I ever see here are other nurses stupid enough to risk their lives on the streets of New York."

"Risk?"

The woman held out her hand. "I'm Johnnie Sappatino. Don't listen to me; I always act like a smart aleck with strangers."

Minna couldn't help but smile as she shook the hand of the thin woman who towered over her. "I'm Minna Goldmich, late for my appointment, so I don't know if I'll ever work here."

"That's pretty funny. That madhouse in there," Johnnie said, pointing at the door that had slammed shut, "will never notice the difference." There was a bounce in her step as she waved good-bye, walked toward the elevator. "See you later."

Minna tried to see through the frosted glass, but everything was moving shadows. She finally walked into the office before she could change her mind. The room beyond the reception desk was not as crazy as Johnnie had led her to believe, but several women uniformed like Johnnie were busy rummaging through doctors' bags, lifting up items to make sure they were where they were supposed to be: stethoscopes, syringes, bandages, tape, medicines. Another group was lined up, in the process of being handed papers, which she assumed were daily assignments.

What on earth was she doing here? With the exception of Ellen, these were not the kind of nurses she was used to working with under Miss Elliott. These women laughed, complained loudly, and seemed to be very independent—the kind of women Pincus always said *she* belonged with.

The receptionist smiled a greeting at Minna. "Good morning! Are you Minna?" Before she could answer, "Got lost, didn't you?"

Minna nodded.

"Don't worry. Annie won't hold it against you." The receptionist rose and started toward a closed door. "I'll let her know you're here ... she was just asking for you."

Too late to leave now.

The receptionist reappeared outside the door she'd vanished behind and nodded for Minna to go in.

Minna's legs turned into hollow wooden stumps, she forced them into motion and tiptoed into the office, her breath yanking hard at her chest.

"Good morning, Minna." The woman who offered a seat was tall and slender, dressed simply in a white blouse and dark skirt, and had a heavy Southern accent. "We are so pleased that you are interested in being part of our group."

Minna stared long and hard, could barely get the words out quickly enough. "You're Annie Langtree, aren't you?

"Have we met?" Langtree asked, looking thoughtfully at Minna.

"Yes. We have. A long time ago, when I first came to America. We talked on the train when I was traveling to Birmingham. I was so frightened and you were so nice to me. The only one who made me feel welcome. I've thought of you so often over the years."

Miss Langtree clapped her hands in delight as her eyes lit up in recognition.

"Well, I do declare ... the Russian girl! Of course!" She leaned forward in her chair. "How did you end up in New York?"

"It's a long story, but I've lived here for many years now."

"Your English is wonderful. You could barely speak when we met."

Minna looked at the woman whose eyes were still the softest

brown she'd ever seen. It was strange to meet someone twice in twelve years, each time at difficult crossroads. She'd always argued with Pincus about destiny. He didn't believe there was such a thing, but if he were alive today, maybe he would have changed his mind.

"Well, Minna … oh, by the way, we're all on a first-name basis here, so feel free to call me Annie."

Minna nodded.

"We can play catch-up later, but for now we've got some serious talking to do." Annie came around and sat on the edge of the desk. "Tell me. Why do you want to be a visiting nurse?"

Minna had composed a pat response to the question she knew would be asked. But when she looked into those soft brown eyes, she knew she had to tell the truth.

Minna shook her head slowly. "I honestly don't know for sure … but I can't stand being cooped up in a hospital anymore. I want to help people, but I need to feel as though I can make my own decisions. I want to spend more time with my patients, yet have the freedom to come and go." She looked up at Annie. "Does that make any sense at all?"

Annie Langtree returned to her chair, her face kind, sympathetic.

"More than you know."

· · ·

Annie Langtree hired her on the spot. Johnnie Sappatino became her preceptor after Minna told Annie of their encounter. Annie said there wasn't anyone who could teach her more than Johnnie. "You may learn more than you ever needed to know," she said with a laugh.

Despite Minna's desire for more freedom, the idea of making

unassisted decisions without the backup of doctors frightened her. At the hospital, doctors took over when things were new or different, or just plain got out of hand. Now she would be on her own.

"Are you ever afraid working by yourself, Johnnie?"

"You're a funny kid, Ruskie. What's to be afraid of? The people you're working on know less than you do."

"That's not what I mean, and you know it."

"Don't get your feathers all ruffled. Next thing I know you'll be cursing me out in Russian and I'll hand out my best Italian 'fuck you'. Then we'll be rolling on the floor pulling each other's hair out."

Minna's laugh was dry. "Okay, so I don't have a good sense of humor."

"Gotta laugh sometime ... life's rough enough. But to answer your dumb question, of course I'm afraid. I don't want to hurt anybody any more than you do."

"Do you ever get over that fear?" Minna said.

"I don't even try. Knowing your limitations, what you can and can't do, can save as many lives as thinking you know everything."

"I guess I'll understand sooner or later."

"Listen, Ruskie, it gets down to this. We've got a lot to offer and those people out there need us ... we're all they have. Dig into that brain of yours and you'll find you know more than you think you do."

• • •

Johnnie knew how to wiggle out of the Harlem assignments, but the last day they were scheduled to work together, one of the nurses called in sick. Johnnie was stuck.

"Goddam coloreds! Meanest people you'll ever meet."

"You're soft as butter to everyone else, Johnnie. Why are you so awful about them? They're just trying to get by like everyone else."

"Save your sympathy. Those people knifed my brother. Damn near killed him. I've got no use for them."

"How did that happen? What did your brother do?"

"What did my brother do? Well, Miss Minna, I'll tell you what he did." She stood with her hands on her hips, tapping her toe. "He was strolling down the street minding his own damn business and some drunken nigger knifed him in the gut. Just like a pig in a pen."

That day when they walked down the streets of Harlem, people stepped out of Johnnie's way. You could spot the white woman with a chip on her shoulder a mile off. Like Minna's brother Moishe, Johnnie hated negroes and nothing was going to change that.

Minna never worked as a team with Johnnie again after that long, difficult day in Harlem. From then on, Minna would work alone and only have herself to depend on.

• • •

It took time to figure out the transportation system, to fully understand the different sections of the city. Most assignments were grouped so she was in one neighborhood all day, but she knew sooner or later she would find herself working at opposite ends of the city in the same shift.

Her first assignment happened to be in Harlem. She smoothed her summer cape and held her doctor's bag firmly as she walked down the streets—a white face in a sea of black humanity.

It wasn't much different than being in the South, but Harlem negroes weren't anything like Birmingham negroes. These people looked you right in the eye and they weren't afraid.

Johnnie claimed the coloreds could be threatening and nasty, but the people she met on the avenues were not only friendly, they were respectful. Most were poor and never saw a doctor or went to a hospital for medical attention. Minna knew they looked forward to nurses' visits. At least they knew somebody cared.

She began to relax as she moved with the syncopated rhythms of the streets. Jazz, the kind of music that Pincus had loved the most, blared out across the neighborhoods. Without Johnnie, folks on the stoops smiled at her. Even though she felt their eyes on her back after she walked by, she sensed no hostility, only curiosity. Children walked up to her and tugged at her cape, then laughed and ran away; adults shooed the children, stopped to see if she needed help.

Minna was happy. She smiled, nodded greetings, and after awhile she came to the same conclusion she'd always had about people—no two were ever alike.

• • •

Minna checked the address of the rundown building against her assignment sheet. This was definitely it. She started up the cracked steps, noticing the stoops were strangely empty.

The minute she stepped into the building, shattering screams vibrated through the halls. For an instant, she wanted to turn and run, but instead, she squeezed by six wide-eyed children mashed against each other on the cement steps to the second floor.

She had barely finished knocking on 2A when the grease-splattered door was flung open.

"What ya want?" said a dark-skinned woman barely out of her teens. "Oh, sorry, nurse. C'mon in," she said, relief in her voice.

"I'm here to see Rufus Washington." Minna checked her papers. "A six-year-old with stomach pains."

"Rufus gon' have to wait his turn."

Minna tried to keep from wincing at the rush of curses and screams from the other room.

"Annie Mae's sick and it's Momma's time. You gon' hafta hurry."

Minna looked around the tiny apartment: peeling paint, torn linoleum, two teenage girls on a large sagging bed whose sheets were crumpled and torn. The girls hugged a little boy in the middle of the bed whose face was tired and gray, and he shook violently with chills under a threadbare blanket.

"Lawdamighty! Where Annie Mae?" screamed a voice choked with pain. "Why ain't she here? Crystal! Sweet Jesus, Crystal! Get in here! You gon' leave yo' momma alone at a time like this?"

Without another word, the girl hurried into the other room.

A strange quietude overtook Minna. Her mind seemed to float in the midst of all the stress and noise.

She undid her cape, let it fall to the floor and grabbed her bag and hurried into the other room.

"I don' need no nurse," the woman in the bed said, pointing a finger at Crystal. "Where's my Annie Mae?" She shook a fist at the heavens. "Sweet Jesus, stop this pain."

Minna rolled up her sleeves, reached for her bag. She pulled up a wooden crate that was used for a bedside table and placed it at the foot of the bed, and then set out a bulb syringe, cord, and scissors.

"Crystal," she ordered, "bring me boiling water, a towel for the baby."

Crystal fled from the room.

"Mrs. Washington—"

"I ain't no Mrs. Washington. Name's Pearl. Where's—"

Pearl's eyes were hostile, then wide and frightened.

"Pearl! Listen to me carefully. Annie Mae's sick. She won't be here."

Pearl began to cry. "JesusJesusJesus."

"Crystal," Minna called out again. "Bring me a glass of water." When Crystal flew into the room, Minna held Pearl's head and gave her several sips. She helped her into a more comfortable position, straightened the bed and tossed away the soaked towels under her.

"How's that hot water coming?"

"It gon' take a long time."

"Go get it. It's probably warm enough now."

Crystal returned with a small pot of tepid water. Minna pointed to some sheets wadded up in the corner of the room. Crystal brought a torn sheet to Minna, who sectioned it into various sizes.

Minna dipped a cloth into the pot of water and began cleaning the moaning woman.

"Crystal, fold that large piece to fit under your Mama's bottom." She watched, nodded. "Good! Now help me get it under her. Yes, that's it! Now hold your Mama's hands tight. She's going to need you."

Pearl let out another glass-shattering scream and began to push. "JesusJesus sweeeet Jeesssus!"

Minna slipped on a pair of rubber gloves. The baby's head was crowning. "Almost there, Pearl. Stop pushing! Wait for the pain or you'll tear yourself apart."

But Pearl wasn't listening to Minna. She grunted with all her might and the baby boy seemed to fly into Minna's hands. Pearl lay sweat-soaked and panting.

Crystal's eyes were large and frightened and the room had turned strangely silent.

"I don' hear my baby." Pearl lifted herself up on her elbows. "What wrong with my child?"

After tying and cutting the cord, Minna had the baby tightly wrapped in cloth and was carefully wiping fluid from his face. There was no sign of movement.

She grabbed for the bulb syringe. "Come on, little one." The hissing sound of mucus being sucked up seemed to bounce off the walls. Crystal stood near her mother with both hands clutching the woman.

"What's wrong?" Pearl screamed. She sat up and tried to grab the baby. "Give me my child, white woman!"

Minna stood with the baby, held it snug against her waist, head down. "Pearl, stop it! Let me do what has to be done! We're losing time!"

Crystal and Pearl both covered their mouths and watched with wide-eyes as Minna turned the baby and massaged his back, turned him over again and again, sucking more mucus from his mouth with the bulb syringe. Finally, she uncovered his feet and flicked her fingers at them. The baby wailed weakly, and in a few moments was screaming.

"Praise be the Lord! Thank you Lord, thank you for saving my baby!"

. . .

Little Rufus Washington had appendicitis. Minna rode in an ambulance with him to the hospital. She was worried about the boy. He was very sick, but he was also very strong. She thought he would survive. When she reported back to the agency, everyone gathered around, shouted her name and clapped.

"Hell of a first day," Johnnie said, now all smiles.

"I'm so proud of you," Annie said, hugging her. "Have you ever delivered a baby before?"

"Only in the hospital."

"You're not a hospital handmaiden anymore, Minna," someone yelled. "You're a woman of the streets."

Everyone roared with laughter.

When Minna rode the trolley home that night, she knew she was a different person than the one who had started out that morning. She was finally in charge of her life.

Minna rushed up the steps of the apartment house, carefully planning what she would say to Ellen and David: Tell them how much she loved them, how important their support and encouragement had meant to her, how she couldn't have gotten through her loss of Pincus without them.

She threw open the apartment door, looked at her friend and her brother, and shouted:

"Ellen, David. I'm moving out. It's time I found my own apartment."

Chapter 30

It was an uphill battle but David finally talked Minna into going to a party meeting—the first since Pincus's death. He'd gone to her apartment and made a damn fool of himself hammering at her. Finally, she agreed to go just to shut him up. Usually, he arrived early to rail with his cohorts about current issues and whatever else was agitating him. But people had continued to ask about Minna, wanting to see her again, and he was feeling very cocky about talking her into coming even if they were late.

He hurried her into the crowded meeting hall. "There're two seats." He pointed and prodded her in the right direction.

A buzz filled the room as several people called out Minna's name. Many heads turned, hands went up to wave. He watched his sister flush with pleasure and he knew getting her to come tonight had been the right thing to do.

"David, why did I let you talk me into this. I'm not ready."

She tried to pull away but he kept her moving. "It's been two years since Pincus's death. Time marches on with or without you, Minna." Before she could turn and run, he had them seated in the middle of a row, enclosed by other members.

"You know how important this is," David said. "There's so much you and I have to do. Pincus would have wanted you to carry on his work."

Her eyes turned a brittle blue and he knew he'd gone a step too far.

"I'm sorry, Minna, but Ellen … we both worry about you. There's more to life than work and sitting around your apartment."

She slumped, placed a hand over his. "Still can't talk Ellen into joining the party or coming to the meetings?"

"She hates communists. Thinks if there were no communists Sacco and Vanzetti would still be alive." He ran his fingers through his hair before firmly resetting his cap, centering it on his head. "She's worldly about so many things, but totally naive about our comrades and the work we do."

"Maybe *she's* right."

He studied her expressionless face. Were those words really coming from his sister's mouth?

"Do you really believe without communists there would be no witch hunts?" he said. "Do you believe, even for a moment that the poor, the working men and women of this country would even have half a chance against the capitalists?"

"Why does it have to be them or us? Can't people just be different?"

"They're different all right. And the difference is: Power! Money!" David heard his voice. It was laced with sarcasm.

The face of his older brother flashed before him and he remembered his visit to Alabama.

Miserable SOB gave him a long lecture on the evils of communism after treating him like a stranger.

"I don't want to hurt you, Minna. You're the only family I have."

"There's Moishe. No matter what you say, he's still our brother."

"Have you seen that *putz* lately? Is that why you're talking this way?" David's chest tightened. Hatred left a foul taste in his mouth.

"I worked a couple of days at his Bronx nursing home."

"You mean that hellhole where he stores the living dead."

"What's the matter with you tonight, David? What happened to all that compassion you spout at the drop of a hat?" She poked him hard in the arm. "Living dead? Those are old, sick people. They have names. They're human beings like all the communists sitting in this room."

"That dive is a warehouse and you know it." His hands clenched into a tight fist and he wanted to hit someone. "They threw Moishe out of that hospital in Alabama, and he bought that terrible nursing home to hide and lick his wounds."

"You can be so cruel, David. The man was sick with malaria."

"You think I'm cruel?"

"I wouldn't be alive if he hadn't brought me to the United States. Give Moishe a chance. He's our brother."

"After our fight in Birmingham, I wanted to resolve our differences. When I went to the Bronx, he showed me around his nursing home. He was proud of it! He didn't see human beings lying in their own shit, begging for water. All he cares about is making money. He's become a true capitalist."

"Change things for the better, David. Instead of complaining about Moishe, change that patient's bed. Give something of yourself. Give hope to everyone you touch."

"Damn it! Don't preach to me! I can't forgive him. I'm not like you."

"No! *You'd* rather rant and rave at the capitalists. But if you turn your back on one individual who needs your help, are you any better?"

He was angry at her for lecturing him. But he knew what she said was true. He tried to calm himself, reached for her hand. "Still with the golden light, Minna?

"Not anymore. I've lost it." Her face became a mask of pain. "It left me when Pincus died. Now I try to do what I can to heal with my nursing skills."

He was speechless. He'd watched his mother, his sister heal, do things he still couldn't believe were possible. Often, when he woke in the blackness of the night and felt alone and frightened, when he questioned his beliefs, his atheism, he remembered the golden light hovering over his mother and Minna. He wondered many times what was wrong with him, with Sarah. Why didn't they have the power? He could witness the power, but he had none of it.

He gave Minna a sidelong glance: her red hair was cut short, but other than that, she looked the same. Yet, she had changed since Pincus died. The old Minna wouldn't argue with him about anything. This Minna was more like the brat he remembered sitting in the peach tree on their farm in Russia, telling him to go to hell.

"Moishe brought me to America. He saved my life. If nothing else, I owe him for that." Her eyes were twin pools of sadness. She rubbed a finger against his chin. "David, you're so serious. I never see you smile anymore."

"Give me a better world and I'll not only smile, I'll laugh my head off."

"You've got Ellen."

David nodded. He had Ellen, yet he didn't. Most of their arguments were about his political involvement. She refused to marry him as long as he was a communist. He couldn't give her up, but he couldn't ignore all that he believed in.

A hush fell over the room as the meeting was brought to order.

This was the second gathering he'd been to since Saul Lubin became president of the local chapter. David didn't know him well, but the man had a fire in his belly and that alone inspired David.

Someone stepped up to the podium and whispered in Saul's ear. He shook his head and looked around the audience.

"I've just been told that Minna Goldmich is here with us tonight. Minna was Pincus Levine's companion for many years. Pincus is one of our fallen heroes, a soldier in the long fight to save our brothers Sacco and Vanzetti."

Cheers, whistles, applause echoed around the room. David put his arm around Minna. "See how important you are to us."

Minna wiped away a gush of tears that spilled down her cheeks.

• • •

The meeting was long. The shaking fists and shouting were even getting to David and he kept shifting in his seat.

"Now for one final item. The International Worker's Order has sent out a plea for funds for Camp Kinderland. For those of you who don't know about this place, it is a wonderful progressive oasis on Sylvan lake not too far from Poughkeepsie. The camp is a summer haven for the children of working men and women, a place where Jewish culture, in fact, all cultures are honored. There children learn to have pride in helping others … helping our fellow communists and socialists."

Groans rumbled through out the room.

Saul held up a hand and laughed. "Now I know a lot of you think socialists are wishy-washy. But remember, they're more with us than against us." He held up a fist. "We need everyone."

People in the room stood and screamed their approval.

• • •

David watched Saul approach Minna. His jerky movements shouted roughness, instability, and it was bourgeois the way he took her hand and lifted it to his lips. Yet the effect was natural, neutralized by the faded jeans and wrinkled shirt he wore.

"I've only seen you from a distance, but I can't tell you how much I've wanted to meet you over the years."

Minna stood awkwardly as Saul continued to hold her hand. The crowd was thinning and David was restless.

"You ran that meeting like a pro," David said.

"After you've dodged the Cossacks, leading a meeting seems simple," Saul said laughing.

"Why were they chasing you?" Minna said, her interest obvious.

"I ran messages back and forth between the Bolshevik groups. The 'Whites' found out. I was only a step ahead of the Cossacks when I left the country."

"Where are you from?" David asked, yawning.

"Minsk."

David watched Saul eye Minna, who was looking intently back at him. "Minsk? We're from Bobruysk."

Saul smiled widely. David thought he was handsome in a rugged way, but pockmark craters in his cheeks and nose marred the total picture. Barely taller than Minna, he still was wiry and strong looking.

"We were destined to meet," said Saul.

When David first heard of Lubin, remarks mostly alluded to his talents at seducing women. One friend described him as a "*schtupper*." Although David admired Lubin's passion for communism, he wasn't sure he wanted a rake hanging around his sister.

David took Minna's arm. "It's getting late. I better get you home."

"Not yet, David. I'm talking to Saul."

She was obviously annoyed at being interrupted, but not nearly as annoyed as he was. First he couldn't get her out of the house, now he couldn't get her to go back home.

236

"I'll take Minna to her apartment," Saul said. "You look done in. Go on. She'll be fine."

David's first response was to argue the point, but it was late and he would get little sleep before heading for the docks in the morning. Minna was a grown woman and she was old enough to make up her own mind.

She reached over and kissed David. "Thank you for bringing me tonight."

David only nodded. He was speechless over the change in his sister. Her eyes were sparkling again. He hadn't seen her this animated in two years and when he turned at the door to look back at Minna and Saul, they were almost the last people left in the meeting hall. They were still holding hands.

. . .

Minna was flooded with forgotten passions as she and Saul walked into her studio apartment. She felt weakened, numbed. *What am I doing here alone with this man?*

The place was small. The single room held her bed, a tiny kitchen area and a thin partition that walled off a toilet and shower. Saul filled every corner of the room. There was nowhere for her to run, to hide.

His lips were soft, his tongue probing as he maneuvered her toward the bed, hands moving across her back, her breasts.

A voice she barely recognized had dissolved into panting whispers. "I'm not ready for another man, Saul."

"Yes, you are, Minna. You're more than ready."

Tired, so tired, she thought as she fell to the soft and comforting bed. She closed her eyes, stopped fighting herself, and let her mind drift as she rolled in the raw sensations that came from the insistence of Saul's touch:

A field of bright orange poppies waved
in the soft breeze for as far as she
could see … pollen floated, bees and
butterflies danced around her … the
sun was strong and warm … Pincus, up to
his waist in flowers, was running to her,
his arms outstretched.
"Minna, it's me."
She crushed him to her.

Saul stripped off their clothes. Their arms encircled each other, bodies twisted and turned.

"Don't be afraid, Minna. Touch me, hold me."

Minna pulled the covers over them and allowed herself to run her fingers through the hair of his chest, across his shoulders.

Minna kissed Pincus's face.
"Where have you been? I've been
looking … so long … so lonely."
Always there … always with you."

Saul rolled her onto her back. He slid up and down the length of her until she thought she was on fire. Spikes of heat filled her groin.

"There's someone else, Pincus. Don't
know what to do."
"Time to live, Minna."
"But how am I to be … who am I
Who will I be without you?"

The sensations of Saul penetrating her left her suspended between two worlds … her mind melded with harsh bursts of purples, reds, oranges, and yellows.

From far away, she saw Pincus wave good-bye.

Chapter 31

Albuquerque

"La Costa Inn, please."

Frieda slid into the back seat of the cab, panting from the shock of hot air that seared her face.

"Sure ya want La Costa?"

"I told you exactly where I want to go."

"Okay, okay. Just trying to earn an extra buck." He hit the accelerator and jerked away from the curb.

God, she was tired of people trying to hustle her for one thing or another because she was a woman.

Rummaging through her purse, she pulled a ten from her wallet, sat back with a heavy sigh. She would not be caught like some frantic chicken fumbling for money at the last moment.

She hated surprises, hated not being ready for every single moment of her life. That was why she loved having her own catering business: it gave her short-term relationships, beautiful results, control over everything. She sighed—the only wild card was having Sophie as a partner. Her daughter would not to be controlled by anyone.

"Hot, huh?" The cabbie eyed her in the rearview mirror. "Where're you from?"

"San Francisco."

"What's it like there?"

"Sixty-eight when I left."

"Been 115 here for the last three days. Just hell!"

Frieda didn't want to talk to him. She wanted to make her way from the airport to her room in blissful silence. But the day wasn't going well. Seated on the plane next to the most talkative man

239

she'd ever met, she'd tried diplomacy, then finally point-blank nastiness, telling him she wanted some quiet. It brought a nod that barely interrupted whatever he was saying.

No, it hadn't been a good day.

She'd told no one she was coming, not even Sophie. She wanted to burrow into a nice quiet room without the hassles she would have to go through for not staying at her brother's, where Cynthia made her feel less than welcome.

The cab pulled up in front of the inn, a small adobe-style hotel with an unusual mix of lush tropical plants and towering cacti. She wondered abstractly how such tropical plants survived the winter. She liked the place because she didn't have to look down on the highway like most of the big-name hotels and the atmosphere was one of Southwestern hospitality. No one rushed to do anything.

She paid off the cabbie and sailed through registration before being taken to her room. After tipping the bellboy, she immediately stripped off her clothes and turned on the radio. Even though the room was air-conditioned, she knew her face had suddenly turned bright red. A wave of heat flashed over her and in a moment she was beyond damp as perspiration ran down the length of her body. How she hated being plagued by these episodes that seemed to attack her like unpredictable invaders.

"Damn it, this is obscene!" She bolted to the shower. The cool water rushing through her hair, on her neck and down her torso was life saving. Soon, her hot flash subsided and she was able to think again.

For the last two days she'd blocked her mother from her thoughts, not much different than their usual relationship. But now the extreme weather and her own surges of body heat shoved her back into reality. Things she tried not to think about broke through.

If her mother died now, Frieda would never be able to tell her how sorry she was for being such a failure, for never making her proud, no matter what she did. Most of all, she would never be able to tell her about the secret. That secret was the one thing she knew would make her mother happy.

Once thoughts of her mother seeped into her head, a pile of unwanted memories surfaced, one on top of the other.

Frieda acknowledged that she probably was not very lovable otherwise her mother would have loved her as much as she did her brother. Even her ex-husband had validated that notion when he left.

"Unlovable bitch!" was what he'd shouted.

Well, maybe she wasn't lovable. But no one pushed *her* around, especially her ex. Still, at moments like this she had to accept she missed him—he was the only one who could make her laugh at life … and cry.

A shiver coursed through her. The same doubts, the same hateful thoughts. "Don't they ever go away?" she asked the walls. She covered her face as her self-control deserted her.

How frightened her mother must be—alone like a lost child in that inferno.

Pain. Thirst.

Frieda forced herself to lie still. The room became cool and comfortable. She let her eyes flutter shut, then quickly opened them.

How weary she was of hiding from a golden light that always found her in her dreams. She'd run from that vision since she was ten years old, refusing to tell her mother of its overwhelming presence.

Her mother would prod, question if she ever saw a golden light. And Frieda would lie. Softness would cut through the layers of silence that surrounded their relationship during those times.

Her mother would tell stories about Frieda, the healer. The grandmother she was named after.

Healing had passed on to her mother and should have passed on to Frieda. But the secret got in the way. The secret that she savored like a raft in a turbulent, empty ocean.

Frieda reached out for her father instead. Someone who would hug her, would love her ... a warm affectionate man who sang like a cantor and thought like a communist.

She grabbed the telephone and punched in her brother's home phone.

"Hi, Leah. This is your Aunt Frieda."

"Oh, I'm so glad you caught us, we were just going out the door. You must want to speak to Sophie."

Before Frieda could answer, Sophie was on the line. "Hi, Mom. Are you managing all right without me?"

"Sophie, I'm in Albuquerque."

There was a heavy moment of silence. "Are you sure you want to be here, Mom?"

"Right now, I'm sure. But I'm in a nice air-conditioned room away from your uncle. Check with me later."

"We're going to look for Grandma. You want to come?"

Frieda wanted to scream, "What kind of stupid question is that?" No, she didn't want to go outside and wander around in that oven. The briefest exposure to that torrid sun had left her breathless.

"Pick me up at the La Costa Inn, but give me a few minutes to get dressed. Okay?"

"I'm so glad you're here, Mom."

. . .

They were waiting for her when she walked out the front entrance. She immediately had trouble breathing in the hot air.

Both Sophie and Leah jumped out of the car and ran to her. Aaron kept the engine running, stayed behind the wheel. He waved.

Sophie's red hair was flying every which way, but what struck her most was how much alike the two cousins were even with a ten-year age difference. Leah's hair was identical in color and curl and both had startling blue eyes like their grandmother.

Sophie squeezed Frieda in a tight hug, then laughed. "I'm not used to seeing you in jeans."

"Aunt Frieda, you came just in time to go with us." Frieda reached for Leah and they hugged a moment.

The three of them walked over to the car. Aaron stepped out and gave Frieda a brief hug. "Thought you couldn't come because of business."

There was that superior tone that made Frieda's skin crawl. "Don't start worrying about me now, Aaron. I can take care of my affairs."

"Then why the hell didn't you get down here sooner?"

Frieda could feel her face and neck turning red as a major hot flash engulfed her. Her legs trembled, but she stood her ground.

"Don't take that tone with me, Aaron. I'm not some little kid you can push around anymore. Either talk like a civil human being, or I'm walking."

People stopped to listen. Leah and Sophie held hands, their eyes beacons of dismay.

Aaron turned away. When he finally faced her again, he said, "I'm sorry, kiddo. It's been a rough two days. Why don't we jump into the car before we roast to death?"

Frieda nodded and went to the back door. Even after several minutes of driving, the car held an awkward silence.

. . .

The sun squeezed Minna's skin with a crawling pain that made her instinctively clutch her robe. But closed, the material created an oven. She was cooking. Braised and battered in caked sand.

She wanted to laugh at the image but her mouth was stuck together. Blisters had popped and coagulated into a crusty poultice.

She crawled into the base of a sage bush where a lacy shadow covered her head and arms.

Her mind was sluggish and dull. She wondered where everyone was.

Water.

If only she could have a sip.

Pond … she and Aaron would throw bread to the ducks.

Water.

Statue of Liberty, where the great lady stood in the river.

GIVE ME YOUR TIRED, YOUR POOR, YOUR HUDDLED MASSES, YEARNING TO BREATHE FREE.

Water.

Scrubbing floors, cleaning patients, birthing membranes flooding everywhere.

Water.

A fly buzzed, flew into her face. She sluggishly waved it away, but in a moment it was back again. She was getting angry.

Flies were dirty, carried diseases. She needed to wash everything.

Water. She needed water.

The buzz grew louder, bombed her ears. Soon she was sitting up, swatting at the air.

"Stay away from me!" Her head grew very heavy, she fell backwards onto the sand.

The fly crawled back and forth over her face. She closed her eyes and no longer cared.

Chapter 32

Saul looked at Minna, his eyes wide with panic. "Pregnant? Again?"

"I'm not a brainless fool. Don't talk to me that way."

"Minna, we can't have another child right now."

"Don't tell me what I can or can't do." Her voice was shrill. "If you didn't want another child you should have thought of that sooner. I didn't get this way by myself."

Aaron ran into the room as fast as his six-year-old legs would carry him, arms outstretched to her.

"Mommy, Mommy!" He hugged her with all his strength, his heart racing against her chest.

"Can't we have a quiet discussion? You scream and scare the child," Saul said. He paced back and forth, the small apartment swallowing his every step.

"You want a quiet discussion about being pregnant?" Minna kissed the boy on the forehead and he settled down, heavy on her lap. "You didn't want him and would never have married me if I wasn't pregnant."

"You know that?"

"I know you! You wanted a woman, not a wife and mother to your child."

"What difference does it make now?"

Minna's voice turned sarcastic. "And what would you be without me, Saul Lubin? A bum scrabbling on the streets of New York."

"Can I help it if there's a depression? What do you want me to do? People have no money to buy clothes."

"Buy clothes from that pushcart?" She wanted to sneer but held back. "You call that earning a living?"

"It's an honest living. Can't you respect me for that?" Saul sat down at the kitchen table, rubbed his fingers back and forth on the flowered oilcloth covering the hopelessly stained wood. "Maybe you could have an abortion?"

"The same solution you offered six years ago." She settled the boy down on a tattered, faded sofa. There were tears in the corners of his eyes but he lay quietly.

"You know I love Aaron with all my heart, and I'm glad he's here. But we're poor and half your salary goes to that lawyer in Germany."

"Do you expect me to stop looking for my sister?"

"That's not the point. How will we pay for another child?"

Minna moved to the kitchen table. "Look at me, Saul. *Look!* at me! What do you see?"

Puzzlement lined his forehead. She noticed his hair had turned dull, looked sparser every day.

"What do you mean?"

"Look at me. *Look!* at me."

"So?"

"What you see is an overworked, thirty-six-year-old woman. Almost too old to have another child."

"Minna, don't talk foolish."

She pulled her dress away from her legs. Her ankles were swollen: ropes of varicose veins stood out like large blue rivers on a map.

"There are days my legs ache so badly I can barely get out of bed."

248

"Minna—"

"I'm tired. Do you understand? Tired of all the sick, poor people who depend on me to take care of them … tired of pounding the pavement in weather that's either freezing or boiling … tired of feeling like an old woman."

Saul stared hard at her. "All good reasons *not* to have a baby."

She wanted to scream at him again. Instead, she looked helplessly around their apartment: the sofa was so rickety it barely held her weight and it had to tolerate both of them when it opened into a double bed. Aaron's room was nothing more than an oversized closet. The only things that made the place bearable were the cheap copies of paintings by Chagall and Matisse, carvings of Buddhas and swatches of oriental rugs Saul found a way to buy over her objections.

She reached out and rested her hand on his. "I've given Annie Langtree a month's notice. I'm going to work for Moishe in his nursing home."

"But that's in the Bronx."

"There's a small apartment in the back, we can have it rent-free if we clean it out."

Saul's voice sounded defeated. "Terrible place to take a child."

"My salary barely pays the rent here. People are living on the streets, begging for food. I don't want us to be one of them."

"Damn capitalists! They control everything. Those vultures are responsible for this mess we're in."

"What's the difference whose fault it is? That's the way it is, and we have to make the best of the situation." She turned away, studied Aaron who was now sleeping. "Don't ask me again to have an abortion, Saul. I won't do it."

. . .

Moishe's Nursing Home

Its beady eyes stared out from the hard shell that covered its body, searching antenna waved in the air, and it seemed to look around before it darted across the floor.

"*Yop tvayu mat!*" Saul smashed the cockroach with such violence the pictures rattled on the walls. "You little *mamza!*"

It had taken a month to clean out the floor-to-ceiling stacks of rotting chairs thrown in the back rooms of Moishe's nursing home. Before they moved in, Saul had scrubbed and rescrubbed the walls and the floors. Still, the place stank of mold and filth. Worse, he had seen that rats had used the area to nest, and no matter what he did the roaches still came.

Saul was now the janitor, Minna the nurse-in-charge. Sometimes they didn't see Moishe for days, off doing whatever he wanted to do. Saul couldn't imagine what Moishe did with his time—but who could blame the bastard for wanting to get away? The place reeked of death and decaying bodies, and no matter how grateful Minna insisted they should be, Saul felt anything but gratitude to Moishe.

Saul argued with his brother-in-law almost from the first moment they entered the place. When Moishe paid him weekly, he made him feel not only like a useless parasite, but less than a man.

"Damn capitalist," Saul muttered, putting down poisoned potatoes to bait the cockroaches. He carefully pushed the chunks between the cracks in the floor so Aaron wouldn't become interested in them. But he still worried.

His mother had had a passion for cleanliness, too. She would clean and reclean their big house in Minsk. Even though his father's vodka factory made him a wealthy man, none of his money went into making his mother's life easier.

"Bourgeois bastard. Let her work her fingers to the bone."

It didn't take much for Saul to recognize that the beginnings of his fervor for communism had its roots in rebellion against a father he knew would despise his connection to the Reds.

One day the factory burned to the ground. His father, already a miserable rich man, turned into an even more miserable poor man. When the old man's cigarette smoke choked him to death during an asthma attack, Saul comforted his mother, but he rejoiced.

Saul checked his watch. It was almost time to pick up the kid from school. He walked toward the front of the building where Minna sat at a desk writing. He noticed her uniform was getting tighter, and it was stained, probably from her lunches the past several days.

"Are you going to pick up Aaron?" Minna said.

"Yes."

"Maybe you should talk to his teacher."

"What do you want me to say ... Aaron is restless and angry because he lives with old, sick people in a dirty, filthy nursing home?"

She glared at him. "I'm tired of the notes asking me to talk to her 'at my earliest convenience.'"

"Then maybe you should take the time to talk to her."

"Can't you see I'm working? How can I speak to some woman at school when I work seven days a week?"

Minna's voice was rising to a higher pitch. He knew the next sounds from her mouth would be loud and harsh—nothing stopped her from screaming, not even the few old ones who were able to wander up and down the halls and stare.

He wondered again what had happened to the sweet, quiet woman who had coerced him into marriage. Over the six years she'd gained a hundred pounds and she'd become sloppy, often wearing clothes that were not only wrinkled but also dirty.

"Will you take care of it? I can't do *everything*." She threw her pen at the desk. Flying ink spatters added more stains onto her gray-white uniform, tossed dark globs on the desk blotter. "He's just a child. How bad can he be?"

Saul turned and left before her voice reached an ear-shattering shriek.

• • •

Saul tightened the scarf around his neck, drew his overcoat closer around him. The clothes he wore underneath were crisp, clean, warm, and a necessary buffer to the frosty air. It would snow for sure, maybe today or tomorrow.

He took his time. It was only six blocks and he enjoyed walking. He inhaled a deep breath, could swear the aroma of fresh roasted chestnuts was all around him.

It was a day like this when his mother died in her tiny apartment in Brooklyn. The same day Aaron was born. The doctor had ignored her complaints, told her it was a stomachache that would go away in a few days. Saul had almost beaten the quack to death when she died of food poisoning. All he had now was his sister Olga, who nagged at him almost as much as Minna.

The trees were all bare: only a few evergreens provided any sense of life among the brick buildings. Even the botanical gardens, half a mile away, were filled with dormant plants. He missed the summer days when potted geraniums lined the apartment fire escapes and porches.

He stood in front of the brick school and sighed before walking up the steps.

Inside, a bell rang and children of all ages came laughing out of the classrooms. He met Aaron in the hall, helped him on with his jacket.

"Daddy has to talk to your teacher. Can you wait outside for me?"

The corners of Aaron's mouth turned down. "Okay."

Saul watched him trudge like a little old man toward the school entrance. He watched until he was outside, out of sight.

"Oh shit, I hate doing this," he muttered as he knocked on the classroom door.

He shook hands with Miss Scott, a short plain woman with intense, searching eyes.

"Thank you for coming, although I expected Mrs. Lubin."

"Can't a father speak to the teacher? Does it have to be a woman?"

"No, no. I'm sorry if I gave that impression."

"My wife is working and is too busy. You'll just have to settle for me."

The teacher was flustered for a moment, but she indicated a seat. Saul looked at a large red apple, a fresh blotter and a pile of papers neatly arranged on the small desk. A whiff of stale underarms filled the air as she reached into the stack of papers and handed one to Saul.

He looked at the paper. Aaron had scrawled his name across the top, the rest was scribbling done with such violence the pencil had torn the paper.

"What do you think of this, Mr. Lubin?" She reached into her bottom drawer and pulled several more papers his son had destroyed with a pencil.

"I think Aaron is not much of an artist or he has a very poor teacher."

"Maybe. But I think Aaron is profoundly unhappy and is expressing his anger."

Saul shifted in the seat. "He's a child. What do you expect from someone so young?"

She tossed the papers in the wastebasket, wove a pencil into her bunched up hair, and clasped her hands in front of her.

"I expect your child to sit quietly at his desk and do the work required of him. I do not appreciate his running around the classroom screaming dirty words and hitting other children."

Saul felt a chill edge up his spine. Now he was worried. "I'm sorry, Miss Scott. I can see you've been very patient with Aaron." He stood as the teacher rose to indicate the meeting was over.

"The child will have to do better or I can't have him in this classroom."

"You would throw my son out of school?"

Miss Scott's harsh voice became gentle, soothing. "I would have to place him in a special group."

"What kind of special group?"

"Mr. Lubin, I'm hoping we can avoid that kind of action. But that particular group is for …" She was trying to reach for the right words, "children who don't fit into the normal classroom setting."

"You mean like retarded children?"

Saul could see the teacher was very uncomfortable. "Some children in the class are retarded. Some have behavioral problems like Aaron."

He reached for her hand. "Please, please don't do that. My family … our family is having a difficult time right now."

She squeezed his hand briefly, her voice was gentle. "Most families are in trouble, Mr. Lubin. My class is filled with hungry kids. Everyone is suffering in one way or another during this depression … these are difficult times. But most of the children in the class do their work and they are mentally present. Aaron isn't."

"Miss Scott, please give me some time to talk to my son, to see if we can make things better. Please, let me work with you."

Her lips were pinched and her shoulders were taut. The room was like a separate presence that remained silent as they stared long and hard at each other. Finally, her face turned soft and vulnerable. "We can try."

. . .

By the time Saul left the building, snow was falling and Aaron had his tongue out lapping up the large, wet flakes. Saul watched for a moment, remembered doing the same thing when he was a kid.

His son looked so innocent, so happy. Saul wondered what he could do to help rid him of a temper that when unleashed seemed to consume everything around him.

When he saw his father, Aaron's face changed from joy to concern.

Saul offered his hand. "Come, let's walk in the snow. It's beautiful, isn't it?"

Aaron skipped next to Saul.

"Stop that, Aaron," Saul said.

"Why, Daddy? It's fun to skip."

"You'll put holes in your shoes, then we'll have to buy you a new pair. They cost a lot of money that we don't have."

Aaron walked, stomping down harder with every step.

"*Boychik*, what are you doing? Why are you so angry?"

Aaron looked up at him with large brown eyes. "Can't we go back to the city?"

Saul heard the pleading in his voice and his stomach turned. He took Aaron's hand and led him into the deserted botanical gardens. They walked along the pathway, the snow melting on their clothes. When they came to a bench they sat down, even though it was wet and cold.

Saul put his arm around his son. "I want you to know I love you."

Aaron nodded, tugging at a tear in his jacket sleeve. "Why are you and Mommy so mad?"

"Life gets hard. We're forced to do things we don't want to do."

The six-year-old frowned.

"We didn't want to leave the city but we have no money. We have to live here for now."

"But I hate this school."

"Why do you hate it?" Saul asked. He reached for his hand.

"The kids push me around because I'm new."

"Are you afraid of them?"

Aaron's face flushed a bright red. "No, I kick their *tuchus.*"

Saul sat quietly and let his son work out what he really wanted to say. It was at times like these that he wished he were rich and could make his son smile with delight over some treat he couldn't afford now. His mind wandered: What was he to do with another child when he couldn't help the one he had? And Minna? He'd never loved her—he was trapped.

"Daddy? Daddy?"

"Yes, son."

"They don't have pictures on the walls."

"You mean at school? I saw pictures."

"No. No. No beautiful tall buildings."

"I'm not sure—"

"Tall, big. Bricks and stone with shining lights."

Saul was puzzled. What did this have to do with anything? Even in the cold, Aaron's face was turning sweaty and he was sputtering, unable to express clearly what he wanted Saul to know.

In a moment there would be no turning back, he would be caught in a tantrum.

Saul remembered their walks around the city. He would take Aaron to the museum and although he was interested in the pretty colors of the various paintings, he would love to touch the stone walls, columns, decorations.

"Aaron, do you want Daddy to take you to the city? Do you want to ride the subway?"

The boy stopped fidgeting and nodded solemnly.

Saul straightened his son's collar. "Do you want Daddy to take you to see the city every Saturday? Just you and me."

Aaron smiled.

"You must do your school work and listen to Miss Scott. No more acting like a bad boy in the classroom. Can you do that?"

The smile faded. Aaron looked off in the distance, his eyes thoughtful.

"Every Saturday?"

"Yes Aaron, every Saturday."

Chapter 33

Germany—*Kristallnacht*

November 10, 1938

Sarah Goldmich covered her ears. The doorbell was jingling, jingling, jingling, jingling.

It made her scalp crawl.

She wouldn't answer it, no she wouldn't, no matter what. She wouldn't.

In the street were sounds of shattering glass, people screaming. It sent prickles of fear across her skin.

Shatter, clatter.

Shatter, splatter.

Stress eased with the rhyme, made her feel like everything was quieter. The broken glass, the beatings, the screams … for a moment all were pushed farther away.

The bell continued to jump back and forth, up and down over the door like a crazy dancing puppet.

She clutched the almost finished dress for Frau Schloss's daughter. It was supposed to be ready tomorrow.

Was it tomorrow? Or the day after? Well, she would have it ready for tomorrow and not have to worry.

"Go away!" she yelled at the door. She wasn't expecting anyone. She would not open the door.

Her fingers danced over the material, the needle clicking against the thimble. Frau Schloss was a very silly woman, had talked in a nervous, high-pitched voice.

"Magda would kill me if she knew I'd hired a *Jude* to make her wedding dress."

"*Ja*, Madame."

259

"After all, her fiancé, Peter, is a lieutenant in our people's army." Her bright red painted nails waved in the air as she talked, making Sarah dizzy. "Good German people honor German labor." A nervous titter. "But you are so competent and reasonable for a Jew."

"*Ja*, Madame."

"Did you see the sign on the tailor's window ... Herr Rosenfeld's shop? *Nue bei Deutjchen. Nich Juden.*" She giggled nervously. "Yet here I am."

Herr Rosenfeld's shop was next to the bakery and candy store across the street. Sarah had worked at both places during the last fourteen years, since her trip back from America.

Her mind picked through memories: the rich smell of yeast in the bakery, the lush dark chocolate in the candy store. Sadie and Irving, Ethel and Sam, the owners of those shops, had been good to her, helped her when she came to Berlin from Hamburg. They were kind when there was no one, nowhere to turn.

The windows of both shops were now shattered. Hours ago Hitler's soldiers had grabbed her friends, yanked them by their arms, thrown them out in the street. They beat them until the sidewalks were covered with blood. When her friends were finally still, the men crushed their skulls with the butts of their rifles.

She'd heard their cries, watched it all, hidden behind the white lace curtain of the large living room window. When she couldn't stand it anymore, she covered her eyes and screamed at the walls.

Jingle, jingle, jingle.

She put the lacy dress down carefully at one end of the sofa and hurried to the door.

"Go away!"

"Fraulein Goldmich, please let me speak to you. It's urgent."

"Go away!"

"Your sister Minna has sent me ... your sister in America."

For a moment, Sarah's heart brightened. Then she paced back and forth in front of the closed door.

Why should she listen to him? Believe him? How could Minna know where she was? Sarah didn't know where Minna was. How could she trust this stranger?

Soldiers, their eyes hard and cruel, had made bonfires of books, had gone into the library and carried stack after stack, pile after pile, created a ferocious fire that threw sparks at the sky. Crowds cheered and the soldiers laughed and flirted with pretty girls.

Why should she trust this stranger?

Jew-baiters who had followed her neighbor to the apartment had tossed her friend Sylvia Toller out of her third story window like a useless rag doll. Good non-Jewish German neighbors had remained silent behind closed doors while the murderers laughed, smashing everything in sight.

Why should she believe this stranger?

Laughing, smashing.

Smashing, bashing.

But no one had hurt her here. Here. Inside. Inside her own apartment she was safe.

She would keep them out.

Jinglejinglejingle.

"Please, *Fraulein*."

Maybe this man *was* sent by her sister Minna. Pinpoints of doubt started her pacing again. Memories of her mother, her sister, and the last time she saw them in America were all a blur. She'd been so frightened she hardly remembered anything.

"*Fraulein*, please."

The man knocked frantically, having given up on the bell.

She opened the round metal peephole and looked at the man:

young, nice black suit, clean-shaven, a briefcase clutched close to his body. A *goy*.

"Please open the door. I must talk to you." His blue eyes stared back at her. Kind eyes. "There's so little time."

Savage Hitler's youth had trapped, raped, spit on, laughed at her, beat her unconscious, all because she was a Jew.

Why should she trust this *goy*?

Sarah hunched her shoulders and with a wavering hand reached for the door bolt. Then her whole body was shaking: it started from the top of her head until her hands would not hold still. Fighting her tremors, she undid the lock and looked up at the man.

"What do you want?"

Even though it was a cold November morning, the man was drenched in perspiration. He looked up and down the hallway as though someone was chasing him.

Screams and shouts from the streets crackled the air.

"Please let me in. I must talk to you."

Sarah opened the door wider and the man stepped inside.

"There is no time to waste. You must come with me now."

Sarah's knees were knocking together. She could barely recognize her own voice as they stood in the middle of the living room.

"Who are you? What do you want from me?"

The man swallowed hard. "I'm Herr Mueller, an attorney."

"Yes?" Sarah said.

He looked toward the sofa. "Is it all right if I sit?

Sarah nodded, watched him pull a handkerchief from his back pocket and mop his brow.

"The world has become a madhouse ... what was right is wrong ... what was wrong is right. Only Hitler and his henchmen forcing Jews to register allowed your sister to find you. That and the usual bribes."

Sarah could barely get the words out. "Do you know my sister?"

"We have written. In fact, she started the search for you with my father. When he died ... well, I have continued."

Her heart was racing. "My ... my mother? And my mother, Frieda?"

Herr Mueller loosened the tie around his neck. "I'm sorry to have to tell you your mother died many years ago."

Sarah covered her mouth. Her mother had died many years ago? Many years?

Years in which Sarah could barely remember anything, years of each day running into the next, years when she worked as a house cleaner in Hamburg, years when she lived in Berlin; lonely, empty years unable to focus on any one thing for very long until one day, as though awakening from a long dream, life made sense again. But she was alone. There was no one.

Alone.

Her mother, David, Minna, and Moishe were somewhere across the ocean in America, and she was by herself. And now this man, this Herr Mueller was saying her mother was dead.

Dead, dead.

My mother is dead.

Dead.

A moan that welled from some inner darkness echoed off the walls of her apartment.

"Nooooo!"

The attorney jumped up, helped Sarah to the sofa. "*Fraulein*! Please! I know this is hard, but we have to get you out of here. Right now the Nazis are grabbing Jews all over Berlin—in their apartments, at their businesses, on the streets. Taking them away to concentration camps."

Sarah wrung her hands, tears smarting. "What is a concentration camp?"

Herr Mueller sat down again next to Sarah. "A place where they murder Jews."

She shook her head slowly. "But my mother … she came to me in my dreams like a golden star … she wrapped me in her golden light. She must be alive."

"*Fraulein.* Please understand, I cannot be found here by the Nazis. We must go. Now!"

"But you are not a Jew. Who would hurt you?"

"*Fraulein*, you don't understand. I could become a political prisoner."

"You're a stranger. Why do you want to help a Jew?"

The attorney became even more agitated, he used his handkerchief again to mop moisture from his neck.

"I'm a good German, *Frauline*. Murdering Jews … women, babies, is a black mark on the souls of our people, a crime against humanity. We are not evil people. I refuse to believe that we are. So I will help where I can, for as long as I can. Someone must."

Sarah looked at the wedding dress at the end of the sofa. She would have to finish it. Then she would go with this stranger.

"I cannot leave now. In one hour."

"*Fraulein!* If I am to keep you safe, you must leave now!

"I must finish my commission."

Herr Mueller stood abruptly. "Can you not hear the soldiers, the people's screams of terror? Look out your window, *Fraulein*. Look at the piles of dead bodies, look at the Jews being herded like animals. Can't you hear their cries?"

"Herr Mueller, I'm safe in here, in my apartment. No one will come in here to hurt me."

The attorney's eyes widened, he mopped his brow again, then shrugged in despair. "Please come with me. I beg you. Leave everything behind and walk out the door with me now."

Sarah was filled with indecision. She'd never failed to finish a commission. How would she find work in the future if she had a bad reputation? Frau Schloss would call her a bad Jew and she would never get work again.

"Can you not wait one hour?

The attorney stood. "I cannot wait one second longer. I will go now."

Herr Mueller's body seemed to droop as they walked to the door. "I will be at this address for one hour ... not one minute longer." He handed her a piece of paper. "I beg you to hurry."

The streets had been so noisy for so long; men, women, children being pushed, beaten—everyday there were cries of pain. But today the screams below rose in a shrill of terror that made her think of the opened eyes of butchered animals.

Safe here.

My space here.

Raped, torn apart, by ten, fifteen men who shredded her clothes and left her naked. Scars from the beatings were nothing, but no matter how much she washed, no matter how hard she scrubbed, tore at her skin, she was filthy with them still inside her.

Safe here. Safe in her apartment. Clients came to her and she paid young Heinz to buy her food and supplies. In here no one had hurt her. Could she actually leave?

She dashed to the window in time to see Herr Mueller hurry away. A high-ranking soldier in leather jodhpurs, uniform pressed and crisp, stopped to question the attorney.

His riding crop slapped a rapid rhythm against his leg. Herr

Mueller pulled papers from his coat and the soldier looked very carefully at them before waving him on.

• • •

Sarah tried to block the sounds growing louder around her. Her fingers flew over the fine material. The hardest part was sewing the multitude of tiny seed pearls around the neck. Each pearl took its own time, as though it had a special life requiring individual attention.

The chimes of her clock struck two. She had finished the dress in thirty minutes.

She held it up and let it float through the air like a banner flying on a windy day, then allowed it to come to rest spread out on the sofa. It was very beautiful.

Loud noises echoed on the staircase inside the building. She hurried to the door, her purse, the piece of paper Herr Mueller had given her clutched to her chest. She carefully, quietly opened the door and listened.

She started to step into the corridor when heavy steps brought the soldiers into sight.

She quickly dropped back into her apartment and locked the door. Running through the middle of the room, she peeked out the window.

Jews were being shoved into the center of the street, forced to march: women, men, children cried out as silent crowds of onlookers lined the streets. Below, twenty or thirty soldiers were grouped in front of her building.

The sound of feet grew louder and louder.

Safe space.

Safe place.

She hurried into her bedroom, flung open her closet, and pulled down the attic ladder. She hurried, breaking out into a cold sweat as she pulled the stairway up behind her.

Safe inside,

Safe inside.

Below she heard her front door crash open, the rush of heavy boots stomping through her apartment. Now they were at the closet right under her.

Her heart froze as she watched the folded stairs drop down. She could barely breathe as she tore the paper with Herr Mueller's address into tiny scraps and stuffed them in her mouth. Her head throbbed but she chewed rapidly. The pieces were swallowed as a soldier's head rose up into the attic. He stared into her eyes.

"*Raust, Jude Schweinhundt!*"

Sarah's body would not move, her mind spun as though she were swirling on a frenzied carousel.

Two soldiers surrounded her, grabbed her arms and dragged her to the stairwell.

"Please don't hurt me." They threw her down from the attic. Stabbing pain tore at her back, keeping her down.

All the loud voices, the shouts made her feel as if her brain would explode. Like an old ball, they took turns kicking her into the living room. She vomited as a soldier bashed her in the head.

It was then she separated, left her body. She rose, floated toward the broken window where the lace curtains reached out like billowing arms. A golden haze of light seemed to draw her, enfold her in a strange, but embracing warmth. Her mother's voice called to her.

Sarah stared back one more time at the Sarah left behind—the Sarah who had always been left behind: mouth distorted in agony, eyes pools of terror, hands clutching her breast. A soldier's rifle rose high above her.

The butt of the rifle came crashing down while Sarah, from up above, watched one of the others grab the wedding dress. Large hands tore and shredded it. The tiny pearls flew, scattered like precious kernels of wheat returning to the earth.

Chapter 34

New York City

Late 1930s

"Another meeting, is it, David?"

"Please don't, Ellen. Not tonight. I'm so tired."

"Not too tired for the blarney the commies hammer you with year after year." She collapsed into a chair and started crying.

"You knew when we met I was a communist. I never lied to you."

"And a communist is all you've been."

"I don't understand. Who could have loved you more?"

"Are you a husband? A father?"

"I could be those things if you'd have me."

"You don't care enough to give up the damn Reds though. They steal you away from me."

Silence made the air thick, so suffocating he could barely breathe. Ellen hugged herself, rocked back and forth. Finally, she stood and spoke again.

"There have been no lies between us, David Goldmich ... and there'll be none now." Her eyes were a stony blue as she turned away. "I'll be leavin' you, lad."

"But Ellen—"

She held a hand up. "There's nothin' more to say, David. Nothin'."

She locked herself in their bedroom and he helplessly rushed out of the apartment. After almost thirteen years of loving Ellen O'Hare, he'd lost her in a single moment, and there was no place to go except the union hall.

. . .

The stage was bare except for a six-foot banner behind the speaker and a print of Lincoln in profile, soldiers surrounding him:

Friends of the Abraham Lincoln Battalion

David's eyes wandered from the banner back to the speaker. The usual dress: jean jacket, pants, sweat shirt. This particular shirt sponsored the United Libertarian Organizations' newspaper, *Spanish Revolution.*

The man on the podium shouted: "We need *you* to go to Spain, to fight Franco. Franco, who devours, strangles the hearts and souls of his own brothers and sisters."

Growling rumbled, echoed through the hall.

In the back of the room a single voice began to sing. Everyone joined in as the speaker continued:

Spanish heavens spread their brilliant starlight
High above our trenches in the plain;

"Why do these comrades rush to die in a foreign land? Why do they leave their families? Their friends?"

From the distance morning comes to greet us
Calling us to battle once again.

"Why are they willing to splatter their blood on foreign soil if they didn't know ... yes, *know* it is vital to save this republic? Spain's freedom is our freedom."

Far off is our land, yet ready we stand,
we're fighting and winning for you. Freiheit!

Wild shouts of "Freedom! Freiheit!" swirled around David.

The speaker paused, waited for the room to fall silent. He lowered his head and stared intently around the hall, his eyes catching, then sweeping past David.

"While you sit in this hall, while I stand on this stage, the people of Spain are being raped, butchered in the name of Christian civilization."

Shouts of "No!" were scattered across the hall.

"Franco says that this is a Christian crusade against the Reds. You believe that?"

"No!"

David was stunned by the screaming voices around him. People were crying out their pain, his pain.

"Spanish priests don't believe it. They fight side-by-side with our brothers. They're all fighting the giant monster called Fascism."

David's head rang from the whistles, the screams. The noise blurred then exploded into a raucous emphasis of his own private hell.

"Fascists are murdering their own people … claim the Reds, the Loyalists are the murderers."

"No!" echoed around the hall.

"It's *not* the Reds who commit murder, rape, mass executions. It is Franco's military, his Civil Guards. And who asks you to turn a blind eye to these murdering bastards?"

"Who?" cried the crowd.

"The United States, Britain, France. These great countries do nothing. Worse, they prevent the republic from arming itself for protection."

"No!" resounded across the hall.

"The republic is a cry for freedom from your brothers and sisters, the people of Spain. We need you! *We* neeeed you!"

David looked around at the audience. Saul was in the back of the room shouting with his friends. He saw many he'd brought into the party—students, miners, fur workers, lumberjacks, teachers, salesmen, dancers, artists.

He turned back to the speaker and wondered if he was ever as young or fiery, stomping the stage with his work boots until everyone pounded the floor into a deafening roar of thunder.

Excitement churned in the pit of David's stomach. Was forty-three too old for all this brimstone and fire?

Maybe Ellen was right after all. He'd given everything he had to idealism, left nothing for her.

Or maybe he'd been right all along and there was nothing else more worthwhile.

Maybe now was his time, time to step up and make a real commitment, throw his life into *this* circle of fire.

• • •

By the time David was ready to leave for Spain, he knew the vital statistics: he would become one of more than 2,000 American volunteers who were going to defend the Spanish Republic against a military rebellion led by General Franco.

Minna, Saul and Ellen gathered at the Lubins' small apartment to say good-bye. Ellen begged him not to leave. He thanked her for her love, for helping him to be strong. To meet life on his own terms.

Minna cried the most. "There's so much to do here," she said. "You're needed here."

"This is an important mission for all of us. I would ask you and Saul to go if it weren't for the children."

Saul embraced him like a brother.

"Ellen, come with me," David said, taking her hand. "We need you, need nurses."

"Have you lost your mind, David? How could you ask when you know how I feel about anything that has to do with communism?"

"You don't understand. Irish, Brits, Canadians, and people from all over the world belong to the International Brigade. We're *all* fighting against Fascism, against Hitler, Mussolini. Many are not even communists."

"Bullocks! It's the communists that have drawn you into this fire. Stay, David. Please!"

"No, I won't! Can't you see that I'm finally doing something important with my life?"

"You poor, demented man, you're throwing your life away. Is it so important to die with a gun in your hand?"

"A world filled with justice is worth dying for."

"Justice, is it? Going to someone else's country and telling them the communist way is the best way. That's a lot of blarney, David! If you want to go, say so, but don't be toying with me, handing me glorious ideals as your reasons."

"Ellen, try to understand. There's a hunger that gnaws at people? A hunger to work, to live their lives based on freedom … not repression."

"Oh, Mister Goldmich. I understand the words they've put in your mouth. Understand you can't even think for yourself anymore."

They parted as enemies. There was no trace of the girl he'd fallen in love with in the hardened face of the woman screaming at him.

Chapter 35

Spain
Late 1938

Daylight was fading and the sound of artillery fire was getting uncomfortably closer. David lay shivering in a muddy trench blending with the earth as the heavy smell of mold clung to his uniform and his hair. The sounds of his stomach no longer tricked him into wanting to eat … there were no rations and they had not eaten since yesterday. The hardest thing to face was the look of defeat on every man's face. Even the brave ambulance drivers had stopped their snake-like maneuvers to pick up the wounded. Men were dead or dying all around him.

He pulled a pencil and paper from his knapsack and began to write:

Dear Ellen,

I came to America hoping for a better world. Oh, yes, I know you're thinking, "He's a bloody fool" and you're probably right. But the execution of Sacco and Vanzetti made me realize I had traveled half way around the world only to find more hunger, human injustice, and fear. The land of the free and the lady with the torch had let me down. And it was time that I did something worthwhile, no matter what the outcome.

I fooled myself into thinking that the uniform I bought from the Army-Navy surplus store, along with the tourist ticket, was an act of courage. In reality, it was only to hide the simple truth that I was performing an illegal act. An American going to fight against Franco. I suppose I should have had some kind of premonition as to how difficult this fight really was going to be. When I arrived in France and met with other volunteers, we felt only a sense of adventure as we boarded a train to the edge of the Pyrenees Mountains. But by the time we trekked through the snow-filled mountains to Catalonia, purpose was the only thing that kept us going.

Finally, at the northeastern border town of Figueras, we organized and received our orders from Albacete, headquarters for the International Brigades. In a few hours we were taught how to use a rifle and I joined a small group of seasoned Americans who had survived winning battles in Saragossa, Belchite, and Tercul. They all spoke of those victories as times past. And it hasn't taken long to realize they were right. Franco and his allies are crushing us.

Isn't it strange that I waited until late 1938 to join the brigades? My determination grew only as the Loyalists were losing heart as well as most of the battles. It seems as though my whole life has been one losing battle after another.

I can't tell you how many nights I stare at the darkness thinking of our terrible last moments together. I've loved you so long that every breath I take is like breathing for you even though we are thousands of miles apart. I hope your bitterness will have passed and you will remember the happiness we had.

I'm glad you did not come with me. Glad you are not here to witness the depravity of man. Still, I would give anything to have you next to me. To smell the freshness of your hair, the perfume of your skin.

Yesterday we liberated political prisoners held by the Civil Guard. These men in their dark cloaks and patent leather hats are the epitome of Franco's Black Spain. Their legacy is death. People see them coming and they run for their lives. If I told you the things these monsters do to torture the human body, you would have the same nightmares I do.

I miss you desperately, sometimes at the strangest moments. When my gun misfires or a bomb explodes in the trenches and flying shrapnel shreds the person next to me. Or as I run toward the fascists, my belly filled with terror. In fields where bombs, not flowers, explode, I don't dare stop, for there is certainly a bullet, a bomb with my name on it, waiting, waiting for me to slow down, stop, so it can catch me.

Yesterday as I walked through a silent battlefield I looked into the eyes of the dead. The emptiness made me feel weak and I fell to the ground. The sky turned very dark and a flash of yellow light blinded me. All at once, a sense of peace and hope lifted me to a place where there were no more dead bodies, only an orchard of soft green olive trees.

It was so beautiful. Although it is winter here, as I floated, voices swirled around me, carried on a soft summer breeze. Pincus Levine and my mother, even Uncle Heshie, were there surrounding me in a warmth that made me feel young and whole. Since then, I'm no longer afraid. I'm finally at peace.

Ellen, I can hear you telling me how insane I've become. Maybe you are right. The dead bodies are still here. And there will be more every day.

But one thing I know without a doubt. You have been my redemption. And you will remain my shield against the horrors surrounding me. It is the thought of you that makes me still feel whole. And on the days when I ask myself why I'm here, you are the answer. I'm here to protect you, and everyone I love.

We are fighting for you!

Viva la Quince Brigada!

• • •

Minna, Saul, and Ellen sat at the kitchen table in silence while Aaron and Frieda ran around the room shrieking in childish delight. The contrasting silence soon forced the children to stop and retreat to the living room sofa although no one had said a word to them.

In the middle of the table was a telegram. No one wanted to touch it, as though that could cancel its reality.

Finally, Minna said, "He's gone."

Saul slashed at the silence that followed her statement. "Don't say that! All we know is that he's missing. He could be a prisoner. He could be alive."

"Don't you hear what you're saying, man?" Ellen's voice was harsh. "I'd rather he were dead than to be in the hands of those murderers."

"I want him to live," Minna said, crying. "I want him to live."

"Have you not read David's letters?" Ellen shot back. "Have they told you nothing? Those people torture their prisoners, and then they kill them. Is that what you want for your brother?"

"Stop it! This is not a time to fight among ourselves," Saul said, tears running down his cheeks.

The room fell still again. Minna stirred the tea in her glass with a spoon, remembered her mother doing the same thing long ago in their kitchen in their tiny house in Russia.

As the silence stretched out, Minna's mind flipped through the pages of her own life. She squeezed, compressed, shaped it all until its reality existed only in this moment.

What did it all mean?

Are we all only accidents? Conceived not to thrive, but to lose each and every person we love until all we crave is our own death?

Last month it was Sarah, this month David. How many more loved ones would she have to lose, how much more pain would she have to overcome until she finally lost her will to live?

She looked at her children's faces, filled with unanswered questions. They were too young to understand the emptiness in her heart and it would not be long before they grew up and left her, probably never to know who she was.

And Saul? The father of her children. He shared the same beliefs, but their relationship was empty. She knew he was sleeping with other women. Even if she had not heard the whispers of others, she had eyes to see what could not be hidden.

A boiling anger in her gut almost doubled her in pain. She pointed a finger at Ellen. "This is your fault! If only you had tried to share his beliefs, tried to understand the importance and depth of his commitment, he might still be here with us."

Ellen's eyes narrowed. "This is my fault? My fault? Minna, don't be trying to avoid your own responsibility in this loss by passing the blame to me."

"There was an emptiness in David," Minna said. "He needed you. Needed you to care as he did."

Saul stood. "Stop it! Both of you are acting like children. Blaming each other will not bring David back."

Minna ignored him. "He wanted to marry you, have a family, but you kept him away with your manipulating, your demands he leave the Communist Party." Minna knew her face was bright red. She was talking so rapidly she could barely breathe.

"You don't know what you're talking about," Ellen blurted.

"You asked him to give up the very ideals that made him what he is."

"Not is, Minna. Was. What he was, was a fool! A fool, do you hear me?"

Saul abruptly left the table and went to the sofa. He sat down next to Aaron and Frieda.

"I would give anything to have David sitting here with us, but I would never have asked him to stop believing …" Minna struggled with the words that would not be uttered. "Stop believing—"

"Talk and more talk about nothing," Ellen said.

"Can't you see that these fascists will swallow the world, if we let them?"

"And I suppose the Reds will save the world?"

"At least they've tried to help save the Republic. What's the matter with you, Ellen? Do you hate the communists so much you can't see the truth in front of your eyes?"

Ellen stared a long moment at Minna. Her body was rigid and she shook with anger. "There is only one truth: David is dead." She leaned down until her face was almost touching Minna's. "Dead! Do you hear me?"

Minna's eyes filled with tears again. "I hear you."

Ellen walked to the apartment door and yanked it open. Before the door slammed behind her, she said, "I will wound you, Minna Lubin. Make you pay for my David's death. Then you'll understand pain. *My* pain."

Chapter 36

Minna slogged through the two feet of freshly fallen snow that led from the trolley car to her apartment. She had left work early with a blinding headache and although her head was pounding, she treasured the stabbing pain because without it she would still be sitting at a desk surrounded by old, decaying people.

She visualized Saul cleaning their place. The children would be in front of the building with Aaron watching Frieda. Instead, Frieda was on the stoop-playing Jacks in the middle of a group of older children. Not a sign of Aaron.

"Mommy, Mommy," Frieda cried out as Minna approached. The little girl ran to her, hugged her so tightly, they both almost slid into the snow.

"Frieda, your brother? Where is he? Isn't he supposed to be watching you?"

"He went away ... told me to wait or he would beat the shit from me."

"How many times have I told you and your brother not to talk like that?"

"Mommy, I good. It's Aaron."

Minna grabbed the little girl's hand and took the elevator to the third floor. As she opened the apartment door, Frieda clutched at her leg, her eyes like huge saucers.

Silence.

No sounds of Saul cleaning.

They walked to the back of the apartment.

Silence.

Minna stood before her closed bedroom door for several seconds. She and Frieda were frozen in one spot.

Finally, she flung the door open. Called out. "Saul?"

The musky smell of sex sent shivers through her.

"Won't that teach you not to pop home without warning?" Ellen said, not bothering to cover her nakedness.

"Minna!" Saul barely whispered.

"You bring this to our home where our little girl can witness what a rotten fool you are?" Minna let her wet coat sink to the floor.

"Well, dear girl, you always said Saul was sleeping around. What's a body to do but help a friend out?" Ellen said, slipping into a blouse and skirt. "Now you know the truth of it."

"I expected this from him, not from you."

Ellen put on her coat that had been tossed on the floor, and as she walked out she stopped, tousled Frieda's hair. She stared with stony eyes at Minna.

"I warned you. Warned that you would pay for my losing David—"

"Ellen, but how could you?"

With a toss of the head, Ellen walked down the hallway.

"We're even now, Minna. You'll see me no more. He's all yours."

But Ellen had been wrong. Saul had never been hers to keep. He'd been trapped into being a father and that was all he was.

Ellen was the real loss.

• • •

Minna crossed the roof of the ten-story apartment building. The night was cold and brisk. Winter breezes sifted through her threadbare coat and she hugged the tattered material to her body to keep from shivering.

She'd missed the freedom of climbing to the roof when they

lived at Moishe's nursing home. Oddly enough, it had finally become the most important reason she'd agreed to move.

Yes, this was freedom.

Exploring the top of the building was a happy ritual she performed most nights when she left Saul and the children asleep in their beds while she stole away to enjoy moments of peace and quiet.

Often, Saul would awaken and yell at her before she left.

"Wandering on the roof after midnight is not a respectable thing to do. Damn it! You're a nurse and a business woman of almost forty, not a street walker."

She ignored him. There was little to be afraid of since the only person she'd ever seen at that hour was the janitor. He wasn't very frightening and he didn't care what she did.

Her shoes crunched into the remnants of last week's late winter snowstorm. She walked to the far end of the roof where the janitor had erected a crude lean-to for his pigeons. The birds cooed softly.

Minna brushed snow away from the roof ledge and sat. The jagged skyline of the surrounding buildings created black shadows and each individual apartment became an integral part of the darkness. Finally, she turned toward the old deserted movie studio next door, imagined what it looked like in the bright sunlight:

Tannish-yellow pockmarked cement sprawled across two blocks, and inside were sagging stages with molding sets and props. Saul had wandered through the building and told her there were very few windows, and those he did see were broken. Aaron and his friends roamed through the place almost daily, bragged about throwing rocks at rats as big as cats. Minna had given up scolding him about his trips into the studio. Aaron did what he wanted no matter what she or Saul said.

Reflected city lights blocked out most of the stars' blinking beauty, but that never kept her from pretending she was back in

Russia straddling a limb of her peach tree, imagining her mother would be along soon to force her back into the house. She'd been gone from her homeland for such a long time. Some days she remembered nothing of her farm, her existence in Russia, but on other days, she could see everything in her mind's eye as though she'd walked away a moment ago.

Tonight, the sky was unusually clear. She searched for her friend Orion: the group of stars winked and sparkled. Maybe her mother and Sarah were in the heavens sitting on Orion's belt, smiling down. Or maybe it was all a fantasy as Saul said.

She tried not to think of her lost sister, but Sarah was a ghost that hovered over her, next to Uncle Heshie, her mother, Pincus, and David. Even the boy she'd murdered, the one who tried to rape her, was somewhere nearby next to her father, tantalizing Minna with memories of her childhood.

It had been months since she'd heard from the German attorney with the news. He'd risked his life to find out what happened to Sarah during the time the Nazis called Crystal Night.

Kristallnacht! What a lovely way to describe such a brutal event, as if glittering crystal in the velvety night could soften the harsh blow of genocide. The attorney felt that Sarah's quick death was probably a blessing, a better fate than the tortures of a concentration camp.

She asked herself again, as she had so many times: Could that be so? Wasn't some chance of life better than none?

But what did Minna know about dying? She was still here.

Tears flowed down her cheeks as she pictured the last time she'd seen Sarah at Ellis Island: Her good-bye wave, her crooked smile, had the flavor of a child's farewell, not that of a thirty-year-old woman being cast away. Minna silently thanked her brother

Moishe again for bringing her to America. Minna had been lucky to steal away from the horrors Sarah and other Jews had to endure.

She sighed. She would have to go in soon or Saul would come after her. The beginnings of another fight.

How did she end up with this man? Most of the time there was nothing good to be said of him except that he was a good father.

No love between them, yet she'd conceived Aaron almost instantly. So many wonderful years with Pincus—someone she loved so dearly—and she'd remained barren. How could anybody explain that?

Now there was Frieda, a sturdy little girl of three. Often Minna would look at her and see the golden light hovering over her. Was there ever a doubt that Frieda would be special, the way her grandmother was? The way she herself once was?

Frieda made Minna feel sad, reminded her that the golden light no longer filled her or protected her.

Loss. So much loss.

The wind whispered in her ear: Everyone dies.

Yes, everyone dies.

And what was happening to her time? She was almost forty and her life was ebbing like the sands of the hourglass she kept on her desk at the nursing home. Grain by grain, year by year her life was draining away.

What did she want?

All she could think of were the things she didn't want.

She didn't want to be poor, didn't want to work with downtrodden, hungry people anymore. Maybe her days of being a communist were over. The workingman didn't seem so glorious, especially now that she worked seven days a week.

And she didn't want any more children. They demanded so much, wanted to know so much, and she didn't have much left to give or tell them.

She definitely didn't want Saul. This man she lived with, supported, still couldn't accept her as she was. Always criticizing, always watching: how she walked, the way she dressed, how fat she was. She would never be pretty enough, smart enough.

Most of all, she didn't want to be constantly humiliated. Saul continued to see other women. She could smell them on him, could taste their presence, even after he promised to stop.

He never stopped.

She poked holes in the snow on the rooftop ledge and a chill seeped through her gloves. What shape would each day take when her children were gone? Who or what would she not want to be then?

Turning her attention back to the stars, she stared hard at them for several minutes, then made up her mind not to think too much about her future.

Ellen used to come to the roof with her. They would giggle and talk about things Minna would never dream of talking about with anyone else.

One night after running into the janitor, Ellen whispered he was nothing but an Irish drunk. She'd snickered when he proclaimed his love for the pigeons. "Everyone knows he eats them regularly."

Minna argued, "How can you blame the poor man for trying to fill his belly, drunk or not?"

Ellen only laughed. "Minna, you're too serious."

Yes, she had always been too serious.

It would be so much easier if she could hate Ellen for blaming Minna for David's death. But how could she hate her for just being human? Don't we all feel someone should be responsible for the losses we endure?

Someone.

Minna choked back a sob. She hadn't understood how vital Ellen was to every single day of her life until she was gone.

Minna bowed her head away from the wind.

• • •

In the Desert

Her face was buried in the sand, her mouth clogged with grit and mucus. Coughing, choking, Minna managed to wheeze in a raw breath before looking around in a daze.

Where was she? Where was Ellen?

"Ellen! Come back!"

She tried to stand up, tried again. Each time she fell back until her face slammed hard into the ground. She lay still, not daring to move.

A distant throbbing made her drag her hand up to her eyes—ripped nails and ragged strips of torn skin barely clung to her fingers. She studied smears of dried blood.

"Buurd."

The sound of her voice was thick and alien, rousing her. She turned toward the sun. The molten ball made her burning body feel hotter. Her tongue pulled at her cheek, felt strange stuck to the back of her throat. With a shaking hand, she forced it out of her mouth. Like a snake, it sampled the hot and dry air before curling back in her mouth.

Tight. Her face was so tight, she could barely move her lips.

"Burrrn."

She gingerly ran a sand-coated finger over crusty blisters on the back of her neck, across her face. She wanted to lift her legs, tried to wiggle her toes but there was no feeling, no sense that anything existed below her waist.

She turned toward the horizon. Something was moving. Far,

far in the distance she saw masses of people walking toward her. As they came closer, light surrounded them like sparks over a snapping fire.

"Here," she whispered.

Men. A solid black horizontal density grew larger, closer. Clots of black-uniformed soldiers with shining boots kicked up the sand as they advanced. Before she could identify them, they were gone.

Her eyes closed in despair, she began to drift off.

"Minna Goldmich Lubin."

Someone was kicking her.

"Minna Goldmich Lubin!"

"Yes! What do you want?"

A man stood over her, dressed in a spotless Nazi uniform, his face frozen in a sneer. "You Jew whore! I want you to die!"

"Go away!"

"The Cossacks couldn't kill you because your kind are like bugs that blacken the earth. You kill some and twice as many take their place."

"Go away!"

"No place to hide now. We will starve, gas, exterminate, until you and all of your scum are nothing but a memory in the history of mankind. Go away? No. It is *you* who will be gone soon."

Minna's chest heaved, seemed sluggish. Pain laced itself around her ribs, stabbed through her middle.

"You will come with me now," the Nazi says.

"I won't!"

"Then die with your sister, Sarah Goldmich."

"No!"

"She is your sister. You are Jews! You will die together!"

Minna looked at crowds of people moving across the desert floor. Thousands upon thousands drifted toward her. As they drew closer she saw they were covered in raggedy striped cloth that clung to the skeletons they had become. Some walked out of and away from their clothes, too weary to hold them up.

"I present the future of the Jews," said the Nazi.

"No!" Minna struggled to her feet, stood next to him and dry-spit his face.

"Nazi murderer!" The effort made her stumble; she fell back down to the sand again.

"Look at you! Jews are so weak, such an inferior organism."

"Leave me, you bastard!"

The Nazi's laugh roared across the desert. "That's why you're out here all alone. No one wants you. Not even your own kind. Where is your son, your daughter?"

"They'll come for me."

She clamped her eyes shut, wanted to cry, but tears wouldn't come. When she opened her eyes again the crowds were marching closer, would soon trample her.

"Go away!" Minna cried out to the Nazi, then began to laugh hysterically.

The soldier spread his legs and kicked her hard in the back. "Jew pig!"

The marching crowds, the masses of concentration camp victims formed a circle around the two of them. Tears still would not come and words were caught in Minna's throat. She studied the women, their breasts and bellies nothing but flaps of wrinkled skin; the men, old and powerless, their heads more skull than a living human. Children like torn ghosts floated above the sand.

"This is *your* gift to humanity?" Minna said.

The Nazi smiled. "What do you know? You're just an old Jew who should have died with her sister."

She pointed a shaking finger at him. The crowd surrounding them pointed also. "You killed six million human beings."

"Not human beings. JEWS!"

The Nazi grinned at the crowd surrounding them and pointed back at them.

It took every ounce of strength, but she finally stood face to face with the Nazi.

"Where is your Hitler now?" She slapped him hard across the face and his sneer melted away. "You and your master race are nothing but dust."

The effort made her head spin and she fell down hard.

A narrow band of a shadow no more than a foot away was under a sagebrush branch. She crawled hand over hand, inched to the gray spot and covered her face. When she looked up again, the soldier was gone.

It was a little cooler in that slim band of dappled shadow. She looked at the horizon again and moaned.

A soft cool hand caressed her face.

"Sarah? Is that you?"

"Yes, Minna. It's me."

Minna looked up into a golden light. It filled the sky, the sand that surrounded her sister. Minna smiled. "I thought I'd never see you again."

Sarah ran a hand over Minna's hair. "I'm with Mommy now."

"Can I see her?"

"Soon." Sarah turned to leave.

"Please don't leave me, Sarah. I've missed you so much all these years." Minna sobbed. "I'm so sorry I couldn't save you. Please forgive me."

"It's not your fault, little sister."

Sarah drifted, floated high above the sand. The golden light shifted farther away.

"Sarah! Sarah! Wait for me!"

Chapter 37

"For Christ's sake, Frieda, it's been two years since you came to see Mom. *Now* you bother?" Aaron jammed a cigarette into his mouth and yanked out his Zippo, refusing to wait for the car lighter to do its job. "You know she's going to die out there, don't you?" he said.

He jammed the car into gear and jolted away from the hotel parking lot. Leah and Sophie remained silent, but they tightened their seat belts.

"Don't guilt me, Aaron. I'm here, aren't I?" Frieda coughed, fanned away the drifting cloud of start-up smoke. "You live in the same damn city…when was the last time *you* saw Mom?"

The radio blasted out the weather report, abruptly silencing them both:

WHATAYOUKNOW WHATAYOUKNOW! OUR METEOROLOGIST HIT US WITH AN UP-TO-THE-MINUTE. GET THIS, GONNA BE THE SAMEOLE, SAMEOLE FOR THE NEXT 48 HOURS. YESSIREE! 115 DEGREES OF THIS STINKIN' HEAT! TELL YOU WHAT, FOLKS. TONIGHT WHY DON'T YOU CURL THAT LITTLE BODY OF YOURS ON TOP OF THE AIR CONDITIONER AND SLEEP THE SLEEP OF THE RIGHTEOUS. OOOOORR BE A MANIAC, MANIAC, MANIAC AND DANCE THE NIGHT AWAY. OHOHOH. THIS IS BODACIOUS ANDY PASTILLO SAYING HASTA MANANA.

"God, I hate that asshole," Aaron said, sucking hard on his cigarette. "I don't know why I turn on that stupid station." He reached over and clicked off the radio.

Without the hammering noise, uneasiness settled around them, only the full blast of the air conditioner broke the silence. Frieda turned away from her brother, stared at the sun on its descending path. Through her dark sun glasses the fiery orb took on a softer, mellower glow and made her feel less edgy.

Frieda was the first to speak. "You know Mom and I never got along. When she finally walked out on Dad she wanted to move in with me. To this day I blame her for his death."

"So you've said."

"Mom, you never said anything to me. I would have loved to have Grandma live with us."

Frieda smiled. "That's why I never told you. Mom and I could never live under the same roof again."

"But, Aunt Frieda, don't you love Grandma?"

Aaron was silent, he puffed away on his cigarette while Frieda dug into her purse for some imaginary items. "Leah, I love your Grandma. But that didn't mean I could live with her."

"I don't—"

"All we do, all we've ever done is fight." She looked at Aaron. "Like your father and I."

"Oh, get off it, Frieda. We fight because we don't like each other. Never have. *That's* the bottom line." He stubbed out his cigarette, grinding it into the ashtray. "All this pussy-footing around is a pain in the ass."

"Daddy! That's mean." Leah leaned forward and clutched her father's shoulder. "Take it back. Say it's not true."

Perspiration ran down Aaron's face. He reached into his back pocket and pulled out a handkerchief to mop his face. "Still the troublemaker, Frieda."

"Where did you ever get the impression that I didn't like you?" Frieda said, turning back to the window. "Until I was twelve, I spent most of my waking hours trying to get you to pay attention to me."

"Yeah, and what happened afterward?"

"You left and never looked back. I got tired of being just a pain in the ass."

They drove up and down the mostly empty streets. The few people they saw carried umbrellas to protect their skin from the late afternoon sun.

Frieda eyed the mesa—the unbelievable expanse of desert that seemed to swallow up every landmark, even the sprawl of the Sandia Mountains. She shifted, a strange tingle at the base of her spine made her uneasy.

"The land here is so uncompromising. It's you and the sun. It might as well be Mars." Her voice dropped to a whisper. "Do you suppose Mom really could be out there? I can't believe the police wouldn't have already spotted her wandering the streets."

"Mom, she's out there. I know it." Sophie said

"That's quite a vision: an old lady in a pink robe and slippers trudging through the sands of New Mexico." Aaron spit the words out. "Shit, even out of her gourd, instinct would tell her not to head out to the desert in this kind if heat."

"She's out there, Aaron."

Frieda shut her eyes against a rush of yellow hovering over the desert—it continued to blind her even with her eyes closed. She tried to will it away, but the unwanted light remained, and for the moment, it brought an eerie calmness. "She's waiting," Frieda whispered.

Aaron stared at her.

Sophie touched her mother's shoulder. "I feel it too, Mom. When I look at the mountains, I see the beauty but it's the desert I'm drawn to."

Leah took Sophie's hand and squeezed it tightly.

"Have you tried searching the mesa areas near the nursing home, Uncle Aaron?"

"Are you kidding? If you think I'm going out there in this heat," he said, pointing toward the vast wasteland, "you're out of your head. Besides, it's probably the first place the police searched."

"Grandma's been gone two days," Leah said. "Maybe it's worth another try, Daddy."

Aaron shook his head and made an abrupt right turn.

"It's nothing but a useless gesture. But if it'll make all of you happy, I'll go along with it ... first thing in the morning."

"Aaron! What's wrong with you? Mom's dying. You don't have to be a rocket scientist to figure that out." She looked at her watch. "It's 5:30. We still have three more hours of daylight. Let's do it now."

He pulled off to the side of the road. "Will you listen to me, please? We're not going to find her on foot ... it's too damn hot to go slogging around in the desert."

"So rent a four-wheel drive," Frieda said.

"Yeah...we could do that," he said quietly. "But getting one right now, gearing up with what we need to survive, is going to leave us damn little time to do anything before it's dark."

He was right. By the time they rented the Jeep and were ready to go, all that was left of daylight was the orange afterglow of another spectacular New Mexico sunset.

• • •

Frieda barely slept.

She stared at the moonlit ceiling resisting the strange sensations the dancing prisms of light brought as they floated above her bed. She knew how to resist their beauty, their message of love and hope. Reason and logic would send them away. Over and over she would weave and interweave, loosen and tighten the threads of her predictable life. Things had to be comfortable, understandable, controllable. *That* was the core of her strength, the center of who she wanted to be.

She deliberately turned away from the moonlight, but the prisms remained.

Emotions rose to the surface and before she could stop the rush, memories overwhelmed her.

For months after Aaron went into the Army, her mother would pace the length of the apartment night after night. Frieda would waken and listen for the steady scuffle of footsteps until she and her mother shared the same internal clock.

One night, staring through the darkness, waiting for the flap of her mother' slippers, she dozed off. When she awakened, it was morning. Her mother had not walked the dark hours away.

There was little mention of Aaron after that. Her father spent most of his nights away from home and Frieda was lonelier than ever. Whenever she asked her mother about her brother, a different voice, one she didn't recognize, answered.

"Never get too close to anyone, Friedaleh. When they leave, all that remains is emptiness ... emptiness that can never be filled again."

Twelve-year-old Frieda understood the words, knew it was not only her brother that had broken her mother's heart. Still, she never stopped missing Aaron, and it was a long time before she gave up the nightly vigil that her mother had abandoned.

• • •

Frieda sat up. She had soaked the motel's sheets with sweat. She pulled her nightgown off, slipped into a cotton t-shirt, and lay down on the dry side of the bed. It was soft, cool. But as she started to doze, the memory of her mother's footsteps in the hallway seemed as real as the very first night she'd heard them.

Aaron had finished his stint with the Army and gone to school in Albuquerque. She was surprised when he became an architect—her memories were of him tearing things down rather than building them up.

At twenty-five she started her own struggling catering business—the same year her brother started his architectural firm.

When they talked by phone, it was always of his success. Frieda often wondered if it had been easy to step away from his dreams of design and settle into creating mundane commercial developments. Aaron wouldn't discuss it.

They rarely discussed anything—their children, their failed personal relationships, or even their mother and father, which was usually the reason for the call in the first place. At one point, he complained about the "Red Threat" to the country and their parents' insane "Commie connections."

"First, it was the Rosenbergs, now they're rallying against this McCarthy guy when anyone can see, he's just a political idiot full of shit," Aaron said.

Frieda would stand up for her parents and their political commitments, even though silently she had mixed feelings about many of the causes they were involved in.

But her brother remained adamant, intense, and endlessly angry. Whenever she finished speaking to him, she was depressed for days. He left a huge hole in the center of her being, and no matter how hard she tried, she could never plug its emptiness.

Staring through the darkness, she searched for some kind of answer to explain her continued devotion to Aaron when he wanted nothing to do with her. But, as always, the night only threw back more questions.

Why was Aaron so angry with her?

Why didn't he want her to be here?

She eased out of bed, paced back and forth before walking to the bathroom. The sharp chill of tile floor distracted her for only a moment.

What did her mother want from her? What had she ever wanted?

And what would she say if she could see her mother one more time? Could she even say she loved her?

Frieda grabbed at her chest, clutched the t-shirt, and tore it off. What was missing inside that made saying I love you to *anyone* so frightening?

A sudden flash of blinding light lit the bathroom like a golden shower of fluorescent rain. She covered her eyes, but the intensity of the light remained.

An old voice, weak and eerie: "Friedaleh. Please!"

Frieda jumped into the shower, turned on the cold water to douse the yellow fire that surrounded her. But the rush of water brought no relief from the scorch of the golden light.

Was this real? Had any of it ever been real?

• • •

Aaron lay in his king-size bed curled up on one small corner of the mattress. Waves of loneliness rippled from the top of his neck to the base of his spine. He wanted to hold, to be held, but his arms and legs seemed heavy and useless. Not even the thought of a cigarette gave him the energy to reach to the side table and grab what he needed.

He stared across the darkness at Cynthia's side of the bed. "Never here when I need you," he whispered.

What was wrong with him? Even when he had money, all the women he wanted, all the trappings of the good life, he remained lonely. Even in a laughing crowd, he hovered on the edges, smiling, but really an observer.

299

Was there ever a time when each day brought a rush of excitement? No, not even when he was a kid—a little scared Bronx kid who only wanted to crush everyone and everything in his way.

That's when he learned to run. It was what he did best to survive.

He had achieved what he wanted—success, respect. He was even feared.

But why was he still running?

The question turned his stomach, but the answer made him want to cry.

Being broke! That was his greatest fear. Without money, no one would want him—he would be totally alone.

He was hot inside. Hot and empty like the long stretches of sand-filled mesa that covered mile after mile of New Mexico.

When he first came to Albuquerque, the open vistas made him feel safer than he'd ever felt in his life. No one jabbed him in the ribs or tried to move into his space.

There was room.

Real room.

Breathing room.

But after a while, he ended up with that same clutching chest tightness he'd had in the Bronx. A steel band that squeezed, tortured his heart with fear.

4:00 AM.

He stared at the red numbers of the electric clock until they seemed to jump out at him.

Could he trade his mother's life for a way out of the rat race?

Did he really want her to die?

He thought of Leah.

Leah, the only joy left in his life. Soon she would be grown, leaving him alone with Cynthia. How would he ever live without his Leah?

Was wishing for his mother's death the only silent legacy he could pass on to the one love of his life?

How sad his little girl had to have him for a father.

. . .

Minna's eyes still burned from the bright glare of the sun even though the sky now held only a cold moon and the pinpoints of stars.

"Where are they?" she mumbled. "Murdered? Innocents?" She jabbed a finger at the sky. "Secret of secrets ... buried." Her fingers dug into the sand.

"Jews ... Julius ... Ethel ... Murdered."

Minna pointed at the sky again. "Diamonds, Mommy."

The same diamonds described to her as a little girl when she and her mother lay on their backs studying the night sky, speaking in whispers of the mysteries of the universe:

"Why do you love the stars, Mommy? You can't touch them. They just hang there ... so far away."

"They don't just hang there, Minnaleh. They are a presence ... the eyes of all creation. And they see beyond anything we know."

"But you can't touch them."

"You don't have to touch something to love it. The fact that it exists is enough."

"Will you always exist? Will you always love me, Mommy?"

"Even when you can't see me, I will be there, and I will love you forever."

Now, Minna wanted to cry, but she wasn't sure why. It wasn't because of pain—that had receded like an ebb tide, gone for a time, but still waiting patiently for the right moment to return.

It wasn't hunger. All she wanted was water.

No, there was something else she wanted to remember, something she wanted to say.

But no matter how hard she thought, there was only a void, an emptiness that would not speak, could not speak to what was in her heart or her mind.

Minna's arm fell back to the gritty mesa. She lay with her legs spread across the sand drawing in the moonlit coolness and watching a cascade of shooting stars race across the velvety heavens.

Chapter 38

Saul was beside himself. He checked his watch, shouted to Minna, "Hurry up, people will be coming any minute."

Dammit! How many years had he been pushing her along for one occasion or another? He blinked, waited a beat for her response.

"If they get here early, you'll take care of them."

Nothing ever changed.

Nothing.

Except that he was almost sixty and still not happy. Saul edged past the five poker tables squeezed into the living room and plopped down on a brocade sofa. He reached out and ran the tips of his fingers across the cool surface of a ceramic lamp—like its Chinese twin at the other end, it sat regally on a dark teak table.

He'd purchased the lamps at an auction two years ago. The decision to buy them took hardly a moment, but the simple white shades had taken months to find.

He rubbed the toe of a soft leather shoe on the oriental carpet. The intricate designs of imaginary blue, red, white flowers reminded him of the never-never-land Frieda loved as a little girl.

Minna mocked his involvement with the furnishings and the expensive clothes he bought for himself. But he liked to look smart and he defended his need to go to auctions as an intellectual pastime. After all, what he bought had its place in history.

She was right, though.

What he saw around him was the remains of the decadence of ancient ruling classes. His desire to possess these things, to hold, to own them was not only a terrible weakness, it was a horrible flaw in his political reality. But like a moth sensing the light, he was helplessly drawn not only to beautiful women, but to every form of beauty. When he walked into a museum, vibrant, sensual paintings jumped out to grab his attention, and it was rare that he could pass a sculpture without a finger secretly following a favorite line or curve.

He grunted as he reached down to tie his laces, noticing an ugly scuff mark on his shoe. He couldn't imagine he hadn't noticed it before—it was certainly past time for a shoeshine. Straightening up, he loosened the pants around his thighs and opened another button of his tan Harris Tweed jacket. He particularly liked this jacket, with its herringbone design. It had been a present to himself when he sold his nursing home to the city to make way for a Harlem housing development.

Again he patted himself on the back for refusing to stay with Minna in the nursing home she bought after she left Moishe. Over the years, he'd saved the salary Minna gave him for doing janitor's work. He'd invested it in his own nursing home, and was finally free of her constant nagging.

But now, the state was talking about buying her nursing home to build a cross-county expressway. What would he do with her when there was no business for either of them to go to day after day?

"What's taking you so long?" he called out, trudging down the long hallway towards their bedroom. What a stupid man he was: he wanted to leave, yet he stayed, slept with her and even made love to her every now and then. Long ago he'd been forced to marry her when she became pregnant with Aaron, but nothing actually made him stay … nothing except Frieda. And if he was honest with himself, it wasn't his daughter that kept him here.

"What are you doing, making the damn dress?" he yelled through the closed door.

"If I don't wear the right clothes, you'll nag and complain. Be patient. Everything is ready and I'm almost finished."

"Well, make it fast!" He stomped back down the hallway, looked into Frieda's room on the way. His daughter was staring out the window, an elbow propped on her desk, a hand under her chin.

"Please change your mind, sweetheart."

I won't," she said, her voice tight, nasty. "There're a million things I have to do, Dad. I'm *not* going to play poker."

"But Friedaleh, it's for the Rosenbergs. You know that's how we raise money for their defense, to help take care of their boys."

Frieda flung a book across the room. It bounced off the wall and crashed to the floor. "Play without me!"

Saul started to pick up the book, then changed his mind. Why was his eighteen-year-old daughter so frustrated? So angry?

"Can't you understand how sick and tired I am of the Rosenbergs?" Frieda shouted.

"Frieda. How can you—"

"Sick and tired of hearing about them, the Cold War, everything." She glared at him. "And you and Mom constantly going on and on about McCarthy and the House Un-American Activities Committee is making me crazy."

Saul sat down heavily on the edge of her bed, forced himself to look away from her fiery eyes. He stared at the walls covered in museum postcards of Michelangelo's sculptures and Marc Chagall's paintings.

The miniatures of Chagall's work reminded Saul of village life in Russia long ago—but that had been a different world than this mystical, romantic place. Saul envisioned pogroms, brutality, corruption—bleak times before the Tsars were overthrown and the people reclaimed their homeland. Yes, Chagall and Saul shared common roots, but each staked out a different Russia as his own.

He studied every detail of one particular postcard. This was the fairy tale Minna longed for, what she wanted to return to: her cows, her peach tree, her land. A simple life without the constant challenges of the many business decisions that had to be made on a daily basis.

Without warning he was unexplainably chilled, and a rise of nostalgia thickened his throat. He shrugged it off. Russia was a better country now—even when Stalin was at his worst, it was better. His stomach turned queasy—thoughts of Stalin always made him uneasy.

Frieda had turned her back to him. She seemed to be working on some kind of school project. Papers were spread across her desk.

"Are you sure there isn't something bothering you?"

"Maybe I just want to take some time to hang around and do nothing ... sit and stare into space." She turned to look at him, her mouth drooping at the corners.

Saul held his tongue for the moment. He was having trouble controlling his temper with his daughter lately. Sometimes he wanted to shake the stubbornness out of her, make her see the same troubled world he saw.

"This is what happens when you lead a privileged life," he finally said. "A life where every meal, every scrap of clothing, the roof over your head is provided for and taken for granted. A world where every heart's desire is given without lifting a callused finger."

"Well, *you* gave it all to me."

"But it makes no sense. You understand injustice, yet you refuse to involve yourself against the criminal things being done to two human beings who have done nothing wrong. The Rosenbergs sit on death row waiting to die. If we do nothing, they *will* die ... and that son-of-a-bitch McCarthy is going to destroy us all!" He leveled a finger at her. "You know that!"

"Daddy, it's not that I don't care about the Rosenbergs or McCarthy—"

"He lies, prosecutes teachers, writers, actors ... has the country in an uproar over nothing. People are chasing shadows that don't exist."

"I understand all of that, Daddy." She walked to the bed and sat down next to Saul. "But I'm a student. If I don't do my schoolwork, I'm going to fail. Don't you want me to graduate from high school?"

"You're a smart girl. You can do whatever you need to do."

"But I only have so much time to devote to things other than school." She reached out and squeezed his hand."

"Are you sure you won't join us tonight?

"Yeah, I'm sure."

"Everything is better when you're there."

"I helped with the cooking, setting up the buffet."

"You did, sweetheart. But it still makes me sad to see such a young, intelligent person not directly involved with something as important as this." He kissed her on the cheek. "All right. So do your homework, but I'll miss you."

He started to leave but she held his arm, looked at him with questioning eyes. "Daddy, the teacher says the Korean War is almost over, but everyone is still afraid of Russia stealing atomic secrets. The Rosenbergs are supposed to have stolen secrets."

"You believe that nonsense?"

"I don't know."

"Julius and Ethel are ordinary people who had no access to atomic secrets."

"Are you sure, Dad?"

"Frieda, even if it's a lie, do we execute a man and woman with two little boys? Where is the justice?"

"But, Daddy! This is our country. Don't you want us to be safe?"

His fingers pressed to his eyes, he rubbed hard in nervous agitation. "What are you? What are they afraid of? This country is never going to turn to communism. The people here love their possessions too much."

"You love your possessions, too, Daddy."

There it was again. His own decadence. He had money now and felt safer than he ever had before, but along with security came the doubts of his true commitment to communism.

"That's my point. Possessions are persuasive. Not a good oven to bake a real communist."

"But what if the Rosenbergs did steal the secrets?" she said.

"So if we execute them, this will make us safe?"

Frieda thought a moment, then answered, "No."

"There is no safety in murder. And the only 'evidence' is testimony from Ethel's brother who claimed they were involved in stealing the secrets … he's nothing but a crook making up evidence to save his own neck. This couple is being framed in the same way the House Un-American Activities Committee members are destroying innocent people. They point a finger at anyone to cause a big splash in the papers. That way they look as if they're really doing something valuable."

"But people in school are really scared."

"They should be scared … locking up innocent people, forcing Americans to take loyalty oaths so they don't lose their jobs."

Frieda returned to her desk and stared out the window. He kissed her on the cheek and left the room.

He was jittery, wanted the evening to begin so he wouldn't have to think anymore. Impatiently, he arranged and rearranged the card tables, finally sat down heavily into the sofa. He thought about leaving Minna again.

Who was he kidding? Days when he could comfortably live in someone's attic were long gone. Where would he go if he left?

He checked his watch again.

"Late," he muttered.

Agitated, his mind jumped from one thought to another.

He didn't even own this place. Minna owned it. Owned it with Moishe, who lived with his family downstairs.

Moishe. Minna's savior.

Moishe, the hero who turned into a rabid Zionist after his testosterone dried up, and whose energy and money now only went to Israel.

Moishe's money *and* Minna's money.

Money.

Materialism— always the downfall.

• • •

Minna was finally ready. She stood at the living room entry. He looked at her carefully: At least she had repaired the hem of the plain brown dress that had hideously draped her fat knee last time she wore it.

But his heart always lurched when he looked into her beautiful clear blue eyes. Eyes that looked at him with distrust. Eyes that never stopped wishing he were Pincus Levine.

After all these years, he still lived in that man's shadow.

She smiled timidly, looking for his approval, but something made him hold back and bitterness overtook a momentary softness. How could there be kindness after the screams of hatred that had passed between them?

"How much money did you give Moishe yesterday so he could buy more orange groves in Israel?" he asked.

"Out of the blue you need an answer to this question? People will be arriving any minute and you want to get into a fight about Moishe?"

"Why do you let him use you like that?"

"There's more to life than money," Minna said. "You of all people should know that. The Jews need a homeland. Israel is a young country in the midst of people who vow to push them into the sea. Without money they will be crushed."

"A lot of religious nonsense, that's what Zionism is about. That's what your brother's about."

"The Holocaust happened, Saul. Millions of Jews were murdered, including my sister. Do you think I could turn my back on the only place in the world that belongs to the Jews?"

"So they have a country now. You need to send all your money to them?"

Minna's face turned a bright red and she tugged at her dress in frustration. "It would be far more useful if you spent your money on Israel than on these fancy things that do nothing but feed your ego."

• • •

Minna was exhausted. It hit her all at once in the middle of a poker bet.

The other people at her table were playing a serious game of five-card stud and she was sitting on top of three threes. She knew if she won the pot tonight she personally would have raised about three hundred dollars for the Rosenbergs' freedom fund, and the night was young. Hopefully, the evening would raise about three thousand dollars.

"Minna, have you got another three to go with that pair?" her friend Marcia asked.

"Yeah, what are you hiding?" Marcia's husband Bill prodded.

"If you want to know, you'll have to pay like everyone else," Minna said sweetly.

Saul was staring at a woman sitting across the room, hardly paying attention to his cards. Minna's stomach flipped in contempt for a man who cried out so loudly for justice but had to look at every slim ankle no matter what the occasion. The only one he really cared about was Frieda.

She continued to study him.

One day soon, at a time and place of her choosing, she would hurt him. Not only hurt, but destroy him in the same merciless way he had smothered every warm feeling she ever had toward him. Then, she would leave him hanging with nothing left to hold on to.

Enjoy yourself while you can, Saul. Nothing lasts forever.

Minna turned her attention back to the game, smiled at Margaret and her husband Charles. They were good poker players, but they weren't there for fun and games and a night out. They were only there to raise money for the Rosenberg's young sons, Robert and Michael. They'd already raised thousands of dollars on their own that had been funneled into the care of the two children.

Minna won the pot with her hidden three. Marcia gathered the cards and started to deal.

• • •

The light chatter and cross talk faded away and a flood of

sadness overcame her: Minna knew Julius and Ethel Rosenberg were going to die. They would lose their final appeal and their children would become orphans.

She'd dreamed about the couple last night: Ethel's moon-shaped face was a ghostly white, brown eyes deep wells of sadness. Julius looked at Ethel through broken wire-framed glasses, his full lips drooping in pain as they said good-bye.

Dressed in black. One by one they were led down a long corridor, their mouths sewn shut. Each was led to a coal black electric chair.

Outside the killing chamber, the warden stood at the telephone. All they had to do was confess and he would stay their execution.

But each died in silence.

She'd awakened in a cold sweat, reached for Saul. The moon shone on the wrinkled sheets of an empty bed.

• • •

Marcia nudged her. "Are you going to bet or daydream the night away?"

Minna smiled vacuously at the mixed image, passed some money into the pot without looking at her cards.

But Minna knew all this effort to raise money, all the world appeals, all the letters from people of renown from all over the planet would not change a thing. Like Sacco and Vancetti, the Rosenbergs would die in the electric chair and everyone would go on with their lives as if nothing had happened.

Chapter 39

Albuquerque

MOOORNING, MORNING, MORNING KIDS. IT'S OLE ANDY BACK AND RARIN' TO GO ON THIS SPEEECTACCULAR NEW MEXICO DAY. CAN YOU BELIEVE IT, WEEER'E GONNA HAVE ANOTHER SIZZLER. BUT, GOOD NEWS ON THE HORIZON. TOMORROW THE TEMPERATURE'S SUPPOSED, I SAY SUPPOSED, TO START COMING DOWN. YES, YES, YES! RELIEF'S ON THE WAY. NOW, BEFORE WE GET TOO FRANTIC, TOO INTO OUR FUN THING, PAY CLOSE ATTENTION TO ANDY FOR A MOMENT AND SEE IF WE CAN BE GOOD CITIZENS. OH, THIS HEAT, THIS HEAT CAN YOU BELIEVE IT? AND IT SEEMS A LITTLE OLE LADY IS WANDERING AROUND OUT THERE. OUT THERE FOR THE LAST TWO DAYS. MAN-OH-MAN. HER FAMILY IS FRAANTIC. SHE'S CONFUSED, LOST AND PROBABLY VERY THIRSTY AND FRIGHTENED. HELP, HELP, HELP US PLEASE. OPEN YOUR EYES, OPEN YOUR HEARTS AND LET'S FIND HER. ANYONE, I MEAN ANYONE WITH INFORMATION PLEASE GET IN TOUCH WITH THIS STATION OR CALL THE POLICE.

• • •

Aaron, Frieda, Sophie and Leah were eating breakfast at the Quick Fix diner when they heard the DJ's appeal. The announcement had been blasting the airways on and off for the past two days and each time it aired, it sent a shiver of fear racing up and down Aaron's spine. Now, the intensity of the appeal, and the blare of the radio hurried, chased them out of the diner.

They arranged themselves in the Jeep Wagoneer as though they had traveled together in the vehicle for days. Aaron fired it up and moaned again about the weak air conditioning, was about to drive away when a police car pulled up. He lowered the window, recognized the officer, as one of his least favorite people.

"Morning, Jake. What's up?"

"Chief sent me on over. Said you were probably here chowin' down."

Aaron tapped his finger impatiently on the steering wheel, trying to get through the long pause that followed. "Have you got something," Aaron finally said, "or are we just going to pass the time of day?"

"You're worried, man, I can see that, but no need to be takin' it out on me."

"What have you got?"

"Well, some jerk of a kid workin' in a local drive-in tootled in a sightin' of your Ma. Said he saw her two days ago."

"Oh, my God! What did he say?" Sophie asked.

The officer bent over slowly and tipped his hat to Sophie without replying.

"What's the chief think?" Aaron said.

"Worth checkin'. He's on it, but it's hard to believe some son-of-a-bitchin' kid wouldn't give an ole lady a drink in this heat 'cause she didn't have no money." The policeman scratched under his hat, riding it to the back of his head. "Takes all kinds, uh?" He looked at his watch. "Chief's probably out there 'bout now."

"Where's the drive-in?" Frieda asked.

Aaron was squirming in his seat trying to stay calm, but Jake's country bumpkin style was driving him crazy.

"Where the hell's the place, Jake?"

The officer's eyebrow shot up into his hat. "It's **BARNEY'S DRIVE-IN**. Some poor excuse of a drive-in at the end of—"

"Dad! I know where it is," Leah shouted. "Let's just go."

"Okay, Jake," Aaron said, hitting the accelerator.

The officer frowned, turned away.

Aaron was not only coffee-high, he was wired from all the sleepless nights thinking about his botched-up life. He couldn't help wonder what else could go wrong even though he knew there was always room for more trouble. He rolled up the window to get some cool air moving in the Jeep again while rivulets of sweat ran down his spine side-by-side with an uneasiness that was making his skin crawl.

He studied Leah in the rearview mirror. Her eyes were lit with anticipation. It was the first look of hope he'd seen on her face in two days.

What the hell was he going to do when this whole mess was over? Frieda and Sophie would go home, so at least he'd have them off his back. But would he still have a mother? Even if she lived through this messy situation, there wouldn't be too many tomorrows, and he still wasn't sure what that meant to him.

A wife? Probably not for too much longer—his marriage was in the toilet. He and Cynthia had not been a good fit from the beginning and the truth was, no woman would be happy with his footloose, fancy-free attitude toward marriage. Getting down to the nitty-gritty, whom could he really trust his soul to? People were too damned dangerous, and personal entanglements demanded too much.

Frieda and the girls were talking. A background buzz. Leah called out the directions.

"Do you know the place?" Frieda asked.

Aaron ignored her.

"Aaron, do you know where it is?" she asked louder.

"Yeah, yeah. I've seen it, but it's one of those dives you try to avoid if you don't want ptomaine."

• • •

The sun was spraying fire. Disconnected images rolled before Minna's eyes. She jumped as shots rang out across the desert. Her mind emptied then spurts of shooting napalm turned her arms a crackling black. She screamed, "Stop!" Her fists clenched, she tried to shake them at the sky. But her arms would not move.

"Please don't kill them."

Behind closed eyes, she dreamed, stared at a horizon, squinted at limping figures coming toward her. Soldiers dragging their weapons cut ruts into the desert floor. They shouted, "Make love not war!"

"Make love, not war," she muttered.

When the figures grew closer, they became silent, the only sound the loud shuffling of their feet. She tried to speak again, but her mouth was too dry, her tongue shriveled and parched. Closed eyes only opened new doorways to violent dreams of terrified young men, of babies, mothers, fathers with their flesh burning.

She awakened with a start and squinted in the bright glare of the sun. She tried to get up, scraping her raw skin against the sand, but no matter how hard she tried, all she could do was move her head from side to side and wiggle her fingers.

Then she remembered the funny fruit pictures.

She stared at her arms. Instead of black, scorched skin, she was covered with broken blisters and a network of plastered, bloodless cracks.

Why didn't they come for her? Why did they let her lie naked? Why didn't they bring her food, her Coke? She tried to swallow, closed her eyes against the bright glare of the sun and soon she drifted away.

The haunting sound of music, of voices rang out across the desert. She stirred:

We shall overcome.

"White man down," she yelled, her voice breaking.

We shall overcome.

Oh, my God! "White man down."

We shall overcome someday.

"Somebody help him! Help the black man! Black man down."

Oh, deep in my heart, I do believe, we will overcome someday.

"Murderers! John, Bobby, Martin, where are you?"

She turned from the blinding sun, searched the horizon. Three men in the distance walked arm-in-arm leaving a trail of blood sizzling on the hot sand.

"Come back," she whispered. "Please come back."

A golden light flashed across the sky and snatched them away.

Chapter 40

Minna eased the placard from her bruised shoulder and propped it against a tall brick building. The sign was large and bold—black letters screamed on a splashed background of chilling red:

STOP THE WAR IN VIETNAM NOW.

She shrugged to loosen muscles that bunched in her neck—the motion threw spikes of pain to the top of her head. But just standing in one place was a relief after pacing back and forth all morning.

The worst part of protesting had been surviving the nastiness of the crowds: spitting, cursing, pointing fingers. One woman had run up to Minna and yanked her hair so hard a gush of tears spilled down her cheeks. Minna had shoved the woman and her snarling face away, but she'd been badly shaken. The shouts grew louder and harder to ignore, so instead, she'd followed the path of the sun rising higher and higher.

Weariness made her heart skip into an uneven run of beats. She leaned hard against the building to steady herself.

August 16th, 1970—her seventieth birthday.

She wondered why she had come here on this particular day. Then her head cleared, her breathing leveled off, and she remembered that being at this demonstration was more important than any one person's birthday.

"You look beat, Minna," Angie said, strolling up to her. "But you're hanging in there a lot better than some people half your age. I'm proud of you."

Minna nodded at the young woman, who looked as fresh as when they'd started walking early that morning. Long and lanky, Angie had dark, curly hair that she'd pulled back and encircled with flowers that didn't seem to wilt even in the midday heat. Glittering strands of colored beads were slung wildly around her neck and a large rainbow-colored button— "turn on, tune in and drop out"—was worn proudly above her left breast.

Angie's smile was sweet as she came closer to Minna—sweet as the wispy aroma of marijuana that surrounded her. They'd only met four days ago but were immediately drawn to each other. They'd paired up, not only to picket, but to share their lunchtime.

"Hey, Minna, let's go eat and get you off your feet."

At first Minna wanted to wave her on, but her head was pounding and the humidity was crushing her chest. She hated New York in the summer, and today the temperature was threatening to set a new record high.

"We haven't checked out that deli on the corner," Angie said, grabbing Minna's sign and carrying it with her own.

Minna was too tired to object; she smiled her gratitude. "You remind me of my daughter, Frieda."

"The one who's a caterer?"

Minna nodded.

"Why isn't she out here with you?"

Minna stopped and pulled a handkerchief from her purse and mopped her brow and neck. "Frieda hasn't decided what kind of person she wants to be, yet." They walked slowly towards the deli. "Someday she'll understand. Right now she's a business woman … idealism is for people like us."

They entered the deli and sat down at an inside table. The air conditioner blew out a half-hearted breeze that made the dirty white streamer on the dust-caked vent barely flutter. After a few minutes of rest, Minna was ready to look at the menu. She told a scowling, impatient waiter that she wanted a Coke. "Large, lots of ice." Angie ordered coffee.

"Lunch is on me today, Angie."

"No way."

The waiter rolled his eyes toward the ceiling but said nothing.

"Give us a minute," Minna said to him, pressing fingers to her skull. Her head throbbed with every syllable. When he continued to hover, Minna said, "Can't you see we're not ready?"

"Make it fast, lady. This is a place to eat, not shmooz in the free cool air." The waiter tapped a pencil on his order pad.

"Angie, please! I can afford to take you to lunch, so do me a favor and order whatever you want. It would make me happy." She reached out and squeezed her hand.

"Well, what would really be groovy is one of those giant pastrami sandwiches."

"Then that's what we'll both have."

The waiter grumped and complained all the way to the order counter. "Get a gander at those *shmegegis*. Oughta toss 'em and their commie signs out. Yeah, toss 'em out on their *tuches*. Sick and tired of hearing about the Vietnamese, Shmietnamese ... so sick, I could vomit."

Just looking at the man made Minna want to walk out, but she was too hot and tired. Tired of people who couldn't see past the tip of their nose about anything. "Don't they ever hear themselves?"

Angie nodded. "Yeah. They're the kind of weirdos that think it's okay to murder the Vietnamese because they don't think the way we do."

"The world hasn't changed much since I was a little girl in Russia. All mankind knows is how to kill one another."

"People like you and me are going to turn all of that around." Angie smiled widely. "Keep the faith, Minna."

The waiter brought their food, almost throwing it on the table. Angie smiled sweetly and said, "Cool, man." He said something under his breath and disappeared.

Minna stared at the sandwich, picked up a sour pickle from the plate and nibbled on it. "All the years when I was a communist, I thought the way you do. I thought I could change the world."

"I'm not a communist, Minna. I just want to do what's right."

"So did I. But each decade brought a new set of horrors."

"The universe tests us all."

"We failed that test with Sacco and Vanzetti."

Angie looked puzzled, took a big bite of her sandwich. "I've heard those names, but I can't remember who they are."

"Oh, they were just a couple of communists, a fisherman and a shoe peddler ... executed in 1927 for murders they never committed," Minna said, picking some meat from her sandwich.

"That must have been a sad time for you," Angie said.

"Yes it was. And it was during a demonstration against their execution that my Pincus was injured ... killed."

"Who was Pincus?"

Minna laughed just to hear his name again, but she could feel the hollowness, the emptiness where her lost love lived. "He was just a man, a sweet man."

"We have to keep believing, Minna."

Minna smiled at Angie, but she could feel the heavy presence of a sadness that never left her. "I believed with all my heart through World War Two. A time when the Nazis murdered my sister, tried to destroy my people." Minna took a long drink of her soda. "I still believed even when they executed the Rosenbergs, and right through McCarthy and his henchman. Even during the fight for civil rights."

Angie looked at Minna with large eyes that reminded her of the cows she used to heal: eyes that were soft, yet with an intelligence that tried desperately to grasp every word.

"Angie, when they murdered the Kennedys, and Martin Luther King ... I felt the universe had tested me one time too many."

The silence between them was heavy, melancholy. Minna had stopped eating and sipped her soda instead. Angie spoke first: "But you're here now, Minna."

Minna nodded. "I'm a survivor, Angie. Life has been hard, even ugly. But I still believe each one of us can make a difference." She leaned forward and grinned. "And I say that not knowing if my life made any difference at all."

"But what would the world do without people like you and me?"

Minna had finally cooled down, her headache was gone, and her heart was no longer racing. Eating and talking made her feel more focused, kept her mind from wandering onto something else. Since she'd thrown Saul out earlier in the year, there were days that she couldn't remember anything that happened.

"How old are you, Angie?"

"Twenty-six."

"No boyfriend, no husband?"

"No way."

Minna smiled. "Do you want to spend the rest of your life alone?"

Angie laughed so hard she almost choked on her food. "Minna, I'm not alone. Four of us share a pad ... and that's when it's quiet. Friends are always bedding down with us ... someone always has a joint to smoke or food to share. I'm never alone."

Minna's mind drifted. She'd had friends and family, yet she was lonely. People provided you with the illusion of comfort and security for as long as you were willing to accept a life without questions. Once you asked the hard questions, wake up to the truth, the answer was simple—we live as singular beings. "Angie, the only one you can trust is yourself. Survival is all that matters."

Angie touched Minna's shoulder. "That sounds so lonely, so sad."

"I was never lonely when I was back on my farm in Russia." Minna swallowed hard. "But that was a long time ago."

"What was it like?"

"It probably wouldn't be interesting to you but life was simple and happy." She sucked hard on a chunk of ice from her drink. "My mother was a healer ... she taught me to be one."

"A healer. Cool! Did you save lots of people?"

Minna laughed. "No. We mostly healed cows with what we called a golden light."

"How did it heal the cows?"

"The golden light became a part of me ... like the blood that runs through my body ... but it nourished not only me ... it healed others." Minna could see Angie was disappointed. "Cows were almost as important as people in those days. We would have starved without them."

"Funny, I think I know what kind of golden light you're talking about. I've seen it." She laughed softly. "But only when I drop acid." Angie's eyes were dreamy and she seemed to be staring at something far away. "It gave me a strange, eerie feeling ... like I could see, no ... like I could *be* everything all at once ... in the eye of God."

"For me, it was a sense of safety. I've been uneasy without it. Every day I wish it would come back."

"But why have you lost it ... how have you lost it?"

"I don't know," Minna said. "One day it was gone."

Angie reached for Minna's hand. "Maybe if you pray, pray real hard, things will be right again."

Minna stared at the young woman and a spark of agitation rumbled her stomach. Angie's face was so fresh, so unlined. Minna wondered if she ever had been as carefree and unafraid as her young friend. "God deserted me a long time ago, Angie, deserted me when I left my farm, my mother."

"Minna, you *have* to believe in something."

"I believe in justice, in survival, we all have a right to that." Her hand tightened into a fist, but she took a deep breath and forced herself to relax. "If it's God who makes life so hard, He should find something better to do. Leave us alone!" Minna shoved a bite of her sandwich into her mouth. "But is it God," she asked, chewing her food, "that's made us the way we are, or is it that mankind is basically cruel?"

"God must have put us here for something better than that," Angie said. Otherwise why are we even alive?"

Minna continued to chew, letting the question hang in the air.

"Years ago when I was a communist, I didn't believe in God. But now, I'm not a communist anymore and it's made little difference. I'm still not sure what I believe or if there's even anything to believe in."

"Feeling like that must be hard. I can see why you're lonely."

Minna sighed. "I was just thinking how sad Pincus ... the man I mentioned before ... how sad he would feel to hear me say I'm not a communist."

"Tell me more about Pincus."

Tears unexpectedly welled up. She'd stopped crying about Pincus a long time ago.

Angie squeezed her hand.

"Pincus loved me. *Me.* Not the clothes I wore, or the money I made. Or what I could do for him. He just wanted me to be happy."

"He sounds like someone I would have liked."

"Yes, you would have. Everyone loved Pincus. He was a noble person. Devoted his life to fighting the injustices that deprive us of our individual destiny."

"What do you think your destiny was meant to be?"

Minna wanted a pat answer for Angie, but instead her memory carried her back to her childhood on the farm.

There, the air was fresh with the satisfying aromas of straw, hay, and manure in the pastures. There, the loamy feel of the dark earth convinced her she could make anything grow.

There, even with the freezing winters, the sun warmed her soul and the stars at night were so brilliant, she could almost pluck them from the sky.

There was where her destiny lay— across an ocean in a place she should never have been forced to leave.

She gazed into Angie's dark, expectant eyes. "I was destined to live my life in peace, surrounded by love."

Angie smiled. "You wait and see: my generation will make everything work. We'll turn people away from war. We'll find a way to share the planet peacefully with all living creatures."

Minna smiled. "And what if it doesn't happen with your generation either?"

Angie sipped her coffee thoughtfully. "Then we'll have to become survivors, too."

Chapter 41

Albuquerque

Aaron, Sophie, and Leah stood next to Chief Ramirez and listened carefully as he described his search plan. The chief's uniform was limp, mapped with perspiration. His fingers pointed here, there, and then his hands flew in all directions. He looked very worried.

Frieda kept her distance. Her stomach was churning from her hurried breakfast, but she concentrated on the voices breaking through bursts of static on the hand-held radios. Far off, motorcycles fanned out across the desert. The riders and their machines seemed to float as they formed a surrealist flutter in the harsh light.

A shimmering glare made Frieda wince, undoing the reality of a coming sunless night cooling the infinite grains of sand. She yanked off her sunglasses to better see the harshness more clearly.

Here the mesa country held no dunes or beautiful waves of shifting sands. Rather, the New Mexico desert was all wiry sagebrush and plates of scalding silica served up to the sun as it stretched into the tall, brooding Sandia Mountains. Yet, Frieda knew there was a rare, uncompromising beauty here, even with the blinding heat.

Leah, Sophie, and Aaron listened to the chief, hanging on every word. Frieda stayed in her own world where the sights, sounds, and realities of the desert flowed through her body.

Her mother was out there. There was no doubt about that. She studied the horizon, watched a dust devil materialize from nowhere before falling to nothingness.

"Aaron! Let's go!"

Aaron looked at her, his eyes a blank stare. She pointed to the dust devil that danced into sight again and again. He shrugged his shoulders, shook his head, but he walked toward the Jeep. Leah and Sophie followed.

The four of them hunkered down into the straight back leather seats. Frieda eyed the drive-in where her mother was last seen: It was a quiet, lonely world; a battered, weathered western outpost at the end of a long stretch of small businesses. Behind them lay the sprawl of a large city, in front of them nothing. Nothing but the blistering desert.

They sat in silence, caught up in a time warp that refused to release them from the knowable past or into an uncertain future. Frieda turned to look at Sophie and then Leah, while Aaron sat in the driver's seat looking useless. He revved the engine, revved it again.

"Do you think Grandma's out there?" Leah asked.

Sophie whispered, "I hope not."

"Let's do it," Aaron muttered under his breath. He released the clutch, and with a lurch they zigzagged onto the sandy floor. A lone, throbbing helicopter circled the sky above them.

They had been in the desert no more than ten minutes when Frieda shouted, "Stop!"

Aaron hit the brakes and Frieda jumped out. Sophie and Leah followed.

Another dust devil rose, wound its way between the three of them and started across the desert floor. They followed the raspy whine.

Frieda glanced at Sophie and Leah. They were walking with trance-like steps.

"What the hell are you doing, Frieda?" Aaron screamed, trailing behind them in the Jeep.

What *are* we doing? Frieda thought.

What had her mother been doing trudging through the desert like this?

With each step they sunk even deeper into the sand and the hot air burned their lungs. Yet, the thought of returning to the Jeep only brought an icy tingling that started at the base of Frieda's spine and made her shiver in the triple-digit temperature.

They trudged slowly through the desert silence ruptured by the rasp of motorcycles, the whine of the Jeep, and the thump, thump of the police helicopter circling back and forth.

• • •

There was a blur of noise.

Minna wanted to speak but her lips would no longer open, bound together as though needle and thread had curled their way through the blistery flesh. She tried to swallow but sand filled her mouth and throat. There was a hum of noise that came close, then went far away, disconnected.

A golden spire shot into the air; yellow tentacles flashed across the sky, then showered down on her. When they settled and covered Minna's face, her mother was there, cradling her head in her lap.

"Mommy, I've been waiting for you."

"I know you have, little girl. But I've been here watching over you all the time."

A soft breeze cooled Minna's face, but her heart was heavy.

"My life, Mommy … it's been so hard. I've been so afraid."

"Everyone's afraid."

"Pain … suffering. Why were we born?"

Her mother smoothed her hair. Minna watched golden flecks of

329

light swirl from her mother's fingers onto her own face. Her skin was cooled, soothed. "We are here to love, Minna."

"But all those terrible things. War. Hatred."

"The ideals you fought for ... they shine like the golden light."

Minna's sadness swelled. "I lost the light, Mommy. Lost it so many years ago I can't remember ever having it."

Her mother laughed. "Minna, your powers have never left you. You *are* the golden light."

Minna looked at her arms, at her body. A glow embraced her. Her mother was right. She *was* the golden light.

A whirlwind of memories surrounded her—her mother, Uncle Heshie, David, Sarah, Pincus, Aaron, Frieda. And then Sophie and Leah. How could she have forgotten?

She looked around and smiled. Her farm was off in the distance. The limbs of her peach tree reached out to her.

How beautiful! Her beginnings were never really lost—they were still there waiting for her.

She took a deep breath, exhaled a perfect circle of golden light and melted in its glow.

• • •

Frieda stopped.

There was an arm half buried in the sand. Minna was lying naked on her back under a scraggly limb of sage bush. Frieda's breath tore at her chest—she rushed to her mother.

"Mom! Mom!" Frieda cried, gently shaking Minna's shoulders.

Sophie and Leah sat down in the sand next to them. They began to cry. Aaron climbed down from the Jeep and dropped down next to his daughter. They encircled the motionless woman.

The heat was retreating, cooling the surrounding sand, but it still seared Frieda's fingers as she raked through the tiny crystals of sand.

"Grandma's dead," Leah said in a whisper, clutching Sophie's hand, then Aaron's.

Motorcycle policeman closed in around them, their loud whispers scattered the facts to the wind.

They all stared at Minna, at her smooth face, strangely untouched by a merciless sun that had left the rest of her burned and disfigured.

Frieda looked up at the sky—it had turned the eerie color that secretly visited her ever since she was a little girl.

Tears ran down her cheeks. She bent over and whispered, "I should have told you, Mom."

Frieda caressed, smoothed her mother's hair. It was silky and soft, as though it had somehow repelled the harsh sun and sand. A finger traced a perfect yellow outline around soft lips that were stretched into a secretive smile. She looked deeply into her mother's eyes.

They glinted with a golden light.

Acknowledgements

This book was written over a period of fifteen years. It has gone through the talented hands of many rotating members in our critique group, as well as other readers who have contributed their ideas and opinions. I want to thank all who have been a part of my creative process with *The Russian Girl*, and hope not to forget anyone, even though I accept that will be impossible.

Thank you Dotti & Bob Day, Katie Velick, Gabe Farkas, Marcia Muller & Bill Pronzini, Peggy & Charlie Lucke, Rita Lakin, Jaki Girdner & Greg Booi, Gina & Bill Thomas for always being there.

Special thanks to my critique partners in crime, past and present: Margaret (Peggy) Lucke, Judith Yamamoto, Nicola Trwst, Rita Lakin, Gwen Kaufman and Shelley Singer—what would I do without you? Also very special thanks to Sue Trowbridge and Eileen Magill & Magill's Quill.

And the star of them all, J. J. Lamb.

About the Author

Bette Golden Lamb is an RN, three-dimensional artist, and writer. She claims to need all of these disciplines to stay out of trouble. Her prize-winning art works have appeared in numerous gallery shows and are held in private collections nationally. Articles featuring her work have appeared in national magazines.

Born and raised in New York City, Bette is the author of *The Organ Harvesters* and *The Organ Harvesters Book II* and the best-selling Gina Mazzio RN medical thriller series, in collaboration with J. J. Lamb. Also written with J. J.: *The Killing Vote, Heir Today...,* and *Sisters In Silence.* Bette lives with her husband in Northern California.

www.twoblacksheep.us

Printed in Great Britain
by Amazon